ACE BOON COON

Bronzeville Books Inc.
269 S. Beverly Drive, #202
Beverly Hills, CA 90212
www.bronzevillebooks.com

Library of Congress Control Number: 2020939249

ISBN 978-1-952427-06-0   hardcover
ISBN 978-1-952427-05-3   paperback
ISBN 978-1-952427-04-6   ebook
ISBN 978-1-952427-07-7   audiobook

10 9 8 7 6 5 4 3 2 1

DANNY GARDNER

ACE BOON COON

THE TALES OF ELLIOT CAPRICE

BRONZEVILLE™
— BOOKS —

DEDICATION

For my ace boon, Rommel C. Shaw.

The only friend my father allowed.

CHAPTER 1

The sky above the tavern hadn't darkened, the familiar smell of ozone was missing, but his bum left shoulder never lied. Sure enough, distant thunder roared. He hoped for heavy rain that would head Southville way. The farm needed a good harvest to make up for the three year stretch of bad that came with Estes Kefauver's war on organized crime. That's why he split the week between attorney Michael Robin, for whom he served process, and his uncle, Buster Caprice, for whom he grew string beans, wax beans, and anxious. When he wasn't serving that mean old man, Elliot Caprice worked hard dragging stumblebums to the courthouse, as he needed the dough to make the mortgage.

He needed a good crop of string beans to make amends.

Before he opened the door, he tapped the court documents underneath his raincoat twice, taking extra care. He didn't want to disappoint the fiery young complainant who arrived to the small, one license firm, three beige babies in tow, none older than seven. In one hand, the coupon for expert advice Mikey ran in the Chicago Daily Defender. In the other, a summons on her wayward beau she wanted to appear in court for bastardy. She put the entire thing together pro se, as every attorney, court clerk, and social worker she encountered treated her like a whore.

"I'm not respectable, like Miss Ann over there."

She pointed to Elaine Critchlow, young Negro paralegal, the mountain climber, who clutched the pearls that made the point. Mikey Robin stepped in, of course, as he was the crusading race attorney. She waved him off. She didn't trust him, off the bat. Her errant beau was white and, up until then, all white folks did was stick together.

"At least you only half," she said to Elliot, as if that half of him wasn't listening.

"Ma'am."

"I see them writing boutcha in the papers. I like how you walk and talk it, Caprice."

She lowered her voice, as if it wasn't everyone's business by then.

"I know where he lives," she said. "With his other old lady. The white one. You could try to serve him there."

"Perhaps a public place," Elliot said.

"He spends most days drinking at the 19th Hole Tavern, out in Rockford, but he's surrounded by white boys."

"Ain't we all."

She shoved the court papers in his mitt, followed with a wad of cash.

"I paid you good money," she said, shaking his hand firmly. "Don't screw me over, like everyone else."

"Wouldn't think of it."

He couldn't imagine a golfer had ever been near the place, or any of the patrons had a tee-time to make. A few dusty odes to the game hung on the walls; old clubs, championship plaques. It was the other glories on display, the Anglo-Saxon trappings, framed tartans, "*Erin Go Bragh*" over the door arch, that was the tell. Lots of fellows wearing flags on their olive drab, and scorn on their faces.

Staring into a longneck of Old Style sat his quarry. Blue flannel shirt. Dock pants. Work boots. As if the region gave him a reason to wear that getup. Area military contracts were discontinued. Agriculture programs were cut by the War Department. An entire community tooled to do one thing, reduced to a legion of day drunks at the stroke of a politician's pen.

"Whatcha having, fancypants?"

The bald bartender with the eyepatch and forearm tattoo had a point. Elliot was slightly overdressed, in his charcoal double-breasted, powder blue shirt and gray tie. He meant to visit the bank later that day to ask for an extension on the mortgage to conserve cash flow through harvest. He wanted to look strong walking back in after clawing the farm from the grip of those bastards.

Elliot scanned the top shelf and found a bottle of bourbon he could stand.

"A couple fingers of Four Roses."

The bartender snorted, found a glass, and poured Elliot his drink.

"Want me to put a cherry in there for you?"

The functional drunks all snickered.

Elliot downed the shot and tapped on the rim of the glass. Cyclops poured him another.

"That's quality hooch, mister," said the fella in flannel. He was reading some sort of pamphlet printed on white paper.

"Best this joker got, anyway," Elliot said.

"Best any of us can afford. Times are hard, what with the furniture mills closing."

"Mills been closed going on a few years, haven't they?"

Elliot sipped his second pour slow as he sized up the mark. Not too big, but wiry, and young enough to put up a fight. And pissed. That part, Elliot understood.

"I'm waiting until that Ford plant they promised during the election opens.""

"Promises, promises," Elliot said. "Good work, if you can get it."

"Better be lined up early." An older drunk seated by a wall of Irish heritage tchotchkes belched. "You know the niggers'll be lined up."

"I blame the big shots hiring them for cheap," the mark said. He waved his pamphlet. "Right, mister?"

That was the tell Elliot wasn't made for Negro. The bar was dark. The mark was drunk.

"I guess things are pretty good in your line, friend."

"No shortage of work lately."

"What do you do?"

Elliot finished his pour, and stood.

"Douglas Hargray, of Rockford, Illinois,—"

The mark's bloodshot eyes went wide.

"Wait a second—" The mark stood. "I know you."

Elliot reached his hand into his pocket. Hargray leaped from his barstool, which fell to the floor.

"Don't kill me!"

"Wait, what?" Elliot waved off the assertion.

"He used to come around with this real tough guy," a drunk said. "Saw my dad almost every payday, for a year."

Another tough stood and walked up behind Elliot.

"I got an older brother who still can't walk good," he said.

He grabbed Elliot from behind. Another brandished Hargray's felled barstool. Cyclops, the Bartender from Olympus, pulled a baseball bat.

"Let 'im go," he said. "I can't have that in this joint."

"It's Izzy Rabinowitz's nigger. He collects for the Roseland Boys."

"You tell that to the Turk," Cyclops said. "That's who I pay up to."

"Oh, Christ on the frickin' cross," Elliot said.

Hargray took off in a full sprint, out the door and onto the rainy Rockford streets, where the gutters ran full.

"I'm gonna carve some numbers in your hide, half-breed," Bearhug said, through the foul breath of a man who long ago gave up on himself. "Enough for the vig I paid to your Jew."

Elliot would have rolled his eyes at the mention of Izzy, but he had to keep one on the asshole with the stool. The bottle of Four Roses was still on the bar. He stomped Bear Hug's foot hard with his heel and threw his head backward, smashing the drunk's nose. Once free, he grabbed the bottle of bourbon, caught the barstool in his left hand, and struck hard with the right. Both men went down hard. Elliot grabbed his hat off the floor and took off after his mark.

"Hey," the bartender said. "You owe me for a bottle."

Elliot reached into his pocket and tossed out a fiver.

"Keep the change," he said. "And your mouth shut."

CHAPTER 2

Elliot ran full speed down Kishwaukee Street until it bisected Belle Place. He made Hargray out the corner of his eye.

"Slippery son of a bitch." He pointed as he ran. "Stop right there!"

Hargray pivoted and ducked into an alley. Elliot pondered yanking his piece and taking some fat meat out of his thigh, which they taught him in the academy, Patrolling 101. Soon he gained on him, but also, from an alley near the dock behind Miss Fisher's Potato Chip factory, he made a man in a black hat and black raincoat, doing his best to conceal himself once spotted. His body language was so sloppy he had to be a Fed, like the kind that had been coming around since Mikey got himself entangled in the movement for Negro Civil Rights, full bore. Some of it tracked back home to the farm, always driven by the Negro press, hot for information on his connection with the McAlpins. Instead of starting a scrapbook, Elliot begged Uncle Buster to throw out the Negro rags, which gleefully printed half-truths and innuendo. All the movement had done for Elliot was distract the local constabulary, make the neighbors more suspicious, and dull his Florsheim wingtips. He played for different stakes than the speechmakers, who rented apartments, and didn't have to make payroll. When you have no desire for your neighbors' want, the government needs no hired help to clear your land.

Elliot heard a gurgled yelp and followed moaning to just the other side of the potato chip outfit. The philandering mark might have gotten away, what not for the good fortune of that clothesline in the alley, otherwise known as Frank Fuquay's forearm. Hargray laid flat on his back in a puddle, the wind knocked out of him. Frank stood over him appearing pleased with himself. He was wearing his field canvasses, standing legs apart, looking every bit the Colored Colossus of Rhodes.

Elliot yanked the papers from the place his .45 would normally be and shoved them into Hargray's collar.

"Douglas Hargray," he said, between big breaths. "You are ordered to report to Winnebago County family court. If you don't attend your hearing, you will be in default and subject to arrest."

Elliot pointed in his face.

"Clean yourself up. Provide for your children."

As they walked away, Frank gave in to uproarious laughter.

"Yeah, yeah," Elliot said. He examined his crushed hat. "That old man tried to tell me I was overdressed."

"We shoulda let me serve him."

"I'm not in the mood for your I told you so's Francis."

"I'm just sayin', I'm the one wearing the canvasses. I dressed for fighting."

"You're dressed for farming." Elliot shook his head. "Which is what you should be doing."

"Hard to farm without enough rain, Elliot."

"Well, regardless, you were supposed to wait in the car."

"And I did," Frank said. "Until the mark gave you the slip. I don't see why you didn't just have me serve him, Boss."

"I told you, as long as that old man needs you, you stay out of the rough stuff."

"Why you have me drive, then?"

"Because we're in Rockford," Elliot said. "Not many friends of Elliot up this way, if you remember."

Frank nodded.

"I asked you to watch my back," Elliot said, pointing his finger instructively. "So you figured you'd intervene, but how do you know whether or not I'm running toward that fella, or away from something else, and a lot worse? Hm?"

"You're right, Boss."

"Or have you forgotten the Short Paper War is on? And everyone thinks I'm still in Izzy Rabinowitz's crew."

"No, Elliot," Frank said. "I haven't forgotten. That's sort of why I made tracks after y'all. Sorry."

Elliot slapped Frank on the arm. "Hey," he said. "Don't shine me on, man. You hop in to be a hero, you get hemmed up, get me?"

Frank grew quiet. Elliot soon felt like shit for taking the Big Schoolboy to task when he shouldn't have even been there but with his face in a book, following the rules: want to stay in Buster's house, you work the land, and you go to school.

"Frank, I'm tired. Run on and get Lucille, will you?"

"You've been working too hard, Boss." Frank trotted off. "Makes you cranky."

"You must be studying rhetoric, all these comments of yours."

Frank found his quiet and found Lucille. Elliot was thankful for some quiet himself. He needed some space. The conflagration in the tavern brought it all back. No matter how much good he did, or the kind of notoriety he and the firm received, he was still Izzy's half-colored thumb breaker. That, or the process server of the Jew lawyer who stirred up trouble among good Negroes. Bill Drury. John Creamer. Kefauver. Uncle Sam. Such an ever-expanding list of white men for whom he schlepped water, like some miscegenated Ganga Din. Elliot had studied the works of Rudyard Kipling at Bradley and found him to be a well-intentioned asshole, of which his life had no shortage.

Frank wheeled Lucille around the corner and Elliot was on the door handle before he had a chance to brake. He noticed the fuel gauge hovered near empty.

"Big man, I seem to remember that, aside from comic timing, vehicle maintenance is your responsibility."

"Nothing changed."

Elliot pointed at the dash.

"Ah," Frank said.

"Ah."

"Well, between lookin' after Uncle Buster, keeping the field hands from stealing us blind, plus add my general equivalency—"

"Okay, Big Man," he said. "I understand. Good work back there."

"Really?"

Elliot nodded. "You're learning how to think ahead. Watch the play. How'd you know where Hargray was gonna dip?"

"Bus station, one block up."

"Smart, Francis."

"Really?"

"You got him, didn't you?"

"Appreciate you sayin' so," Frank said. "It's not always easy to tell how you feel."

"I feel like you staying out of trouble," Elliot said. "Get me?"

"Okay."

"I promised your mama, now."

"You did."

"Good work back there, tho."

"Thanks."

"If we don't run out of gas."

"Aw, man."

"Fence mending is hard, ain't it?" Elliot laughed. "Nail one board in, two more pop out."

As an angrier rain began, Elliot made a black sedan, piloted by the soggy legman, who seemed to be new at his job, what with direct eye contact and everything.

"Something wrong?"

Elliot thought to say something about the tail, but kept his quiet.

"It's coming down nasty. Let her out slow, Frank."

"Always do, Boss."

CHAPTER 3

As the service man filled up Lucille, Frank availed himself of the men's room. Elliot stood outside the station underneath an awning. He fished a hand-rolled out of his pocket, reached for his Zippo, and had the remainder of his morning ruined.

"Well, well. If it ain't Elliot Caprice."

Elliot's stomach sank. Chester Gant stood before him. He was ebony wood-black, with smooth, clear skin and piercing, almond eyes. A godawful black bowler hat covered his close-cropped haircut. He wore no facial hair aside from a patch underneath his bottom lip. He had on a black raincoat. He didn't take his hand out of his pocket, the tell he held a sawed-off underneath. The first time they tussled was in grammar school, when Elliot learned bitterness makes a child a bully and picked on the wrong kid in the schoolyard. Chester gave him as good as he got, and in front of everyone. It was a lesson he'd never forgotten.

He offered a light. Elliot accepted, and silently timed Frank's restroom break.

"High Yella seems a long way from Southville, don't he?"

Gimp was Chester's ace pally. He stood over six-foot three, a full inch over the Big Fella. He wore the same hat and coat. Elliot wondered if they all went shopping together.

"Shol' is." Chester grinned. At the sight of his gold tooth, for the second time that day, Elliot felt the urge to shoot someone.

"Where's yo flunky, that fool Big Black?"

"I hear you haven't learned my name."

Frank walked out of the bathroom and arrived full of tension.

"It's Fuquay," he said.

"Big Ugly, more like."

This provoked an exchange of physical semiotics between the two mighty colored men who carried danger in their bodies and malice in their hearts. It was a silent debate in a language that no one seemed to teach, yet every Negro learned at one time or another, and always from their fellow man.

"Chasin' down philanderers seem like hard work for a man as stylish as you, Lightskin," Chester said. "The drought got you down?"

"I didn't know the Turk owns the 19th Hole."

"It's what the banks call a collateralized asset."

"You shoulda done some checkin'," Gimp said, and he took a step closer. Without a flinch, Elliot finished his square, stamped on the butt and looked up at Chester.

"I'm here on the court's business. Didn't mean to cause a ruckus."

"And yet, you did."

"No one wants me in Rockford less than me."

"Except Douglas Hargray," Chester said, through that goddamned grin. "Next time, call before you come. I coulda taken you over Hargray's house. Introduced you to his wife and chirrens."

Chester flashed that gold tooth for a third time.

"His whiter chirrens."

The service man raised his oil rag.

"Let's pay the man and get on, Frank."

Frank slowly walked away. Gimp then menaced Elliot, who rolled his eyes toward Chester.

"At the Texaco? In the rain?"

"Aight, nah, Gimp," Chester said. "Elliot is just passin' through."

Chester turned and walked away. Gimp followed. Elliot walked over to Lucille. Frank was in the driver's seat. He seemed disappointed he didn't get to scrap. Elliot climbed in the passenger's seat and closed the door.

"Boss, I hate those sum'bitches."

"You must," Elliot said. "To be cussin'."

Chester walked right up and tapped on Elliot's window. He rolled it down.

"Too many of our boys wind up dead in the fields of Southville for you to be passing into Rockford without announcing yourself, Caprice. Wouldn't want anyone to figure you're still working for the Jew."

"Izzy says the Turk muscled in first."

"What's he going to say?"

Chester finally stopped grinning. He tugged his hat brim. "Careful in all this rain."

Elliot tugged his brim in kind. Frank started up. As he pulled away, Elliot checked the rear view. Chester stood stock still in the rain, glaring death at him through the mirror.

The fat cats at the bank didn't treat him as nice as the friendly patrons of the 19th Hole, denying Elliot an extension on the mortgage and demanding either more collateral or a bigger monthly payment after harvest. As he transferred more of his savings from the Costas Cartage affair to the farm account, he felt badly about dipping into it again, but he wouldn't survive another winter eating out of cans and praying over the soil.

As he left, he saw a sign in the lobby about the County meeting, where they'd discuss some new Harvest Protection Ordinance, as well as real estate development in Southville. These were the moments Elliot truly hated his hometown, where landholders were presented the old problem as if it were new, and the old evil as if it were the best solution, marketed right where everyone's money lived, all but printed on the free calendars.

He sat on the front porch in Uncle Buster's rocker watching the sunset.

Once the rains ended, it was a slim reward for a hard, wet day. At least he had better bourbon in the house than Four Roses. Elliot was halfway to morose when Frank stepped out the front door, a bottle of grape Nehi in hand.

"Mind if I sit?"

Frank took his quiet as yes. Elliot took another sip of his bourbon. Frank sipped on his pop. He rolled his Nehi bottle in his hands in the same manner as Elliot distracted himself with his own glass. It wasn't a conscious choice to emulate. More how, after a while, men take on each other's stink.

"We can discuss it if you want, Frank."

"That fella we hemmed up," he said. "Chauncey Ballard. He's getting life."

"The whole stretch, huh?"

"In Stateville Penitentiary. Chicago Daily Defender reported it today," Frank said, before he caught a lump in his throat. "They're holding him in Cook County Jail."

"I'd rather Stateville." Elliot chuckled.

"Why didn't you do it?"

"What?"

The Big Man was the kind of quiet that grabbed the moment by the collar.

"What, Frank?"

"Why didn't you kill him, the night we found him, and Alistair Williams?"

Elliot held his stare against the young gent, then looked away to witness the dazzling watercolors. Some silver. Some bronze. Lots of red. A bit of blue.

"I'm sorry, Boss."

"Why ask me about the bad stuff, Frank?"

"They're your stories, Boss. I learn from them. I keep them to myself."

"I caught you telling your sister, on the phone. You sound like an old radio show, carrying on about me."

"We're all proud of you, Elliot."

Elliot rolled his glass again. As he watched the sky, he wished something would fly down and carry him away from Frank, who was like a dog on a bone when he wanted.

"I've been a criminal, and a cop, and now I'm praying for rain. Crime of one stripe or another will always be here, Frank. That sunset has maybe three more minutes before it's gone forever."

Elliot patted Frank on the knee. The Big Man inhaled slowly and deeply and stretched and exhaled. Elliot sipped.

"When's the last you spoke to your Mama?"

"Well, she's near the church phone most Tuesdays, so that's when I call. Spoke to Francine, though. She's alright."

"Francis and Francine. Still cracks me up."

Elliot winked and Frank laughed. The sky darkened, adding marigold and burnt sienna.

"Imma go study."

"Okay, Big Man."

Frank stood and grabbed the doorknob.

"It wasn't in my guts."

"Beg your pardon, Elliot?"

Elliot turned toward him.

"I didn't kill Williams because he didn't come for me," Elliot said. "I didn't kill Chauncey Ballard because there's the state's killing, and my killing, and I know the difference."

Elliot didn't leave Frank any room to reply.

"Good night, Frank," he said. "Don't study all night. We need to get up in the morning."

"G'nite, boss."

Frank went inside and upstairs.

Magic hour ceded to indigo blue. Stars twinkled. Night birds made conversation. Accepting there'd never be enough bourbon to fade his dread, he flicked the rest out over the porch rail, turned and walked into the house.

CHAPTER 4

Molly Duffy caught up with him halfway up Main Street. He wasn't running full speed anyhow, but she was, in the cutest brown sweater, yellow chiffon dress, and laced sandals, like something out of the Saturday Evening Post. He didn't figure she could run in those things, but Molly could cuss, and pitch pennies, and fight as well as any colored boy in Southville.

He took a few. He wasn't afraid of Moses, but most kids were because he was dark, bigger than all the other kids, and came up in the Migration from Cleveland. No one had ever seen a kid from a big city before.

The Midwestern rain seeped into the scrapes on his face. Laced with hair pomade, and lead and nickel carried upon the winds from Chicago, it burned, as did his anger, at everything.

"Elliot, wait," she said. "Where are you going?"

"Nowhere," he said. "To Doc's, I guess. I just want to get out of the damned rain."

"Wait up."

She ran to him and grabbed his arm, stopping him in the middle of the muddy walk on Main Street. He saw her knuckles were cut.

"Who'd you hit?"

"Moses," Molly said. "Right after you did. Before his mama came down the street."

Molly made a sneaky grin.

"I'm sorry I let Moses' fool self ruin the show."

"It's alright," Molly said. She kicked around the water. "You really cracked his mush."

"What it look like, I let him say those mean things to you? You ain't deserve all that."

"Your uncle is gonna be mad you were fighting."

"Once I clean my hand up, he won't know."

Elliot marched through the rain until he made it to the front door of the clinic.

"Keep watch," Elliot said. "I'm supposed to go around back. It's shabbos."

"It's what?"

"I'm supposed to come and go around back on the sabbath for Jew folk because I'm not a Jew. I'm not gonna, tho', because those crazy drunks from Sugartown cut through there."

The lock remained stuck. He dropped the keys again. "Oh, motherfuck."

"Elliot Caprice," Molly said. "You better quit cussin'."

"Why you say my name that way?"

"What way?"

"Both my names," he said. "Together. Why you say it like that?"

"Like what?"

"Like how that lady said it to that man, on the picture screen. Like you singing it."

Molly smiled. Her big, bright eyes, each with a tiny ocean inside, twinkled. Eyes so big, it was easy to see how Mose Boysaw's words about her family problems hurt her. He was sweet on Molly, just like all the colored boys were, even those who wouldn't admit it. She wasn't like anything the colored kids said about white folks, that they stink like dogs when wet, or they don't believe in God down at the Catholic Church but the Devil, and she was going to hell. That they didn't raise their children, except Elliot watched Molly raise her own daddy with her mama gone. Once Moses got going on Sean Duffy's struggles in the bottle, same as all the Irish in

Southville, Elliot couldn't help himself, and he punched his running buddy square in the yap, knocking him on his ass. Mose got up, swung on him, and Elliot knocked him down again. He then cussed Moses' mama, Earline, who told him she'd tell his old, angry uncle. Elliot hated Earline Boysaw almost as much as Miss Betty, both of whom wouldn't mind their own damned bid'ness as each acted like they wanted to be his Step-Auntie.

"He ought not to bring your pap into it," he said, working hard at the lock but also staring at his cut knuckles. "Cappin' ain't supposed to be personal. It's supposed to be jokes."

"It wasn't so bad," Molly said. She looked away.

Elliot felt bad for bringing it up again. Distracted, he dropped the keys into the rain puddle outside the door. He looked at his hurt hand, figuring he probably hit Mose harder than he needed. He certainly didn't mean for his hand to fly, but it was Mose who got tough in front of everyone else. He was the one who puffed his chest out, like he was bad. Elliot couldn't back away, especially once Moses went in on his skin tone, and his parentage, and began saying private things about the Caprices only he would know, as his mama and Uncle Buster had private business, which always caused Elliot a grand bit of embarrassment. Mose spoke on things he wouldn't know. Bearing false witness is what Father Reilly called it. Nasty little made-up things to make other coloreds distrust him, which turned the tribe against him, for the white girl, who made him look even more white to them, and rarely did the colored kids resist making his miscegenation the issue.

First thing Doc told him that day was no fighting, but Moses Boysaw needed something for that nasty mouth of his and his burr-headed mama wasn't gonna give it to him, not as much as she loved her only baby boy. Now he'd get slapped around the office, same as he'd get slapped on the farm, for doing what he had to when no one was around to see how mean everyone else was.

"And what were you doing?"

Slap.

Fat lot of good it did Elliot to be raised by so many men, but never a woman.

He finally opened the door and pointed inside. Molly stepped slowly into the alcove. She hadn't been in Doc's office but once since he met her, on the day she got her first period something awful and the sisters at St. Margaret made her afraid of being knocked up by a demon or some such. Her mama had been dead but a few years prior. Sean brought her to Doc's during one of Elliot's less harsh punishments, where he could escape Uncle Buster's mule strap or torturous field chores by being useful in the clinic. Since that day, he held a tremendous ache within his insides over Molly. He never quite understood it, but it led him to Doc Shapiro's waiting room with her, with the lights off, on Shabbos, and after punching out a boy for her, although she didn't want him to do it, which made him really want to do it.

Molly shivered. He ran to the linen cabinet, snatched a blanket and a few white towels for her hair, too many, but then overdoing it was the theme on the night, what with the pomade, and Mose Boysaw's teefus. As she covered up, he dried her hair with the same speed he would dry the mule.

"Ouch," she said.

Molly took his hand and guided him in making the smallest, softest strokes with the towel. He wondered if he should turn the light on. They were alone. Just who did he think he was, on Main Street, during harvest, kicking around with Molly Duffy like she wasn't a white girl?

He was taken off guard by her scent, rosewater and beer nuts, which her pap let her munch right out of the barrel at the tavern, where she worked, yet did not quite exist. The Midwestern air smelled funky, mossy, and lovely. Elliot looked down to the freckles on her perfect nose.

"Molly," Elliot said.

Before some truth he didn't recognize escaped him, Molly reached her slender arms around his neck and kissed him. A true kiss, one that puts a claim on a man's soul for ages. His guts felt funny. He never figured a person could smell and taste of so many things. Elliot's consciousness was awash in contradictions. Molly was white, he wasn't, except kinda. They were friends, but more, maybe. It was Shabbos, he came in through the front door.

He loved her, and he'd never figure out what to do about it.

"Molly," Sean Duffy shouted from the street.

It was after closing time at Duffy's Tavern that Saturday. Sean needed to find his one and only daughter and get home and he was screaming on the streets of Southville to find her. Normally he wouldn't come anywhere near Main Street, being from Sugartown. She recoiled at the sound of his voice, sat on the waiting room couch, and drew her knees to her ears, holding her legs with her wiry-strong forearms. Elliot stood and closed the shades. Sean called out again. Elliot could make out his drink-addled, slew-footed gait through the vellum screen's translucence. She shivered. Elliot didn't know what to do so he sat next to her and wrapped his arms around her. He held her until the back door to the clinic sounded as if it was kicked open. A huge commotion broke out. Foul language was being spoken by two men. With the harvest on, it could be anyone.

"Stay here," Elliot said, and he leaped to his feet, got the shotgun from the coat closet, cocked it, and ran into Doc Shapiro's examination room.

CHAPTER 5

Lightning and pale amber utility light backlit a root-colored Negro, six-one, standing in the back doorway. The floor was wet. Another thing Doc would yell at him for. His face seemed far angrier than his eyes, which were reddened and weary. He wore blue jeans, a leather jacket, and a black leather eight-panel cap. The floor wore his blood. Before he collapsed, Doc Shapiro's cousin, Isadora Rabinowitz, ran up and supported the colored man's weight as best he could. He was shorter than Doc by at least a half-foot, but broad shouldered. He looked like a prizefighter. His nose was crooked at the bridge, with a scar across. He had been coming around the past year. He always put Doc in a worse mood.

"Alright there, Tommy," he said. It sounded like he cared. "Goddamn crazies, these farm people."

Sheets of water cascaded down Izzy's fine wool gray fedora and matching trench coat. Elliot thought of the pulps he'd get from Saperstein's. The Shadow was his favorite. A bad guy, beating up on worse guys. As he helped Tommy inside, Izzy saw him, shotgun in hand.

"Holy—!"

Izzy recoiled, let go, and Tommy collapsed on the floor. With the hand speed of a close-up magician, Izzy produced a Saturday Night Special at the end of his left hand. Elliot knew that was it, the moment he was going to die and save his mean old uncle the trouble.

"Drop that shotgun, you mother—"

"You're Doc's cousin," Elliot said, frozen in place by fear and the thrill. "From New York."

"Brooklyn," he said. "You're that *mischling* he has working here."

"What that mean, *mischling*?" Elliot couldn't stop thinking about where the gun may have come from. He had never seen anything like that in his life.

"Help me get him on a table, kid."

Elliot dropped the shotgun and helped Tommy by hoisting the other shoulder. That's when he noticed he was the same height as Izzy. He couldn't stop looking at his clothes and hat.

"My cousin taught you how to do any of that field medicine shit yet?"

"Field medicine?"

"Move your ass. He's bleeding everywhere, yeah?"

Elliot helped Izzy take the moaning bruiser to Doc's exam table and laid him down.

"I told you these farmers don't mind your Jimmy Cagney bullshit," Tommy said to Izzy. "This Southville. These folk kill you like they dun killed me."

Tommy moaned. His voice sounded gurgled.

"Just pipe down, Tommy. Let this kid help out."

Tommy Eight-Panels bled from the gut something terrible. Elliot grabbed an armful of clean towels and brought them to Izzy.

"Here," Elliot said.

"He's not takin' a steam, you little nitwit."

"Use 'em to sop up the blood. You can wring it out. Saw Doc do it for a field hand once. Won't last long. Dies quick, the blood."

Elliot looked at Tommy.

"You know Tommy here?"

"We don't all know each other, ya know?"

"I don't mean it like that, ya little shit." Izzy shook his head. "Around town, I'm asking."

"Oh." He made Tommy as no one special and went back to work. It felt weird to bicker with anyone but Uncle Buster.

"I know this little light-skinned motherfucker," the goon said. "His uncle fired me off his farm two seasons ago."

"Fired me, too," Elliot said.

Tommy chuckled, which didn't help the bleeding from his gut any. He cursed with his next breath.

"It's alright, Tommy. I'm pretty sure my cousin taught this kid something."

"Well, where the fuck he at?"

"It's Shabbos," Elliot said instinctively, reflexively. "Ain't Kosher to treat nobody."

"Anybody," Izzy said.

"Anybody," Elliot said.

"Get it from his uncle," Tommy said. "He ain't learned, neither. Know enough to work a man half to death, tho'. Buster Caprice is a hard screw."

"Ought not to speak of my uncle when he's not around to defend himself." Elliot stepped toward the phone on the wall. "I'll try Doc at home."

Tommy coughed, let out a groan, and the red from his gut grew. Izzy snapped his fingers. Elliot hung up the phone and spun around.

"The hell you snappin' at?"

"Oy," Izzy said. "This kid's mouth. Do something already. Tommy's bleeding to death."

Tommy and Izzy's bickering continued as Elliot ran to a cabinet and found Doc's suture kit. The steel clamshell box with the catgut and needles. He wondered, could he do it, having seen Doc fix up field laborers tens of times.

"You ain't gonna wash hands or nothin'?"

"Who's doin' this?"

"Alright," Izzy said, shaking his head. "Have it your way. Just do what you can. Tommy's got a family."

It was different than when his uncle whipped him for the slightest infraction on the farm, or when Doc chewed him out and slapped him upside the head. It made Elliot feel capable, knowing what to do in the presence of another man's blood.

"A boy, your age," Tommy said. "What you about? Twelve?"

"Thirteen," Elliot said. He prepped the suture with catgut. Izzy backed away and fished through his pocket for a smoke. Blood everywhere, dying Negro on the table, and he was creepy-calm, blood all over his hands, smoking in an exam room, with no regard for the environment or circumstances. He was exotic. Hypnotic. Nothing like the jamokes around Southville who give him grief all the time.

"My youngest boy is seven," Izzy said. "Fat kid. Likes his sweets. Smart, though."

"Your uncle is an okay fella," Tommy said. His eyes shifted. "Ain't normal, a colored fella have two plots of land in Southville County. How'd he happen on it?"

"In a card game," Elliot said.

"Bet you living real good off that much land."

Tommy Eight-Panels' top lip rolled into a sneer. Elliot sneered back.

"Almost as good as the mule."

The boy heard angered Yiddish coming from outside.

"Shit on a stick," he said. "Doc's back."

He ran into the waiting room, on the wet floor where the towels lay. Where Molly sat, mortified. On Shabbos.

Elliot's heart rate doubled as Doc Shapiro walked in, his lanky frame wired with tension. He didn't take off his brown canvas hat, or rain jacket. He had his leather medicine bag with him. He took off his wireframe eyeglasses and wiped his wet face with his hand before putting them back on. He always wore his glasses. He reeked of cigarette smoke, which Elliot wondered if it was Kosher.

"Doc," Elliot said. "Your cousin—"

"*Shtum*," Doc said. "Too many injured. Get ready."

"What happened?"

"Coloreds and veterans are fighting over day labor. They're rioting as far as the tavern. State police are coming. Five dead already."

Elliot looked out the waiting room door. Flames tickled the gray clouds above Pettingill Road. The mobs would soon arrive at Main Street, same as every harvest, but especially since the migration hullabaloo began. Even kids his age read the headlines from the Chicago Daily Defender and the Negro Digest, carried across the nation by Pullman porters, imploring colored folk to abscond their former owners with their dignity and bring their willingness to work for what they wanted north, Chicago way.

Except Southville was the last stop before the Windy City, and northerners preferred their railroads underground. Too many farm workers. Not enough segregated accommodations. Certainly not enough jobs for those who fought the wars of the fat cats. The fight over labor had first brewed sometime around his uncle's first boon harvest, when he was seven. At market, he heard other farmers plotting against him. They spoke about the nigger farmer who made so much money each market day, not recognizing him as Buster's nephew, or he was colored himself.

Sean Duffy ran into the waiting room, tears in his eyes. He looked gaunt and fidgety. He reeked of his own supply of Sugartown's finest.

"Molly, honey," he said. He reached his hands out to her. "C'mon."

Sean didn't seem angry at Molly, or Elliot, but grabbed his one and only child and pulled her hurriedly out onto the street.

"We gotta get home."

"My uncle," Elliot said.

"He's still out to market in Crete," Doc said.

Elliot walked out onto the clinic's front step to watch Molly be dragged off in the rain by her pap. He pondered the kiss that felt like she had been saving it a long time. He still tasted roses and beer nuts.

As father and daughter angled toward the corner, he realized he had blood all over his hands and his shirt. Before he could recoil, Molly looked back at him, like a real girl and not his little white play-cousin. She smiled that soft smile again, filled with sunshine and magic that glittered, even in a Midwestern thundershower. Elliot's heart broke into a thousand teenage pieces. The sirens of the trooper cars got louder. As Sean dragged Molly around the corner by her arm, she locked eyes with him. She wasn't afraid.

Doc Shapiro snatched the boy by the arm and pulled him, harshly, toward the exam room.

"Get over here," he said. "Clean your hands."

He marched Elliot to the sink and turned on the water. His wireframe glasses fell down the bridge of his nose. He pushed them back up, leaving a streak of blood on his face.

"I told you, not here," Doc said to Izzy, as he strung catgut. "These are good folks."

"We didn't start it," Izzy said. "When *goy* lose, they fight back dirty."

"Shol' in the shit do," Elliot said.

Doc whacked him across the back of the head and continued to work on Tommy.

Elliot heard the doorbell ring.

Through the blinds, like a shadow play on a cave wall, he watched as the mobs of drunks pushed through the line of state police, who arrived in the nick of time to protect the business quarter, no matter property and citizenry for the working man were already afire. Colored heads would be split on general principle. A few Irish and German heads, too, if they were poor enough, and fool enough to be out there counted with the slaves. When he wasn't anticipating the carnage, Elliot noticed Izzy Rabinowitz staring at him with what Uncle Buster called "hungry eyes," the moment when someone figures out what makes you valuable, without telling you. He longed for the farmhouse he hated, and that old black dragon who never understood anything, if only because everything there was as he left it, unlike the remainder of the world which changed before his eyes, right after Molly's kiss. The racist skirmish would spare Elliot the hassle he'd get from his Uncle's best friend, the kindly Jew who came from nowhere, whose cousin was the most dangerous and fascinating man Elliot Caprice had ever seen.

The wounded began to shamble inside the waiting room. Colored or white, all cried out in suffering. Some were children. Behind them, in his raincoat, yarmulke on his tiny, balding head, was Abe Saperstein, the druggist from down the block. He pushed through the crowd of Negroes, now panicked.

"Ira!"

"Call Sheriff Dowd—"

"I did that already. I'll get triage supplies."

Abe ran back out into the noisy gray and orange night. The streets filled with smoke, which occurred whenever the poor folk's shanties constructed along the edge of the county seat were burning.

"Prep the cots, boychik," Doc said.

Elliot ran to the closet and pulled out canvas cots to handle the overflow of wounded. As he set one up in the corner, Izzy pointed to him.

"His hand," he said. He pointed again. Elliot realized what Izzy meant and his stomach dropped to his knees.

"Kid's a killer, Ira."

"Not him," Doc said. He looked at Elliot through the wireframes. "We'll talk about your hand later."

"Moses Boysaw went after Molly, Doc."

"I said no fighting."

Outside, angry bodies locked in futility with the Illinois State Police.

The ringing sound, now loud and long, filled Elliot's ears.

Tommy clutched at his gut. His breathing was shallow. His lips were turning blue. Elliot pointed to him when a hail of peacekeeping bullets flew through the windows of the clinic. The crowd began to wail. Doc yanked Elliot down to the floor and crawled atop him. Izzy pulled his piece and yanked Tommy down to the floor. The shouting and screaming outside got louder. Elliot trembled inside. Doc held him tighter. Men outside ran past the windows. Some tried doors, only to be shot in the back. The state police kept firing. Everyone in the exam room and waiting room began screaming.

Doc held him tighter. Elliot stared into Tommy Eight-Panels' eyes as he gave up the ghost not five minutes beyond cursing his uncle. His tongue looked thick in his mouth, now hanging open, nothing smart coming out of it.

"Stay down, Elliot."

The ringing was relentless.

"Christ on the cross," the boy said. "Someone lay off the—"

CHAPTER 6

"—goddamned doorbell."

He opened his eyes from his nap in front of the darkened fireplace. He pulled off the hand-knit throw Molly Duffy gave him for his birthday and laid it in Uncle Buster's matching red leather easy chair to the right. It was the more worn of the two, from the years Nathan Caprice would sit and worry about the boy after he ran off to enfranchise himself with George S. Patton, one of far too many ambitious Negroes who took up the fight with Tojo and the Krauts, only to return the enemy of the whites they risked life to defend. He intended to close his eyes only a moment, as that old man fixed him a plate of great northern beans with ham hocks and rice and, with the house filled with so many hungry farming Negroes, he had better eat lickety-split. As he rubbed the pain out of his addled seed-planting knees, he chuckled to himself, thinking it was only right he suffer through his own torment in that chair, having tormented that old man from that very same spot for so long.

He opened the door for Deputy Ned Reilly, who stood lanky in his Sunday best; green wool blazer, collared shirt, boots, badge on the outside. His not quite brown but you wouldn't call it red hair was cut in Illinoisian po-lice-man style. Deputy Good White Folks was dressed to arrest, and, perhaps, impress the Illinois State Police, out in force in the burg, helping to keep the peace during the growing season.

"Ned," Elliot said. He kept his voice down.

"George sent me to run you over to Saperstein's Pharmacy. There's a dead body out back."

"Christ on the cross. Lower your voice."

"Sorry."

"As if I need to worry him during planting season."

"How's he doing?"

"How's your mama?"

"Old," Ned said.

"Well, him, too."

Elliot snatched his eight-panel cap from the hat rack. Buster Caprice, farmer and collector of Negro orphans, emerged from his bedroom in the burgundy velvet robe Frank Fuquay gave him for Christmas. Gray-maned and backlit with the hall light, he looked like Moses, come to plague the grain hoarders.

"What's the matter?"

"Nothing, Unk," Elliot said. "Uh, Ned just needs a hand with something."

"Something down at the pharmacy."

"Shut it," Elliot said.

"Want me to wake Frank?"

"No, Unk. We got it. G'nite."

Elliot pushed Ned out the door. As they walked to the cruiser, George's voice came over the radio.

"Ned."

Ned picked up the handset. "We're just leaving Elliot's, Georgie."

"Hang tight, Reverend," Elliot said.

"You better hurr—"

The sound of an angry mob shouting came over the radio before the mic went out.

Elliot and Ned looked at each other. Ned floored it down the access road, hit the left onto Main Street hard, and put the hammer down toward town proper. Elliot grabbed the Oh, Jesus-strap in the cruiser and held on as they tore gravel. Stray vegetation from the side of the road slapped hard at the car body.

"You think he's alright?"

Ned put his hat on and turned on the siren. Elliot watched the road.

"This isn't his first growing season," he said. "Ours, neither."

The cruiser's hi-beams cut through the darkness of the two-lane pass into town proper. Ned looked worn down as the only actual law during the Short Paper War, which had stretched the two-gun sheriff's department so thin the Illinois State Police had returned to Southville. Moreover, George yearned for the call to service in the movement, and he policed Southville like it, diving into civic matters, such as the nuisance ordinances that plagued Negro migrant workers. This left Ned to be the sole inheritor of the shit police work. Elliot knew policing was thankless. Order meant calm, not comfort. The community cop was the neighborhood king no one ever really wanted around.

They pulled off Pettengill Road into Sugartown. During the harvest, Sundays were more sinful than Fat Tuesday. The streets were filled with poor whites drinking away their field pay. Many were harassing Negro migrant workers, openly accusing them of taking their jobs, jobs they never worked until the war dollar dried up. Ned and Elliot hopped out of the cruiser and came between a drunken Negro in his field canvases and a white boy in an olive drab woolen who looked as if they would kill each other. Elliot got the Negro and his friend to disperse. Ned wasn't so lucky, so he pulled his baton, and the white drunks shuffled off.

Down the block, Elliot noticed Illinois State Troopers holding four Negroes on the curb, one of whom was his Uncle's field hand, Eugene Brophy. He froze his rear on the spring-cold pavement with three other Negroes. He was thin and strong, with a good attitude about work, but was always ready to scrap. Elliot watched him say something flippant to a Statey who kicked him in the back. Elliot trotted over.

"Elliot," Ned said. "Wait!"

"That's my uncle's hand," Elliot said.

The Stateys pulled batons.

"Whoa, now," Elliot said. He raised his hands. "I don't mean any harm. Elliot Caprice. My uncle is Nathan Caprice. Caprice Family Farm."

"Nig farm," a Statey said.

"This is my field hand," Elliot said, pointing to Eugene.

"Three dead bodies in three weeks," a mad-looking Negro said. "No one says nuthin' about that, tho."

"Ain't that Elliot Caprice?" a woman across the street said. "You know this his old boss's mess. Damned money lender owns the po-lice."

An older cop walked over. He had a strong gait. He was solid voiced, using clipped vowels that resonated high in the nasal passages. He had a perfect cop mustache. He smelled like a career man.

"If he works for you, you pay his fine."

"What did he do?"

"Public drunkenness."

"Eugene," Elliot said. "You been drinkin'?"

"He knows I haven't," Eugene said.

Elliot reached for Eugene's arm. Mustache's hand went to his gun. Elliot backed away. Ned stepped up. Mustache's hand didn't move.

"Ned Reilly," he said. "Southville County sheriff's deputy."

The state cops laughed again.

"You got coloreds dropping like flies in Southville, Deputy," the Statey with the fat mouth said. "State decided to crack down on vagrancy."

"This isn't the way to do it," Ned said.

"Ned," Elliot said. "Be easy."

Ned, who wasn't listening, pointed in Mustache's face, and Mustache got nose to nose with him.

"I know your type, Reilly," Mustache said. He looked at Elliot and then Eugene, with a sneer. "You caught the disease."

"You think we don't know you, Caprice," Mouth said. "We read the colored newspapers, too. The brass makes us. Plenty of stories lately about you, and your Jew, as if the two of you are some kind of good guys now."

"The loan shark's son," Mustache said. "Champion of the darker race."

"He's my citizen." Ned put his chest in Mustache's face. "He comes with me."

Ned pulled Eugene away. "I'm bringing you up to your area commander."

"I am the area commander," he said, laughing. "Put the name Meyer in your report."

A bottle crashed on the wall behind the cop with the fat mouth. Another soon followed. Ned pulled his service revolver. The Stateys backed away to save themselves. Cars on the street began rocking. The sound of glass breaking filled the air. Someone threw an ashcan that collapsed atop the state police wagon. Ned opened the rear passenger door. Eugene dived in. The Stateys huddled themselves inside their squad cars. Elliot hopped in, and Ned peeled away with his sirens blaring. He made a left into an alley, then a right back out onto Main, where they watched as George held an angry crowd at bay, with the power of Jesus, apparently.

"Lord, bless the speech makers." Elliot opened the back door. "Mind if I borrow a shotgun, deputy?"

Ned nodded. "Rock salt."

Elliot pulled the shotgun from the rack in the back seat. "Imagine that."

The front window of Saperstein's Pharmacy shattered.

"Stay back," George shouted. He had his gun pulled.

"Eugene," Elliot said. "Run on home and sleep in the covered porch. Don't wake up my uncle."

Eugene left the cruiser and took off down the road.

"Be careful when you go back for them State boys, Ned, 'cuz I know you gonna."

"Someone has to police Southville."

"How about someone paid to do it?"

Ned whipped a U-turn and sped back whence they came. Elliot sprinted the entire eighty yards to Abe Saperstein's family-owned business praying that his best friend, the Reverend Sheriff of a crooked farming town, wouldn't be strung up before he got there.

CHAPTER 7

While not quite sure he was the best person to hold off the crowd of angry drunken Negro field hands, at least a third of whom had been fired by him at one time or another, Elliot pushed through the bodies with the shotgun. When the butt of the gun hit a few backs, the crowd thinned, but the gab thickened.

"Fool think he a cop again," one said.

"High yella used to collect for the Jews in Roseland," said another, an angry woman who picked up a rock. "Y'all got a finger from my daddy once."

A dark, red-eyed Negro who missed a few haircuts raised the bottle of corn he had been nursing and stood behind her. Elliot pickled them both with one blast of the rock salt. Much of the mob ran off. Others left ruefully, especially as the Stateys rolled through, ten deep, swinging batons.

"Y'all, disperse!"

"Fuck you, High Yella," someone said from the crowd, which kicked off more taunts, many the old classics, such as crazy, bastard, criminal, and so forth. Listening much in the way one chooses to stand in the rain without an umbrella, he almost forgot George was in up to his neck. He turned to rescue him and noticed, across the 4-way stop, a green Buick Skylark speeding away, driven by a dark-skinned, bowler-hatted individual. The thought of the Turk's goons reaching as far into Southville as the business quarter unnerved Elliot more than playing lawman.

He walked over to George and took hold of him by the arm.

"You gonna have to ask for a budget allocation, Reverend," Elliot checked his shells.

"You're understaffed."

George tipped his hat with his large, judgmental finger and wiped his brow with a handkerchief.

"Where's the body?"

"Behind the building," George said. "Abe covered it up."

"You're not supposed to let him do that."

"I know, Elliot."

Elliot followed George inside.

Saperstein's was quaint back when no one knew any better and would have accepted any old shack to sell them aspirin. It had a soda fountain, with a coin-op jukebox with rhythm and blues hits. Abe was stocked full of nifty little colorful toys sourced from the many different Jewish tchotchke merchants he knew off Maxwell Street in Chicago, the western end of the Black Belt where Jewish immigrants once found shelter and opportunity amongst Negroes. Many a poor parent found a last-ditch birthday present at Saperstein's, purchased on credit if necessary. It served as Southville's first library. He kept the largest selection of books and periodicals outside of Rockford, even those meant for Negroes. Abe wouldn't separate them, but stacked them in alphabetical order, so Newsweek would stand somewhere near the Negro Digest.

Doc Shapiro practiced at least one day per week out of the druggist counter, delivering tetanus shots to everyone during growing and harvest seasons. He birthed emergency babies in there at least twice. More than a few folks have crawled along the asphalt to make Abe Saperstein's the last face they saw on the unforgiving prairie. Abe was good Jewish folks, even if he charged too much for colored folks' hair care products. Fancy green awnings that were nicer than any other business in the district. The orange Rexall sign that lit up the dark off Pettingill Road. Saperstein gave a care.

Abe was seated on a stack of the early edition of the Chicago Daily Defender. He held a red hand to his head. Elliot snatched a bottle of hydrogen peroxide from one aisle, searched for an applique, found a box of feminine napkins, and ripped them open.

"For the life of me," he said, grunting. "I'll never understand what gets into these sorry sons of bitches."

Elliot ran over to Abe, pried the peroxide bottle open, and irrigated his head wound, catching the run-off with the gigantic maxi pad. He dabbed at the cut, checking for glass and debris.

"I saw you in the paper," Abe said. Elliot bristled. "You look good."

"That's some of Mikey Rabinowitz's nonsense. He can't keep in enough trouble, that one."

Abe winced. Elliot smiled kindly and patted him on the knee. He made sure to keep his voice low. George used the phone behind the soda counter to call Doc for medical assistance, which was close enough to overhear them speak of dangerous things the sheriff of Southville County shouldn't know about the Jews of Roseland.

"What happened here, Abe?"

"How am I supposed to know," Abe said. "I come in the back, I see a dead colored."

"We's considered Negroes now, Abe."

Abe squirmed in his seat and averted his eyes. Elliot irrigated his wound again, and it stung him again.

"Uncle Abe," Elliot said. "Always used to let me read the bad magazines."

"I keep a stash in the back," Abe said, and then he spoke Yiddish.

"You see them, across the street. Those Walgreen's people? Izzy wouldn't have let them break ground so close before."

"Bold," Elliot said. "Like the Turk's play on Izzy. You wouldn't be borrowing from the competition, would you?"

"Shtum," Abe said.

"Tell me now, Abe." Elliot lowered his voice even more. "Izzy cut you off after a bad streak at Balmoral again?"

"It was the White Sox." Abe looked away. "And, no, I'm not in with the Turk. I'm not nuts, boychik."

"Who bets the Sox, Abe?"

"They're winning this year."

"Abe, I just saw one of the Turk's goons nearby, and they've never come this deep into Izzy's territory. You haven't noticed there's a short paper war on?"

"Hey," Abe said. "It ain't me. I'm off ponies, and the Sox."

"Gonna get yourself killed betting on the White Sox." Elliot stood and walked toward George.

"Best team in baseball," Abe said. "We had Negro players, too, same as the Dodgers. Sam Hairston—"

"And Bob Boyd," Elliot said, under his breath.

"And Bob Boyd," Abe said, wagging his finger after Elliot as he and George stepped out to where death came and went.

CHAPTER 8

The bedsheet was bloody where the head would be. Abe was kind enough to cover it up, although whatever a bedsheet was doing this close to Sugartown was best left unexamined. Instinctively, Elliot traced foot paths for signs of egress.

"Shame to see Abe taking a dip in his fortunes," Elliot said.

"Good Jew folk."

"Mm, hm."

Members of the drunken elite stumbled past. George held them off with a stern look and they made tracks. He snatched the bedsheet off the body with a preacher's indignation, revealing the bloodied hump of a scowl-faced Negro. His skull was bashed in at the left temple. His eyes were wide open, as was his jaw. His tongue dangled. Everything was black and blue.

"Lord Jesus," George said. "I'd bet there's no wallet on him by this point. Coroner Shaffer is on the way. He may be able to identify him somehow, but it's Sunday."

"George, that's Mose."

"Mose?"

"Boysaw?"

George drew a blank.

"He was my running buddy before Uncle Buster made me come to church with you."

George looked again.

"Oh, Lord," George said. "That is him. The bad one."

"Everyone was bad compared to you, Georgie-Boy. We lost touch. Always wondered what happened to him. I'll be damned."

"He and his mother came to church for a while."

"Maybe they should've kept coming."

Elliot noticed something, knelt down, and lifted Mose's dead chin from off of his dead neck. He was garroted.

"If we didn't already know it was a short paper war on."

"What is all this?"

Elliot lowered his voice.

"If you shabbos goy for Izzy, you don't go around the front when you pick up from Jews. I'd come get it from them out the back."

Elliot walked over to the garbage receptacles, looked behind, reached, and produced a small, white pharmacy bag.

"Keeps up appearances," Elliot said. "They got the jump on him there."

Elliot pointed to where the gravel was most distressed. When examined, heel impressions pointed away from the door, toward the alley.

"He was ambushed, by person or persons who understands how Izzy operates."

Elliot looked at Mose's left hand.

"Aw, naw, Georgie." Elliot pointed to Mose's wedding band.

"Who did he marry?"

"Prolly Corretta Williams. I was friends with her, too." Elliot grinned.

"That nice girl who stayed off Pettingill Road?"

"Same."

"I always wondered how she's doing."

"When you ruin her morning tomorrow, ask her."

Elliot turned to walk away.

"I need you to talk Rabinowitz into voting down the ordinance."

"My name is Bennett, and I ain't—"

"Elliot."

"George, these mob types don't take over small towns to actually govern them. Besides, I got no rapport with the man."

"He just helped you with the farm."

"In unincorporated county," Elliot said. "Where you don't exactly patrol."

"Elliot, if the state police department comes this harvest, with tensions as they are, Southville will explode."

"I remember your father and the church supporting the Stateys shooting up the town in years past."

"That was before law enforcement became the strong arm of segregationists."

"I think I liked you better when folks weren't coming to church."

"Elliot, you used him to enlarge yourself—"

"I asked him for help to save my uncle's life."

"Now, ask him to save your uncle's town."

"You asshole. I'm out here working as your deputy, for free, during this harvest and all you have is judgments."

"Elliot, step up."

"Georgie, I am even with Izzy Rabinowitz. Do you understand what that means to me?"

"I know it doesn't mean you should get away with it."

Dead Mose watched as Elliot lost the argument.

"Fine, I'll try."

"Appreciated."

"They teach you low blows in divinity school, Reverend?"

He walked past Dead Mose and back into Abe's pharmacy, where Doc Shapiro assisted Abe. They bantered about the Sox's chances. Elliot patted him on the shoulder as he walked out the door, away from the crazy, and headed for home on foot, content to have a long think, if not a good night's rest.

He remembered the night they fought. Buster Caprice didn't expect to find Elliot in the tack room of the barn. He should've been down at Bradley Poly, learning, instead of tending the land that provided for him all his life. Asleep, hung over, bloodied and battered by the Champaign-Urbana police, he woke up with the business end of the shotgun from the kitchen in his face.

"You light-skinned, arrogant, mess of a boy," he said. "You vile, wicked child."

Again, he brought skin color into it, that dark, old man. Always making issue of the difference. He especially hated to be showed off as his little light-skinned nephew. Come, look at the pretty nigger read and write. Do your homework in front of them. Speak good. Part your hair in the middle, like a white boy.

Be a token.

White distributors and grocers came to check in at market regularly. Buster Caprice's bushels moved faster than his white competitors. Same string beans as everyone else, but it just felt a bit better to support the colored man with the adorable, fair-skinned child.

The quality of the product should have been enough, same as making the grade at Bradley should've. He was just so tired of being theirs, for the taking, whenever they wanted to change the rules. That old man may have abided it, but he never could. The one time he tried, the Champaign-Urbana police department beat him into unconsciousness.

The mule strap dug harshly into the palms of his hands as he pleaded for Uncle Buster to stop hitting him. A harder whack across the forearms as he protected himself, then two more for protecting himself. It was in the shouted demand for Elliot to move his hands, he could hear it. The will inclined to more than discipline. The sense that someone strikes not at you, but at something inside you.

Elliot snatched the mule strap right out of Nathan Caprice's hand, rose to his feet, and pushed him out and onto the barn floor. Buster fell hard. Elliot stood over him, shouting. Buster wasn't listening. Elliot kept screaming and gesturing with that strap. Buster shouted back and kicked away from him.

Buster raised the shotgun.

Elliot raised the mule strap.

"You struck me," Buster said. "I got the right to kill you, boy."

"You been killing me, old man."

Elliot tossed the mule strap into the tack room. He walked out the barn with his back to his uncle, pulled forward to destiny by the rage in his belly rather than backward by regret and sorrow. He didn't quite know where he was headed leaving that barn, but then not knowing is how most young fools wind up heroes, and so he kept walking, same as he walked in from a harsh night, took to his covered porch, and went to sleep in the house of that same old man he once hated to love, but now loved enough to tend his fields.

CHAPTER 9

The yellow Westclox Moonbeam Buster had the nerve to gift him for Christmas, with a straight face, sat noisily atop the upturned wooden onion crate he used for a nightstand. He fumbled for its off switch, gave up, and slapped at it until the vile wail of morning ceased. Breakfast wafted in from the long hallway. Elliot hoped it wasn't scrapple.

Through the cold walls of the unfinished covered porch, he listened to field hands complain about the workload, as in the lack thereof, and the string beans that were slow to yield. Elliot found his corduroy house shoes, walked down the long hallway, and stepped into the kitchen.

"Morning."

Uncle Buster stirred grits as scrapple fried in bacon fat inside a cast iron skillet. Elliot kissed him on the cheek anyhow. He looked out the back door. Buster already had the field hands picking from the wax bean field, which had come in a week earlier. On the table, the day's edition of the Negro Digest. On the first page, something about the McAlpin Family Fund's control over Negro land on the south and west sides of Chicago.

"He's relentless," Elliot said.

Frank walked in from the outside.

"Wax beans are still coming up fine." He shook his head. "Nothing popping just yet, Uncle Buster."

"The string beans will come in, Unk," Elliot said.

"They better."

Elliot reached into the painted cabinet for the bottle of Jim Beam.

"Don't forget me."

Elliot grinned as he made his old uncle a cup of Irish coffee, their private tradition which marked the beginning of harvest. Elliot handed his uncle the cup and they toasted.

Elliot answered the phone.

"Caprice Family Farm, Elliot speaking."

"Elliot," said Mike Robin.

"Whatsatchasay 'dere, Mikey?"

"The firm needs you in St. Louis today."

Mikey had that sound in his voice.

"I'm preparing for harvest," Elliot said.

"I wouldn't ask, but—"

Elliot cupped the receiver. "Unk, are you able to spare me today?"

"That's fine," Buster said.

"Okay, lay it on me." Elliot pulled a pencil and a notepad from the junk drawer.

"Do you remember our discussions about DeSoto-Carr?"

"Not gonna lie, no."

"It's a neighborhood in St. Louis, basically all Negro. The city wanted to raze the slums for years, but it wasn't until the Feds coughed up a gazillion dollars to build new homes for the white, middle-class adjacent area, that they got their chance."

"Go on."

Frank Fuquay walked over to the stove and looked in the pot.

"Take it," Elliot said.

Frank took a fork and Elliot's former breakfast to the table.

"We have a colleague, Frankie Freeman," Mikey said. "She's going after the city of St. Louis over it. She's building a solid case, and I think there's overlap between her action and one I'm considering against Chicago's

Housing Authority."

"What about Chicago's Housing Authority?"

"The City of Chicago needs to give up land for a new campus project for the University of Illinois."

"Your alma mater."

"The ballrooms in Navy Pier were a bit drafty."

"Where will the campus go?"

"The Greek Delta," Mikey said. "And parts of Maxwell Street."

Elliot put down his coffee cup before he dropped it. He lowered his voice.

"Mikey, are you insane," he said. "The Greek Delta is damned near under the control of the McAlpin Family."

"We can't help that," Mikey said.

"We can't help not paying the rent if John Costas pulls up stakes. Think about it."

"They've planned a development at the easternmost edge of Bronzeville to accept the first folks who lose their homes to that bullshit. Giant cinderblock buildings. Courtyards. Egress and transportation."

"Sounds like something Negroes would want," Elliot said.

"Until the Feds take away the money, as they did in St. Louis, and Negroes are left in public housing. In a few months, the liquor stores come,—"

"Alright, Mikey. Alright."

Elliot's heart raced, which meant getting involved was a stupid idea. Over the line, Elliot heard him close his office door.

"What don't you want Elaine to know?"

Mikey sighed. "The Chicago Bee is running a new story on us. It won't be flattering. There'll be ink on my connection to organized crime."

"They're coming after you about your pap."

"Finally."

"Who tricked on you?"

"Name's Marion Bradshaw. An old classmate, incidentally. He'd never admit it, but I've heard things he's said behind my back in movement circles."

The line went so silent, Elliot thought Mikey hung up.

"What's the matter?"

"The Bee's gotten some old rumors on you, related to the Black Belt, and your connection to Bill Drury. They want to make the point you sold the Negro underworld to Kefauver."

Elliot ran his fingers through his hair.

"I have friends over at the Chicago Daily Defender. They've offered to help."

"No more propaganda, Mikey."

"The Defender is exposing organized crime in the Black Belt. Mattie Smith is the lead crime reporter over there. Her footman you may know. Vernon Jarrett."

"Christ on the cross."

"You tangled with him."

"When I was stealing dirt on the cops and giving it to Bill Drury. He came after me for a scoop. I don't like him, so I wouldn't give him anything."

"He hasn't forgotten. They want you to verify a few leads they have about law enforcement initiatives, not against Negroes. Early rumors."

"No, Mikey," Elliot whispered.

"I'll sit with you, as your attorney. Anything that's privileged to Kefauver or our office, I'll squelch."

"Mikey."

"We need this, Elliot."

Elliot thought of the string beans that were late coming in. He drank more Irish coffee to wash down his sick feeling.

"So, for some poor Negro land holders, we're taking on the University of Illinois, our keystone client, and the Negro Underworld?"

"Yes."

Elliot shook his head.

"Give me the address."

CHAPTER 10

Earlier that week, the harvester's timing belt slipped, for the second time. Uncle Buster was so attached to it, Elliot's only option was to track down the parts for the ancient thing through the manufacturer. Just another thing to do.

Property developers came around to casually discuss selling. The bastards checked around town. The Seed and Supply told them the family's account was past due. The bank man mentioned the recurring fines for the county ordinances that choked off the labor force. Elliot shut the door in his face, although he couldn't shut out his words. In his zeal to win back the farm for his uncle, he had forgotten the barely hanging on part of being a landholder. The pride that goeth before the fall, the season where man learns land is lure, and what one owns also owns them, for generations.

As he traveled westbound over the Eads bridge, across the mighty Mississippi River, he felt a tickle of fear in his gut. Perhaps it was the sudden return to St. Louis, where he almost bit it in County Jail as Sheriff George and Mikey rescued him. Where he learned the young Frank Fuquay was his karma. It just may have been motoring through the South. Laclede's Landing was the Plymouth Rock for French folks who claimed St. Louis for themselves, although they forgot to bring along enough *liberté, égalité,* and *fraternité* for colored folks. Most likely, it was the tail he shook off in St.

Louis. Black sedan. Dark hat. Maybe a raincoat. They were easier to spot than the Klan, the Feds. Someone was turning up the heat on him.

He pulled Lucille into a parking space out front, stepped from the car, put on his gray sport coat and matching fedora and walked in the building. So many sheepskins adorned her hall; Hampton Institute, Howard Law, prestigious private academies. Frankie Muse Freeman was intimidating before Elliot found her in her office, in her close-cropped bob and horn-rimmed glasses, poring over documents atop her desk, which included a large area map of St. Louis's neighborhood quadrants.

"Ma'am," Elliot said.

He gave her a bow of the head, out of respect. He knew a librarian that made him feel this way. Miss Morehead, who once spent a half hour with him during detention teaching him how to properly turn pages.

"Caprice, come in," she said. "Have a seat as I get these files in order. You understand I was reluctant to share, as we have our own planned action against St. Louis. Your man Rabinowitz doesn't take no for an answer. He's tenacious. I'll give him that."

She tapped atop a stack of green accordion files.

"He's happy to receive them, Miss Freeman."

"He's happy to seek a judge's action," she said. "I don't need the grief."

"He figured you for a colleague."

She laughed before she pointed to the chair. Elliot imagined it falling down and playing dead. He sat.

"Elaine Critchlow and I, until somewhat recently, traveled in the same circles. Business socials. Community meetings. Lovely woman. Negro professionals have to stick together, you know."

"Yeah," Elliot said. "Like the Daughters of the American Revolution."

"The attorney, however, is something of a nuisance."

"Nuisance?"

"His action against Marion Bradshaw's community redevelopment project in Chicago—"

"Ah, I see." Elliot eyed the file stack.

"We've butted heads on a few occasions where we sat with the larger movement. We're also butting heads here, on his planned action against the Near West Side Improvement Association."

Freeman took off her glasses.

"I felt stupid for not seeing it. How did he get Robin out of Rabinowitz?"

"Seems like you have a stake in that new Chicago Bee article."

"The Chicago Bee sent me their story for comment. I only mentioned if it's true, his involvement harms the movement by casting a pall on his finances."

"That sounds Shakespearean, Miss Freeman. Fawning publicans, 'n all."

"Helpful attorney, comes from out of nowhere, colored office girl, eager to meet everyone important." Freeman shook her head. "The press began to ask questions."

"Around the same time this Bradshaw fella gets angry with the attorney."

"Marion Bradshaw is a friend to the movement, in many ways."

Freeman pulled an edition of the Chicago Bee off her desk and handed it to him. It was folded to an article on Life and Style. Elliot skimmed through the article, where Marion Bradshaw was likened to men in his money network such as Dr. T.R.M. Howard, and the Honorable Elijah Muhammad, fat cat Negros who were standing up for the little man and woman in the ghettos of America. The coverage went on and on about new, state-funded business initiatives as if they'd save every kid with a grandparent what once picked cotton.

"An influence peddler," Elliot said. "How grand."

"The movement is made up of all kinds."

"I'm seeing that more, every day."

"Caprice, I'll get to the point," Freeman said. "Somewhere, in these files, is information on a scheme to defraud hundreds of Negroes out of their homes in St. Louis. It's backed by dirty money in the region. It's damned near indecipherable."

"What's that got to do with me?"

"You once collected for Rabinowitz's father, didn't you?"

Elliot held his cool, same as he did whenever he heard a question about Izzy, after the first time he was asked by Uncle Buster, and had the beige beat off him for telling the truth.

"Miss Freeman," Elliot said. "I couldn't tell you the first thing about how Izzy Rabinowitz hides his money."

"Although you could once," she said. "According to Elaine."

"Elaine?"

"That's what she said. In fact, the way the Bee has it worked out, more than a few of your known associates slipped past Kefauver. Still, others didn't."

"Kefauver already had what he needed on the Outfit. They were using me to purge dirty cops."

"As if Chicago produced any other kind."

"You seem to know a lot about things that got me shot, and my friend Bill Drury killed." Elliot leaned back in his seat.

"Drury, and his columns, was good to Negroes," Freeman said.

"So good, my shoulder still doesn't work right. I'm not sure I care for you poking around after something Elaine told you in confidence. Even if she shouldn't have."

"Negros have a powerful network, Caprice. Same as you have your powerful white friends in Chicago, like investor Jonathan Costas-McAlpin, the biggest client in your office, who opposes Marion Bradshaw's sway on the Campus Planning Committee."

"I wasn't aware they tussled."

"Near West Side Improvement Association controls a lot of property that's adjacent to the new University campus. Adjacent to McAlpin family property. Perhaps you weren't aware of that, either."

"Lady, I'm the office hoi polloi."

"Is the hoi polloi invited to Margaret McAlpin's society mixers for the Chicago Police Department's women's bureau?"

"Wouldn't know."

Freeman walked around her desk and toward Elliot, wagging that finger.

"I'm betting you helped Rabinowitz skate past Kefauver," she said. "Years later, his money shows up in a land grab deal that destroys hundreds of Negro families in St. Louis, and you can help me finger him."

"Why would I?"

"To prove you aren't the white man's nigger."

Elliot stood straight up.

"I ruined my life fighting the Chicago Outfit, dotsie."

"You spent two years under the heel of Senator Estes Kefauver and the Special Agents assigned to him because you had a criminal record going back to when you were thirteen, when you first took up with Isadora Rabinowitz, the attorney's father. How are your crops, Caprice? The bloodiest harvest in Southville history, if the Chicago Bee is to be trusted."

"I bet you get the Bee delivered to your front door."

"Listen to reason. You've seen things others wouldn't have been able to. That's why you're valuable to Kefauver. Now, be valuable to Negroes, before you begin to pass through the inevitable intersections."

Elliot stood and put on his hat.

"Pull Mikey off Bradshaw. Rat on Izzy Rabinowitz. Next time you need a linchpin in your gambit, Miss Freeman, don't ask me."

Frankie stood, walked around her desk, and confronted him.

"Alright," she said. "I'll buy you wouldn't know how Rabinowitz hides his money." Her eyes quivered. "Listen, get your man off Bradshaw. He's connected, and powerful, even for a Negro. Especially for."

"Mikey says Bradshaw is bad news."

"If you let a Rabinowitz tell it. Think for yourself."

That was all Elliot could take. He snatched the files from her desk.

"If there's anything you can make out in there," Frankie Freeman said. "Feel free."

Elliot walked out of her office, out onto the street, hopped in Lucille, and rode like a bat out of hell to Springfield.

CHAPTER 11

Elliot could relate to a Negro woman in the law who had to scrap for everything she had, only to be compelled to cede space to a white boy like Mikey, who figured he had every right to fight on behalf of Negroes because he dared love one. Frankie Freeman desperately depended upon the backing of the Marion Bradshaw's of the world, who had an up with power message, and long green. And why wouldn't other Negroes be interested to know who paid for Mikey's University of Illinois tuition? No one complained about the Chicago Bee's regular stories against Negro organized crime.

What he wouldn't abide was her shallow offer to fall in line with Negroes who didn't have questionable racial allegiances. It reminded him of the bank's evil. Once that old man was on the hook for their easy money, ordinances against Negro migrant labor passed. A few months later, property developers come knocking with tales of doom and gloom. Sell to us, they say, and you can be free of the fear of losing it all. Join us, Frankie Freeman said, serve the elite Negro order, and you won't have to be around when Mikey Rabinowitz loses everything.

He sat in courthouse traffic reflecting on the David and Goliath days of Michael Robin and Associates, when they'd lay into a guilty white business concern over something innocuous, claim disproportionate hurt because

Negroes suffer enough, and leave with thousands of dollars for their clients, the bigots fuming in their wake. Since his uncle took him to his first harvest market, he knew the only way to get white folks off you was to hurt them in the wallet. He missed those days, when he could make fighting dirty cost more than playing fair.

He parked in front of the nondescript office building with the limestone façade on Grand Avenue and walked inside. Still running on the fumes of his anxiety, he bounded up the marble until he reached the second-floor offices of Michael Robin and Associates, Wills and Probate. Except the sign painter was there changing the name of the firm to his given name, Rabinowitz. He was leaning into it, the feisty ess-oh-bee. Outed as the son of the Rainmaker, Isadora Rabinowitz, the man who stood against New York, Chicago and St. Louis as short paper king, and he was going with it.

He looked at his name at the bottom of the glass.

ELLIOT N. CAPRICE, Service of Process, Investigations

It was still there, although Mikey had threatened to take it off once Elliot could only be in Monday through Wednesday during the harvest. He opened the door to the main office, which bustled with activity. Elaine ran back and forth across the hall to the storage closet. Her shoes were off. Her attitude was up. A new associate from Mikey's law school was hired to assist with case preparation. Charles was thin as a rail and a nebbish, if a colored kid could be such a thing. He dressed as if he didn't have someone at home who cared about what he looked like, with a plaid shirt, an unmatched tie, and a worn beige sweater. Elliot handed him the stack of files.

"He's been hot for these."

"Charles, I'm taking you shopping."

"So I can look like a gangster? You have messages."

"From what folks I won't be calling back."

"John Costas-McAlpin," Charles said.

"Conflict of interest. Don't want to get yelled at by Mikey. Toss it."

Charles did. "Margaret McAlpin."

"Did she say what she wanted?"

"She's prepared to settle her fee?"

Elliot thought about scrapple.

"Tarbaby," Elliot said. "Toss it."

"The seed and supply called and said you're right, you were overcharged. They'll take it off your bill, which is past due."

"Mm, hm." Elliot took the message and balled it up.

"Earline Gray. Gettysburg 4-5789."

"Who's that?"

"The lady you served for in Rockford? She said he's defaulted again. She may need you to track him down."

It hit Elliot in the ribs.

"And if you're looking for the attorney, steer clear. Marion Bradshaw, from the Near West Side Improvement Association, is in the attorney's office, threatening to sue."

"You're kidding."

"Certainly not kidding," Charles said. "And he's fuming."

Shouting from Mikey's office bounced off the ceiling.

"I want to get a look at this guy for myself."

Elliot walked past Charles, through the stacks, and into Michael Rabinowitz's sparse, yet now larger, office, where within stood a smooth, brown Negro, tailored black suit, starched white shirt, cufflinks, the sort who looked like he knew the commuter train schedule by heart. He had a Duke Ellington-mustache. Waves were hard-brushed into his hair. Silk tie. Class ring.

Talented Tenth.

"I beg your pardon," Elliot said, as he walked in mid-argument.

"Elliot," Mikey said. "This is Marion Bradshaw."

"Caprice," the slickster said. "Your name precedes you."

"As does yours." Elliot looked to Mikey. "Frankie Freeman loves this guy."

"Marion thinks I'm going to be convinced Negroes who lose their homes to wealthy institutions are somehow better off, as long as they're Negro institutions."

"You've seen the planning and development budget for the housing projects in the State Street Corridor. That's thousands of brand new homes for the Black Belt," Marion said, stretching out his arms in appeal. "That's far better than most of them live right now."

"Negroes were doing fine in the corridor before the university's planning agenda started," Elliot said.

"It's unpaved Maxwell Street property."

"Because it's home to the poorest of the city, who've been kept that way."

"We're not all as fond of Jew Town as you, Caprice."

Bradshaw squared his shoulders, claiming more space for himself in the room. Mikey walked around his desk. His lips were stretched across his face from tension, little pink streaks of rage across his angry mandible.

"The legal action is fair, Bradshaw. We were contacted by the families whose rights your improvement association violated. They hired us. Talk to them."

"I can't, now can I, since you represent them, through your ambulance chasing in the Defender, and your false promises."

"You're doing a double-end run on these people's land rights by herding them into cheap land deals."

"And getting away with it, because he's every Negro's brother," Elliot said.

"They're getting fair profit compared to the Belt. Don't thwart Negro progress at the expense of some poor, dirty-soled, country Negroes you Jews can intimidate."

"I better leave," Elliot said, gripping his hat as if it were Marion Bradshaw's neck. He rose from his chair and flew out the door so swiftly, the pompous octoroon had to pivot before he was flattened. Elliot could hear them over the wall of Mikey's office as he marched down to Elaine's.

"Your legman is jumpy, Rabinowitz."

"It's his backbone," Mikey said. "Sometimes it gets to him."

CHAPTER 12

He walked into Elaine's office. It was once Mikey's office, but shit rolled downhill at the Law Firm of Michael Rabinowitz and Associates.

"I expect it from Mikey," Elliot said, as he closed the door. "Not from you."

"Don't come in here with all that," she said. "I have my own problems."

Elaine stood before maps as tall as herself as stacks of papers lined her desk. It was stifling hot. One window was boarded up the last time a brick sailed through it. The other was cracked and nailed shut. The building management insisted if the firm didn't change their clientele, namely the civil rights folks, repairs wouldn't be timely. It wasn't out of spite, but vandals arrived weekly. The firm was becoming a bad pony, even to the landlord.

"I just came from your hero's office, Frankie Freeman, where she beat me over the head with the fella I used to be. She insisted I speak with Mikey about dropping the action. She also had a lot to say about my past, which she says she got second-hand, from you."

Elaine sighed and leaned back in her chair.

"Elliot," she said. "I'm sorry, but you have to let them see you."

"I got a bullet in my arm for each time I did, hon. I told you, I don't want any part of it." Elliot plotzed in one of the creaky mahogany chairs. "Jeez,

Elaine. I told you that stuff about Mikey's father in confidence. I trusted you."

"I know, and normally, I wouldn't have spoken about it—"

"But the movement?" Elliot fished into his pocket for a hand rolled. "So, some Negroes want something, all other Negroes gotta pay for it? Is that the thing?"

"You know how Michael is, Elliot."

"I do, which is why you can't prepare that filing. He doesn't understand us. Just what he loves about us. It makes for bonkers decisions, every damned time."

"The case is legitimate, Elliot. These eight families—" She tapped on the stack of documents on her desk. "—are being railroaded into public housing with their land stolen underneath them. We need Frankie Freeman to make that case stick on the Federal government. I needed something to offer her."

"I'd have never done that to you."

"This work thrives on sacrifice, Elliot."

"I'm a person, Elaine, not your currency."

"It won't stop in Chicago. They'll continue to reduce the value of these folks' land until they give up."

"Then they should just sell," Elliot said. He squirmed in his seat.

"That sounds odd from someone with a string bean harvest to get back to."

"Wax beans," Elliot said. "String beans aren't in yet."

"What are they waiting for?"

"Water," Elliot said. "Got a drought on."

"The weather has been lovely."

"Exactly. One person's lovely puts another person's farm out of business. That's what y'all movement types don't consider. Always want the sun to rise, never wonder who gets left in the shade."

Elliot shook his head.

"What about the river?"

"String beans need more water than that," Elliot said. "Just another thing to worry about."

"Another thing you get to decide for yourself." Elaine smiled.

"None of that implies permission to feed Frankie Freeman, or anyone else, my secrets. She's no friend to this office, whatever y'all figured. Mikey is really blowing it, especially with this Marion Bradshaw nonsense. Don't prepare that filing, Lanie. This one stinks, so bad."

"Tell that to the colored families getting chewed up and spat out by their own."

"Elaine, Chicago has been disputed territory since DuSable conned the Indians out of it. I ran those streets. I policed those streets. The folks crying for their fair share won't care half as much once they get it. Same as it ever was."

"They don't get to drive Negroes to the bottom of Lake Michigan just because they want us out of sight."

Mikey walked into the office.

"When can you get to Chicago? Bradshaw has agreed to open his transition files to us, so we can verify housing is allocated for the families."

"Will that stop it?"

"That'll half-way stop it," he said. "We'll back off completely if the Maxwell Street eight get fair market value for their land in cash."

"Cash, that this firm gets a cut of."

"Exactly," Mikey said.

"You're in the lion's den, bargaining with the lions." Elliot shook his head. "It won't be until next week. Say, I don't know if you remember Moses Boysaw. You were a few years behind in school."

"Kinda, sorta. Lettered in sports."

"And being ugly. Abe Saperstein found his body behind the pharmacy. He died collecting for your pap. Looked like retaliation."

"Oh, goddamn it," Mikey said.

"I see you're all broken up."

"I got Mattie Smith from the Defender on her way with Vernon Jarrett.

That pen of hers is a viper. I don't need this bullshit."

Elliot stood up and pointed toward Mikey's chest

"Now that you're getting the big press, the underworld is an inconvenience for you. It's a bit more so for Mose's wife and kids."

Each met the other with a hard stare.

"Attorney Robin," Charles said, yelling from the next room.

"Shit," Mikey said, and he walked out.

"I'm sorry," Elaine said. "It wasn't my idea."

"It was your reasons, Elaine."

Elliot turned and left the office.

CHAPTER 13

At the front desk with Mikey and Charles stood the journalist Mattie Smith, shortish, with the biggest eyes Elliot had ever seen. She had three whites, as the Japanese called it. Her pupils, limpid pools, filled with accusation. There was a bit of cream in her coffee. Something indigenous in her nose bridge. Maybe a Louisiana gal. Her green and black jacquard head scarf came off with a subtle twirl and she shook out her short, manageable style. She was all business, with her pencil and notebook in hand before she opened her coat. Though she was little, Mattie Smith took no shorts.

"Elliot Caprice," Mattie said, extending her hand. "Lucky for you, our photog was thrown off a train somewhere in Joliet for being colored."

"Imagine that."

Behind her entered a tall drink of lemonade in brown gabardine. Lighter-skinned than Elliot by a full shade, his face was as narrow as a crowbar. He was long and lanky, and tall enough to feel justified in leaning over folks and asking the most inappropriate questions, especially when they had been drinking all night, like that fateful night in 1949, when Vernon Jarrett—high-yellow, Negro press-uppity, and one of the fiercest commentators the Black Belt produced—learned every fair-skinned Negro wasn't interested in going to the social club ball, much less winding up on the business end of his opinion columns.

"Caprice," Jarrett said. He extended Elliot a handshake. "You'll be joining us for the interview, I understand."

Jarrett and Smith walked into Mikey's office. Elliot sat on the credenza behind Mikey's desk. Smith adjusted the hem of her skirt and leaned forward, on her haunches. She jutted out her pencil at Mikey as if she were in a duel.

"You said you arranged for Caprice to give a statement on his activities in the Kefauver Committee."

"Past activities," Mikey said.

"So, he's not involved in the rumored new committee?" Jarrett flipped his notebook open and began scribbling.

"That's what I keep telling everyone," Elliot said. "I hoed one row, and that was the Outfit's reach into the police department. Once that stuffed suit in Washington pulled up stakes, they left me out there to rot."

"May we print that?" Smith scribbled.

"Not unless you want me to die," Elliot said.

"Elliot," Mikey said. "You can confirm that."

"I can confirm that, as an Assigned Detective of the Chicago Police Department, I was contacted by special agents under the control of the Kefauver Committee on Organized Crime as an informant on other police officers who may or may not have been involved in organized crime, racketeering, extortion, gambling, prostitution, narcotics trafficking,—"

"Money lending," Smith said. "Short term, specifically."

He looked to the floor.

"When I was a youngster—"

"From the time you were thirteen years old," Jarrett said, checking his notes. "Until you were an adult."

"I worked, in various capacities, for Mr. Isadora Rabinowitz, known as the Rainmaker."

"We are aware," Smith said. "Your days with the Roseland Boys put you in connection with varying members of Chicago's Negro criminal underworld, did it not?"

Elliot's mouth went dry. He looked to Mikey.

"That information would be privileged to the Committee, and to my client's counsel, representing him against the government, should they come calling about the manner in which they abandoned Elliot Caprice after using him to drive a wedge between the corrupt CPD and the Chicago Outfit."

"We're printing that," Vernon Jarrett said, fiercely scribbling.

"Fuck me," Elliot said. "Right in the face."

"Is Caprice willing to go on record about the existence of the FBI's General Investigative Intelligence Program?"

Elliot shook his head.

"No," Mikey said.

Smith sighed.

"Does Caprice have any information about the newly announced FBI Top Hoodlum Program?"

Elliot thought of the conspicuous tail he picked up driving to St. Louis, and the body man he made as he served process in Rockford. He hadn't felt any heat on him since Costas Cartage went up in flames, figuring all was square with the Feds, at least until Kefauver would ring his bell again.

"Theodore Roe, numbers king." Jarrett pointed at Elliot. "You knew him?"

"Everyone knew him," Elliot said.

"You were known as his friend," Smith said, her eye line and jawline set.

"He was an ostentatious kingpin, as they tend to come."

"Jarrett here is ostentatious," Mattie said. "He's not saving my life down in the basement of Joe's Deluxe Tavern, in Bronzeville."

Elliot's throat closed, likely to spare him the danger of making any sound to confirm a thing no one should have known. No way Mattie Smith is waggling that fact in front of him unless she had someone giving her the truth.

"I knew Teddy from my work with Izzy Rabinowitz," Elliot said. "I was a kid."

"Teenager," Jarrett said.

"When I ran short paper for the Roseland Boys, I made drops to certain members of the Negro underworld, Roe among them. Ask me about any of them, I got nothing. I was a bag boy."

"For your father," Mattie said, to Mikey. "You're on record."

"I'll confirm I knew Elliot Caprice was once under the thumb of the Roseland Boys outfit, which, like all criminal organizations, preyed upon the young and impressionable. I can attest he is a model citizen, and his service record with the Chicago Police Department can prove that."

"His arrest record is impressive," Mattie said.

"He knew who all the criminals were, what they were up to, and where to be to get them." Jarrett threw his hands up.

"This is what I'm telling you," Elliot said, to Mikey. "It's all cheap shots and low blows with these types."

"I didn't invite you here to railroad Elliot," Mikey said.

"We just want him to be on the level," Mattie said.

Jarrett pointed at Elliot. "He's a cagey guy."

"You level with me," Elliot said. "Who'd you squeeze back in Bronzeville, Smith?"

"That's from the kind folks at the Chicago Bee. They're running it on page six. How the FBI's Top Hoodlum Program is being used against Negroes, underworld, and otherwise."

The urge to leave consumed him, so he angled toward the door. Mattie Smith stood and faced him at his back.

"How this works, Caprice, is we have the information we need to be a trusted source, should the lies come. You say the Chicago Bee is lying on you? Get your truth out there. That's what the help of journalists gives you. The public's trust. Right now, no one trusts you, because they don't know you."

"You're the second sapphire today who thinks she does, sister," Elliot said, marching forward, finger out. Mikey hopped in at the nick of time.

"Unfortunately, that's all the time we have." Mikey grabbed Elliot's arm and opened the office door.

"I'm sorry," he whispered.

"You should be," Elliot whispered back.

"We need more," Smith said.

Vernon Jarrett stood, fuming.

"Going to find a white boy to sell your story to again, Caprice?"

Elliot slapped Jarrett's pencil and notebook out of his hand. Jarrett put up his dukes. Elliot walked out, listening to Jarrett complain.

"Caprice, you jackass," he said. "The Negro has a right to know!"

CHAPTER 14

He stood in the backyard of Izzy's large, first-story ranch bungalow, waiting alone in his nicer church clothes, those Uncle Buster made him pick out with Miss Betty, over at the five-and-dime. Before then, he'd wear them to church with George's folks on Sunday—each and every Sunday—until Elliot found repentance for cursing Father Reilly, referring to him as a 'mackerel-snapper,' and saying aloud the Vatican was all a con. The Caprice Family Farm hadn't enjoyed a plentiful harvest, and whatever the fat cats called the Depression was on. If the boy had opinions about the papacy, he should've perhaps kept his quiet until he was finished chewing the post-Mass free breakfast in the basement of St. Margaret of Scotland.

He stood outside, alone, while other folks were inside Izzy's fronchroom. They didn't look like his family, or Doc's kind of people. They were men Elliot saw from around town. Dark, quiet men, who only ever spoke with each other. Men who walked ahead of the women in their lives, not like Uncle Buster, who often worked with them, and took his orders from them, like Miss Betty, and Mamie Roberts, who cooked in the kitchen at Molly's dad's place four nights per week. The Jews around town were nice to him, at least more than colored folk were, and mainly because Doc was his *enkel*. The Irish were occasionally nice. The Germs were nice, always, but real mean about it, especially those who ran the school, all the Weitzs, and Schulzes, and folks who gave a care, and a full stack of detention slips, and raps of the ruler on *ze* knuckles. The boy had his issues with just about everyone in Southville, but it was the Jews who never gave him the business, except now he's the half-colored kid not allowed in the house. It wasn't as if any of those mopes were the Southville Chamber of Commerce. Elliot wondered what was the deal. Izzy walked out the back door and gave him a black felt, eight-panel cap.

"Very funny," Elliot said.

"It's cold out here," Izzy said. "You got the truck."

"Yeah," Elliot said. "We're going and coming right back, yeah?"

"Trust me, kid," Izzy said. "Leaving is the only part of Maxwell Street you want to see."

The drive was for shit. It was cold and raining, and the farm's truck barely made it through the slog to the west side of Chicago. It looked like Sugartown. Same damned mud, at least. Same lost souls. What was different was presence. Maxwell Street teemed with Negroes, none of whom gave a care about the white folks in their midst. Colored folk arrived to Southville mainly to get flush in farming, so most found their act right quick. Those who didn't found Sheriff Dowd's cell, or worse. In Southville, colored folks were pushed around by whites who, although they suffered the same ills, jeopardies, and injustices as Negroes, somehow imagined themselves superior.

On Maxwell Street, Negroes folks did the pushing. Black faces wandered the shops and ramshackle roadside booths along the main row, openly taunting shopkeepers over their prices and selection. Colored shoppers boldly shouted racial invectives at white faces. "Don't Jew me," this and that. "I heard how y'all folks do Negroes," and so forth.

Elliot made a copper, an actual policeman, as colored as he wanted to be. A Negro woman called him over to a booth selling housewares, shouting something about the shopkeeper's inherent capacity for dishonesty. The cop pushed through the muddy walk and entered the fracas. The white folks seemed nervous. Colored cop, making white folks tap dance. He'd have to tell Georgie about it when he saw him next.

Jewish shopkeepers leaned in their doorways side-eying their colored competitors. Colored and Jewish women hung out of their windows, catcalling and jiving. Uncle Buster refused to travel to Chicago, not even for baseball. Now here Elliot was, watching the world grow up from the mud underneath his feet. As they walked, Elliot made a colored hooker in a dirty dress and coat as she was followed into her tenement by a john so dirty it was hard to tell his race. The hooker stepped back and let the john in first. Elliot sucked his teeth. Izzy glimpsed his line of sight and patted him on the shoulder.

"You saw that?"

"Yeah," Elliot said. "A fella in Sugartown got hemmed-up like that, once. Doc couldn't save him."

"You're only as safe as your habits," Izzy said.

Elliot mumbled it to himself, silently, like practice. He wanted to feel how it would feel to say the same words.

"You remember Tommy the other night," he said.

"Yeah."

"He looked the wrong way, at some tail, and a mark gave him the slip. When he reached for him…"

Izzy stabbed the air with his thumb.

"Tough guys bleed, same as poor stiffs. Keep your wits. No fighting over something stupid."

"What's that supposed to mean?"

Izzy grabbed Elliot's right hand.

"You got a bad temper, kid. That'll get you killed anywhere, but especially here."

Elliot made three well-dressed colored men outside a frantically busy saloon. Outside was a painted wooden sign which read Porges Hall. Each man wore a purple tie. They mean-mugged Izzy.

"Go on ahead, kid," he said. "Tell them we're here."

"Why not you?"

Izzy looked at him. "It doesn't work that way. Hop to it."

Elliot trudged through the mud to the first step. Each man had an attitude similar to ol' Tommy Eight-Panels. Rugged, scarred, menacing, yet convivial.

"What you need," said one man, who never let his hand leave his breast pocket. Elliot couldn't take his eyes off him. He was smooth, in every way, like a drink of water. His mustache was perfect. His clothing matched, from top to bottom. The other two covered him. They were button men, Elliot figured, just like in the crime shows on the radio. Colored button men, guarding a colored tough. Never in his wildest dreams would he have imagined.

"I'm Izzy Rabinowitz's—"

"Tell my brother the Jew, and his nigger, are here."

"Aight, Aitch-tee."

One of the toughs walked off.

"We been needing that money, Izzy," H.T. said. "You got my brother in there with his *schmeckle* in his hand."

Izzy smirked at the sound of Yiddish out of H.T.'s mouth.

"You try coming here in this shit and making it on time."

"I gotta live in this shit, and I'm here on time."

"Because you Jones Boys own the place."

"Not for long," H.T. said. "If you keep Jewing me with the green."

Elliot followed Izzy into the saloon, which was nothing like Duffy's Tavern. Most tables were packed with thick-bodied, business-suited, colored men with a few white fat cats sprinkled in. He watched faces and tuned into bits of conversation all seemed about something dangerous. "Unions," this and that. "Voters," and such. Everyone was loud, until they were quiet, with their hushed tones and exaggerated gestures. On many of the men, their suits and ties looked top-notch, but their shoes were cheap.

Elliot and Izzy ventured up the large staircase to the second floor.

"Wait there," Izzy said, before he entered the ballroom, which hosted the fights that night. Izzy backed one of the guys, some punchy Irish pug named Doyle.

For what seemed like forever, he stood by the male head holding the bag. It stunk like the Middle Passage up in there, but he hung outside it, like a shlep, because that's what Izzy told him to do. Elliot didn't quite understand why he dealt with the colored folks by himself, on the colored side of the saloon, where Chicago's colored elite consolidated power, but he'd do it, if only for the chance to see the city for himself. Except it really stunk in there, and no one was coming for the money.

Fierce men, possessed of strength and cunning, wandered the shadowy halls, backslapping each other and speaking loudly, with coarse language. Everyone spoke over each other. No one walked. Everyone barreled forward, abruptly shouting passionate invectives. A slap box fight broke out. A circle formed. A few mean-mugged Elliot as they crisscrossed the sawdust floor. He'd never seen colored men so cocksure. Scarred hands adjusting boutonnieres, pinky rings glistening under the pot lights. Two white men beating the snot out of each other in the ring in the next room as black big shots negotiated openly with politicos and organized criminals from the colored power elite.

His nervous, and finally queasy gut compelled him to enter the fight hall. Elliot imagined what the waiting room to Hell must've looked like. Everyone in attendance was coarse, and rude, and drunk, and dirty, and hopeful. He heard their slurs, and not just for his own skin tone as he pushed and shoved to get through the crowd, but those of the Jewish set who were in full attendance watching Art Lasky pop the snot out of the Irish. Izzy said the fight wasn't supposed to go four, but "Dangerous" Amos had the nerve to be on his feet in the eighth, sustaining the pummeling he was taking from the toughest Jew ever in boxing. Black and white, screaming, howling, tearing up their betting slips or rejoicing. Pushing, shoving.

Elliot walked up to Izzy.

"I thought you said someone was coming for this money?"

Izzy stood and shushed him.

"Don't say it aloud."

"What else they gonna figure is in here?"

Elliot shook the bag. Izzy grabbed it from him.

"Ugh, that frickin' mouth. Go wait where I told you." He threw the bag back.

"It stinks out there," Elliot said.

"Stinks in here. Now, beat it."

Elliot turned and stormed back out into the hall. As he returned to his putrid post, a tough stepped to him. He was sharply dressed in black wool, with a pearl tie pin stabbed through the green, silk plume around his neck. His skin was somewhat pale himself.

"Fuck me, right in the face, it stinks over here." Elliot cased the halls hoping to find his mark.

"Hey there, lightskin," he said.

"Who you callin' lightskin, fair as you is?"

"Whatcha lookin' fuh?"

He had a stubby nose, with eyes which sloped at the edges and cast downward. He stared at Elliot with his chin in his chest. He had tough guy features like a Negro, but he was so pale, they didn't fit. His lips were thin, much how Elliot's were full. He could pass, for Jew at least, especially with his big ol' ears, like Doc's, which heard everything, including Elliot accept Izzy's job offer. Doc wouldn't look at him as he left. It made him nervous.

"I'm supposed to stand here and wait for George Jones."

"Giveadam?"

"Do I give a damn about what? Bother someone else."

The tough laughed. His big hat flopped on his head. "You don't know Giveadam? You don't know George."

"I know he ain't you," Elliot said.

"Who's the bag for?"

He reached for it. Elliot snatched it back and gave him some face.

"Not you. Hands off."

"Alright, alright, lightskin."

He needed that money to reach Jones, so he'd get his fee. It was supposed to be easy work, until the mud. He needed Izzy to feel compelled to pay, as a white man's promise during the Depression was nothing to depend upon. He needed to perform. He needed to eat something other than beans and salt pork.

"Hands off."

"Teddy!"

Teddy with all the mouth straightened up quickly. The man speaking was large, dressed in gray, pinstripe, with a chain that draped out his vest pocket into his trouser pocket. He looked like a banker. He was coarse, and strong. No one could take their eyes off him, their reactions a mixed bag of jeers, sneers, or cheers.

"Where the hell is Jones?"

"Which Jones we talkin' 'bout, DePriest?" Teddy took off his hat and wiped his balding head. "Kid's right. It fucking stinks over here."

"Aitch-tee," DePriest said. "It's too many of them high yella sons of bitches. That sister they got is fine."

"As may wine."

"Who the fuck is this?"

"The Jew's nigguh," Teddy said. "Here for Giveadam."

"Oh," Elliot said. "I get it."

DePriest pointed in Elliot's face. "This little muthafuka? What turnip truck did he fall off? Got a name, high yella?"

Elliot didn't want to give his real name. He already stole his uncle's pickup truck to make the job with Izzy, who didn't want to drive his own car. He couldn't have a secret trip to Chicago get back to him, even if it would help them make the bank note.

"Nate," he said. "Nate…White. Yeah, Nate White, and I guess you ain't George Jones neither, so kick rocks."

The Negro big shot grabbed Elliot by the collar. "You want to get smart with me?"

"Oscar," Teddy said.

Elliot flicked his wrist. Out came a small caliber pistol. He looked at his hand. He'd been practicing it, over and over. He hadn't figured he'd do it. Sure, he pretended with it a hundred times, and even got it right in the mirror once or twice, but just then, he did it, same as what Izzy did at Doc's. He laughed, and realized everyone in that hallway pulled a gun, too.

"Be easy, lightskin," Teddy said. "Don't do nothin' rash."

"Boy," DePriest said. "You know who I am?"

"This here is King Oscar DePriest," Teddy said.

Elliot looked him up and down.

"King of what?"

"Everywhere you walked through to get here, little pink muthafuka. I'm a Congressman."

"I got your kingdom all over my new Florsheims," Elliot said. "Maybe pave some of it, your highness."

Teddy Roe's face broke. He laughed. "This boy is insane."

Inside the hall, it was fight waffles, and everyone's blood and skin went in the batter, race be damned. Amos Doyle, that dumb Irish nutjob, was still on his feet taking Art Lasky past the tenth, seven rounds more than promised. A guy in the hallway got into a fight with a man over his bet. The fight ended when the man who owed made the man who took his bet eat his own lit cigar. Izzy stood up ringside.

"Pull up stakes, kid!" He drew his hand across his neck and pulled his gun. "Get out of here!"

"No."

"Hey," Izzy said, as he ran toward the door. "Scram, I said. Take the bag and get back to the truck."

"Bullshit. I need that money."

Elliot marched off, yelling as loud as he could.

"Which one of you is Jones?"

He made it to a doorway that was cracked open, stopped, looked inside, and was startled as a shortish, red man fell down the stairs into the vestibule. Two large, menacing colored men, one caramel, one deep mahogany, ran down the stairs, seized him and yanked him out the stairwell and into another room. Double-doors swung open, and closed, and open, after they put his face through it. Elliot followed. Two colored men inflicted horrors upon that third colored man the likes Elliot hadn't before witnessed, not even in Southville. It was the look of panic on the man's face that shook him. The certainty in his eyes his goose was cooked. His backpedaling did nothing for him. His pleas to be regarded as kin of the same skin, ignored. The shiny, slick fat cats that followed behind the bruisers, all colored and powerful, encircled him, descended upon him, and devoured him.

Also inside was another man strapped to a chair—black wool suit, purple tie, carnation in his lapel—he sweated his prayers all over his perfect grooming. He just didn't say a word. He couldn't, what, with the knotted handkerchief across his mouth. He watched in quiet panic as they put a bag over the pleading man's head and cut him stem to stern with a knife, slowly, deliberately.

"You next, tough guy," Mahogany said to the dapper man, shaking toward him what seemed to be a fillet knife. "We hear about you and your brothers and how wild y'all are, but we ain't studdin'—"

"Which one of you is Jones?" Elliot blinked in disbelief at himself.

"Beat it, unless you wanna end up like this fool here."

"Aight then," Elliot said. "So much for the dough Izzy Rabinowitz said give him."

The poor fool strapped to the chair craned his neck and murmured indecipherably. Elliot walked over to him and yanked the gag.

"Which Jones you say you lookin' fuh, young fella?"

"George Jones. Goes by Giveadam, I guess."

"That'd be me."

Elliot thrust out the bag.

"As my hands are tied," George Giveadam said. "You gonna have to hand them fellas the bag."

Elliot handed the one tough with the threats the bag. The other tough checked him up and down as if he was crazy.

"It's all here," Caramel said.

"This street rat saved your life, Jones."

Mahogany took a few wrapped bundles of cash out the bag before tossing the skin back to Elliot, who shoved out his hand. Everyone laughed, exempt the dead colored man.

Mahogany untied Giveadam Jones with the fillet knife. He stood up and mucked with his outfit. Nearly filleted, and the first thing he did was fix his clothes.

"When I say beat it, you little shitheel—" Izzy said, as he kicked open the doors. "Holy shit."

Izzy watched as George "Giveadam" Jones walked past the living, and the dead, as if he wasn't just nearly killed.

"That's seven points," Izzy said, to Giveadam.

"You said five," George said.

"That was before we had to risk our lives delivering it to you." Izzy pushed Elliot on the shoulder. "Let's go."

"You said they'd tip me," Elliot said.

"Shtum," Izzy said, shoving him forward.

Giveadam fixed his boutonniere before slipping back into the ruckus as if nothing ever happened. He glad-handed and played up his power, even with the Chicago coppers teeming in, pulling the poorest and least connected onto the muddy walk and arresting them, or beating them senseless. Izzy and Elliot evaded scrutiny by exiting through a fire door and out into the alley, where Uncle Buster's pickup sat.

"That's a tough little crazy muthafuka, Rabinowitz," Teddy said, calling out from the back door. "See you around."

"I should fire you," Izzy said.

Elliot looked at the mud all over his shoes.

"You should pay me those two extra points."

CHAPTER 15

As soon as they pulled away the back window of the truck shattered, the rocks thrown by the mob of angry bettors who bounced around the cab. Amos Doyle hopped out and pushed them through the mud as Elliot steered. Face still bloodied and battered, mud all over his back, openly scolding himself over the loss as every hot-blooded colored on Maxwell Street chased after Izzy's money, and Amos's neck, for not taking the dive.

"*Mischling*," Izzy said. "You got a hard fuckin' head."

"What I tell you about that *mischling*-shit?"

Amos was outside the truck, laughing, watching as about twenty angry colored men slogged after them. Running two-miles per hour. Angry. Slipping. Izzy hopped out the cab and helped push.

"Floor it, Kid, for fuck's sake!"

Elliot put the hammer down. He watched in the rear view as Izzy and Amos were splattered with the mud that'd soon be the death of them. Amos grunted, dug deep, and pushed hard, laughing and shouting encouragement to himself, like a cornerman, or madman.

Finally, they reached Archer Boulevard, where they'd follow the railway out to where white Southside money kept everything smooth and pretty. Izzy hopped in.

"Get in here, you dumb Mickey!"

Amos stopped pushing and fell into the mud before getting up. He hopped in the truck, therefore smashing Izzy against Elliot, who looked in the cab. Mud was everywhere. Mud, from Chicago, the city that killed his pap, Uncle Buster's brother. The city he had no permission to be in.

"It's the mule strap for me," Elliot said.

Elliot looked out the shattered window and noticed immediately all the colored men stopped running. There was no reason, as far as he could tell. The pickup was moving nearly walking distance. Amos's body weight wasn't helping. This menacing crowd of sore losers, who meant blood and ruin, just slowed down and stopped as Izzy crossed some imaginary line.

"This is Amos Doyle," Izzy said.

"Pleased to meet you."

Amos grinned. It made his lazy eye twitch. Elliot thought he was the weirdest guy he'd ever seen, but then he thought that of Izzy too.

"I'm sorry about blowing the match," Amos said. "You think—"

"They're gonna be sore at me, and want you dead?"

"I was thinkin', if they'd just give me another fight."

"You're punchy," Izzy said.

"I know I was supposed to go down," Amos said. "I just couldn't, ya know. Lasky is the toughest, Jew or otherwise. Before the bell, he looked me in the eye, like, hard, ya know? Like, maybe he wanted a real fight. Tough fella. Smart in the ring."

"You nitwit," Izzy said. "We had it all arranged."

"But I could take that guy," Amos said. "You can get me a fixed fight with him, why can't you make a clean one, Iz? C'man. The Outfit knows I'm good for it. How many guys have I broken for you fellas already, huh? C'man, Izzy, just set up another fight."

"If they don't kill us both."

"Relax, Punchy," Elliot said. "Bubbie there will just nag you to death."

"Shaddup, you. You're not in the clear. Amos, you better just come out to the sticks with us. I'll straighten it out. You ain't getting another fight. It's ovah. Besides, your eye is half out your head, as it is."

"What I know is fightin', Iz." Amos was sad.

"Didn't I say I'd figure something out?" Izzy shook his head. "Now, you just got your face beat in and you pushed a truck through the mud. Figure you'd had enough, already."

"I'm hungry," Amos said.

"He ain't stopping," Izzy said.

"Take him to Duffy's," Elliot said.

"Sounds Irish. Where's that?"

"Where there're a bunch of Mickeys like you. You'll fit in. Good food. Maybe they'll sing you a limerick, like your wee ma did, you goon."

Izzy tried laughing. Elliot did, half-heartedly. Amos dropped his chin. Everyone knew the Outfit were going to be sore, and that would cost Izzy, dearly.

"I'm really sorry, Izzy."

"I said I'd take care of you, Amos. Stop talking about it."

Elliot stared out the window, transfixed on the gaslights they passed, one by one, as the pea-soup from Lake Michigan's night tide began swallowing the streets. Miles of mud. Every face an angry one. Chicago seemed like a ball of pain and suffering for anyone, but especially someone colored.

Elliot found it beautiful.

Once they reached Sugartown, Elliot parked in back of Duffy's Tavern and let Amos and Izzy out of the pickup truck.

"Don't forget my money," Elliot said.

"Just give me a second to get this meathead situated."

"Now," Elliot said. "This frickin' truck is gonna be the death of me, Izzy."

"Fine," Izzy said. He snatched a leather pouch from his inner coat pocket and tossed it to Elliot. "Take it out of that."

Elliot unzipped the large wallet and looked inside. It was plenty more bills than he would have seen, both with his cut and Giveadam's extra two points.

"What's this for?"

"Capital," Izzy said. "Keep that safe. I'll explain later."

Izzy walked Amos, now slowed and hobbled from the effects of the day, into the back of Duffy's, where Molly, standing at the back door with her father, Sean, helped Amos inside. She looked back at Elliot. She didn't seem happy to see him, standing there, covered in mud, delivering criminals in the back door of her father's place, where she had her own fucking problems. He waved to her. She waved back. Sean called to her. She disappeared.

Buster Caprice was on the front porch with the mule strap already in hand when Elliot pulled up the gravel road. He asked questions and didn't wait for answers, swinging harder whenever Elliot would articulate, or gesticulate. He grabbed Elliot by the collar, marched him outside, and into the barn. He told Elliot that, so long as he wished to behave as an animal, then with the animals he'd sleep, until he learned his place in his house. That's when Elliot Caprice realized his place in his uncle's world.

At least he didn't cry out. Uncle Buster may have gotten tears out of him, but he wouldn't hear his voice in anything but protest to his old, blind, calloused ways. Everything hurt across the swath that mean black goat laid on him with that strap. As he rubbed away the pain in his backside, he felt the wallet Izzy gave him for safe keeping. Told him he'd explain later. What if Buster found the wallet? What then? When Izzy came for it, if his Uncle had it, what'd happen?

The mule brayed. Her black eyes against her dark coat caught moonlight from the hopper in the roof. He remembered the fella at the Seed and Supply selling her for cheap, since she was black and would overheat out in the sun if left in the fields for too long.

"Sorry I woke you up, Betty."

He hid things there he'd stolen from Saperstein's from time to time, underneath the hay, where the mule would shit and piss. Buster made that his job, as punishment, for his stubbornness. Elliot led the old girl out into the barn floor, grabbed a shovel from the hook on the wall, and cleared away the hay and feed and shit. He stuck the shovel in the ground, pondering how wild his day was, its perils, and its potential. No one pushed him around. He pushed, and the world of men, far older and stronger than he, saw him. Someone finally saw him.

Harder and harder he shoved the earth on his uncle's land into the corner where the mule once took her naps. For hours he worked, with each farm implement he could find, making the perfect hole, four feet by two feet by three feet deep. He found the old barn door that fell off the rusted hinges he never hauled out and tossed it atop. It fit. He lifted it, tossed the money sack in the ground, and covered the door with hay, at least until he could figure something better. He led the mule back inside, made her comfortable, replaced her feed and water, and closed her door.

He couldn't have been asleep long before Uncle Buster opened the barn door.

"Get up," he said. "Clean that damned mud outta the truck."

Buster grabbed him by the collar and swatted his rear.

"That's for the back window."

"Boss," Frank said. "Boss, wake up. It's late."

CHAPTER 16

Elliot woke in his bed on the covered porch. Frank Fuquay stood over him.

"Sorry, boss," he said. "The harvester is completely dead."

"Well, we knew it was any day now. How's that old man taking it?"

"Haven't told him yet."

"Now you're learning, Francis."

Frank left for the kitchen. Elliot rose from his bed and took to the long hallway. Uncle Buster was in the kitchen enjoying coffee and reading the day's edition of the Defender.

"I see you're alive," that mean old man said. Elliot grunted something to the contrary. "That's what happens when you don't sleep, boy."

"I'll sleep when you Negroes let me."

Elliot found the coffee pot. Buster turned the page.

"Whaddya know?"

Elliot looked over Uncle Buster's shoulder. In the Society section of the Chicago Defender was a puff article featuring the exploits of Michael Rabinowitz and Associates, crusaders for Negro suffrage. It dominated the entire right margin, prime real estate for anyone in the western hemisphere with an agenda involving America's cast-off slaves. In the accompanying photo, Mikey looked smart in his wire-frame glasses which hung onto his slightly Sephardic nose, banker's haircut, perfectly cut suit, same as his daddy.

"Is he running for president?" Buster shook his head.

"He's fiddling, as Rome burns."

Although the Civil Rights Movement was commonly depicted as a boy's club, Elaine made it into the shot. Smart white dress. White gloves. Notepad and pencil, standing at Mikey's desk as he sat in his chair, the both of them looking serious about Negro equality. Her face was strained. Her smile was proper. Her eyes were vacant.

The phone rang. He reached for the call.

"Caprice Family Farm."

"Elliot, it's George."

"Whatthatchasaythere, Georgie-boy. Everything alright?"

"You're attending the wake for Moses today?"

"I am," Elliot said. "Aren't you?"

"I can't," he said. "I have business out in Quad Cities."

"Business involving your movement, I take it," Elliot said. "At least tell me you questioned Chester."

"I haven't seen him."

"Because you have to go find him. Georgie, you're killing me, as dead as I wanna be."

"I'm reminding you about your promise to talk to Rabinowitz."

"It was Izzy what got Mose killed, George. I'm not asking him to fix a vote over the man's dead body."

Elliot felt Buster in his business.

"The vote is this week, and the bank has sway over the county board," George said. "Without Rabinowitz, it'll pass. You know what that means."

Elliot remembered the harvest, and pondered the ordinance, and its value to his own family's struggling farm. He thought of harvests long ago, where police bullets flew.

"Look here." Buster handed Elliot another paper. It was the Chicago Bee, the same edition Mattie Smith portended. First up was Mike and Elaine's relationship, once again, depicted as wanton, and salaciously intended.

"They didn't believe me," Elliot said, shaking his head. "Georgie, I gotta scram."

"Talk to him, Elli—"

"You're a stunning example of a hypocrite, you know that, George?"

Elliot hung up and sat at the table. He continued reading the short piece on his involvement in the firm, played like a Notable Negro piece, but with well-blended smears of his character. It detailed his reputation as a good cop in the Black Belt with some accuracy, contrasted against his life as a teen member of the Roseland Boys gang, and what that particular gang meant for Negroes, which was never anything good. They had intimate understanding of Izzy's rise to power in Illinois, and how he once held some sway over the Jewish crime contingent of Maxwell Street.

The next paragraph shook his bones. It was suggested Elliot spared himself persecution for the death of two crooked cops after the assassination of Bill Drury by handing over to Kefauver Theodore "Teddy" Roe, numbers kingpin of Chicago, and Robin Hood to the Black Belt. It included an insinuation he had Izzy Rabinowitz spared as well. A photo of Teddy's funeral parade ran at the bottom, reminding everyone in the ghetto who they had lost to the bullets of Sam Giancana. Nothing mentioned how Teddy was responsible for his own corruption, and the pain and trauma it dealt the Black Belt. Only that he was, once, a well-intentioned man of the community despite white society's confinement of him to a life of crime.

The final paragraph made him reach back into the cabinet for the bottle of Beam. At the same time the murder of Teddy Roe was being plotted by Giancana and other confederates and associates of Tony Accardo, reigning power of the Chicago Outfit, Elliot Caprice was running around the streets of Chicago like a fiend, doing the leg work of none other than Jon Costas-McAlpin, head big shot of the University Campus Neighborhood Planning Commission.

At the bottom was an old snap of him in uniform. He was thin, around a buck thirty-five, and lean. Perfect coif. Cop mustache. White shirt. Yearbook photo.

"Christ on the cross." Elliot sighed. "I look like a straight."

"I think you look good." Buster took back the paper.

"What y'all got there?" Frank closed the ice box. He was chewing. He looked over Uncle Buster's shoulder. "Dare I say you're looking rather *Untouchable* here, boss?"

Frank raised his eyebrows. Uncle Buster laughed and took back the paper.

"Don't talk with your mouth full, Francis. And maybe don't use up all the hot water in the shower this morning?"

"Church clothes? Or fighting clothes?"

"Funeral clothes."

"Gotcha, boss."

Frank walked out of the kitchen. Elliot sat in his funk. His morning coffee hadn't even kicked in and already he was eating it.

"Funeral today?"

"Wake," Elliot said. "Moses Boysaw. Remember him?"

"His mama was sum'n," Buster said. "How'd y'all fall out?"

"America," Elliot said. "I feel bad I'm only going to the burial so I can talk to Izzy about the ordinance."

"The state police have never come down here for anything but to hurt us, boy."

"Half the violence in town is due to Izzy, and he has the vote to get the Stateys to do the other half."

Buster looked at Elliot, stood up, went to the junk drawer, and returned with scissors. He cut out a part of the page.

"What are you doing?"

Elliot rose and followed his uncle into the living room. Buster sat on the gray and purple velour couch they discovered together at a fire sale. Elliot sat next to him as he opened the chest inside the wooden coffee table. He retrieved a leather-bound book, then carefully opened the cover.

"Which one o' y'all moved my rubber cement?"

"Frank needed it for his schoolwork."

"I'm tired of y'all touchin' my stuff."

Buster found the small roll of tape. He opened the scrapbook, with the few photos they had, and taped it to a page inside.

"Unk," Elliot said. "Don't. I"

"You what?"

Elliot turned away. Uncle Buster grabbed Elliot's hand. He spoke slowly, in a low tone which always made Elliot's guts rumble.

"You grew up doin' thangs you prolly wouldn't have, had you more time to think on it. Colored folk don't get time to think. We gotta think with our feet. You follow?"

Elliot nodded, silently.

"You thought on your feet, came up short, and did some bad. Ain't no other way to regard it."

"I helped folks who murder our neighbors for money, Unk."

"Yeah, but you also did this," Buster said, and he pointed to the clipping.

Buster squeezed his nephew's hand tighter. He was old, but he had that old man strength. The kind one develops over a lifetime of doing their own dirty work.

"I thought to invite you to my graduation," Elliot said. "It was in Chicago. I figured it was a lot to ask."

Buster nodded. He ran his fingers across Elliot's photo.

"You look good."

"I look like a dope." Elliot got up. "I got the wake to attend. After, I'm off to Chicago on law business. I should be back before dinner."

"Stop by Mamie's and pick us up some catfish."

"Okay."

"Get there before everyone else, so we get good pieces."

"Okay."

"I would've been there," Buster said. "Your graduation. I'd have made it."

It stopped Elliot in his tracks, the sound. Tenderness, underneath all those callouses.

"I know."

He walked back into the kitchen. In the skillet, covered with a plate, was an overcooked egg, some slab bacon, and a mess of scrapple. Elliot sipped some coffee, ran to the covered porch, and got dressed despite the ache in his legs telling him the worst had yet to come.

CHAPTER 17

Southville's only cemetery was in the field outside Saint Margaret of Scotland, the oldest edifice in the county. There in the unrelenting Midwestern rain, near a tall green ash tree that lost its leaves, stood the faithful and damned alike. The turnout was good despite the weather, and Mose's reputation. Mose's wife Coretta was in the rain carrying on. Even under the veil, she was fine. Elliot and Frank smiled earnestly as they approached. Mrs. Boysaw carried on as if her and Mose didn't fight like cats and dogs going back to their youth. Instead of dancing upon his grave, she leaned on the tree trunk screaming queries to the Lord about why her husband had to die.

Elliot knew why.

Miss Betty approached in a peach raincoat over a rose dress, with a smart matching pillbox hat. Percy, her clueless brother, held a matching umbrella over her perfect bouffant.

"Whassatchasay there, Miss Betty?"

"What brings you out in this dreadful weather, Elliot Caprice?"

Elliot glanced over at Mose's casket.

"History," he said. "Sorry for your loss, Coretta."

Coretta fell out, all the way, leaving Frank to catch her as she cried out to the heavens.

Miss Betty pulled Elliot to the side. "We got a collection going for the family."

"Not sure how much help I can be. We're still waiting on those string beans. They may not come in."

"Back in '37, it took even longer."

"No kidding?"

"You'll see some things, if you live long enough, Elliot Caprice." Miss Betty lowered her voice. "Mose didn't leave her with anything."

In the front row, Mose Boysaw's mother, Earline, in the second veil, where she looked after two children, a boy, and a girl, neither veiled. They sat beside her, crying.

Elliot made eyes with Izzy, who stood under his own umbrella thirty or so feet behind Mose's mourners. He looked almost sullen in his gray Italian raincoat and matching fedora. To the right of him, Amos Doyle stood, no umbrella, his cauliflower-face soaked in the rain, and perhaps a few of his tears. It was he who took care of Izzy's toughs, teaching them in the arts of grift and pain. Amos's older brother act was a con Izzy pulled on the young Negroes who ruined their lives collecting and paying upstairs to the Roseland Boys. It was all bullshit, but it still felt good having an older brother.

"What you know about this ordinance?" she said.

"Reverend Sheriff sent me to speak to the man, for his vote against."

"Do you want to vote against?"

"You see how other Negroes do us. Same with you, and the roadhouse."

"You do too much for folks who ain't your kin, Elliot Caprice." Betty jutted her thumb out at Percy. "My brother and me, we don't love 'em. We just give 'em a place to sleep until they can't pay."

"We're not white folks, Miss Betty." Elliot put his hands in his pockets. "We should want to give our own a little more."

"Nobody respects free, Elliot Caprice."

"Miss Betty, seems to me, no one respects anything."

On approach, Elliot silently rehearsed his first words. He and Izzy had rarely spoken since the entire affair at Costas Cartage, and never about that night. His critical assistance in a difficult hour endeared Elliot to him all over again and brought him closer to Mikey. As he listened to his wet footsteps, Elliot looked at Amos Doyle. The old Boston softie started bawling.

"Hiya, Elliot."

"Amos."

"I see the Big Fella with you," he said. "How's he doin'?"

"Just fine," Elliot said. Elliot hugged him and patted him on his wet back. "He just cleared the eleventh grade on his general equivalency."

"Fast," Amos said. "He wants it bad, huh?"

Elliot nodded. Amos tried getting Frank's attention with a wave. Izzy nudged him on the shoulder.

"Go say hello, will ya?"

Amos left him with the umbrella and walked over to Frank, Miss Betty, and Coretta, who turned up the waterworks as soon she saw Amos, which made his tears start up again. Elliot looked toward Izzy, standing in the rain, witnessing the destruction his greed had wrought.

"Kid." Izzy never smiled, but his eyebrows were ear to ear. "Funerals were never your thing."

"Mose was a friend, once."

"He said he didn't like you."

"What's he going to say? He's doing the job I invented."

Izzy changed hands on his umbrella. "He didn't do it as good as you."

"Obviously."

Up front, the parish priest murmured about Saint Francis of Assisi, and accepting things one cannot change, and so forth.

"Reinhold Niebuhr," Elliot said, softly, to no one.

Coretta left her seat and lunged forward, toward the casket, collapsing atop it in a teary heap. Everyone tried to comfort her, but she was having none of it. Elliot glanced at Izzy.

"What's Mose make? Four now?"

"You countin'?"

"Someone should."

Izzy glanced back at Elliot, then looked away. "Nice view you got from the straight and narrow. Saw you in the Negro Daily."

"You read the Defender, Izzy?"

"When you're in it. Nice photo."

Their eyes met. Izzy's jaw tensed.

"If I had anything to say, I would've. A long time ago."

"I know how the coloreds get chatty," Izzy said.

"We're all chatting about the dead bodies you're leaving in the fields."

"They struck first."

"One of the Turk's goons says you did," Elliot said.

"You knew, kid, as soon as I got strong again, I'd hit back."

"Izzy, Mose Boysaw was the closest thing to a civilian casualty yet."

"He was a good man."

"He was a lout." Elliot shook his head. "No way you hired Mose if things were on the level."

"No way I'd hire him if you listened to me."

"No one needs me to be the next Mose Boysaw. Or Amos, who I see is back on the job."

"What else is Amos gonna do?"

"Have a choice, maybe?"

Neither man said a word. Coretta tried crawling into Mose's casket with him. Frank and Amos tried to pull her away, but she was too formidable for both bruisers.

"Is it killing Mikey to be known as my son again?" Izzy looked down in the grass.

"It's killing him you won't accept his lady." Elliot swallowed. "And that you won't stop the short paper war."

"It didn't start with me."

"It could end with you, man."

Izzy breathed deeply of the dead and exhaled slowly. The two watched

Frank practically sit atop Coretta to keep her from going in the ground with her man. Amos returned to sobbing.

"Have your fixers in the county seat vote down the ordinance."

"Harvest is here, kid."

"Exactly, and with the way you, the Turk, and the State dicks put colored bodies in the ground, I won't have anyone to help when the string beans come in."

"That's a new favor between us, Misch."

"Name your price," Elliot said.

"Let me know what else Frankie Freeman asks about," Izzy said.

Elliot was stunned into silence. He remembered months prior, when Izzy had the telephone at the farmhouse turned back on. Perhaps he tapped the line. More like he was just Elliot's wet blanket, always wrapped all over him.

"I trust you, kid," Izzy said.

Elliot stood stock still for a moment, feeling the clutches of the Roseland Boys outfit. That comfortable squeeze of paternal warmth, followed by the sting of the whip.

"I'll let George know he has your support."

Elliot nodded in Izzy's direction. He turned and walked to Amos Doyle and patted him on his back.

"Be careful out here, Elliot." Amos wiped his tears. "And watch your back from the bowler hats. I feel it coming on. Like the old days."

Coretta Boysaw fainted in a chair. Miss Betty gave Elliot Caprice a strong nod in his direction. Frank made their goodbyes as Elliot silently watched a kid who was once his ace boon coon be lowered into the ground.

***

He pulled Lucille up the gravel access road and parked in front of the farmhouse.

"Boss," Frank said.

"Yeah, Frank?"

"Are you okay?"

"Don't make me lie to you."

Frank wouldn't stop staring so Elliot looked away. Toward the fields, the workers harvested wax beans, Uncle Buster amongst them, picking, advising, communing with his own. The sun honored them. A gentle wind gave them succor. They laughed and commiserated as they toiled. His uncle was right. He came from something. He grew from the ground his family owned, same as each and every bean.

"My past is at our door," Elliot said. "It's not leaving until I answer it."

Frank and Elliot watched as Uncle Buster led Eugene Brophy, and others, through the proper picking and sorting of wax beans.

"Once we had this old cow. She was already fallow, but she chewed the cud, so she could work the land. It floods in Mississippi, especially in the lowlands, where colored folk are forced to farm. The cow got caught in the creek. Bigger Frank didn't like to lose anything, not even a fallow cow, so he got me out of bed, grabbed a rope, and somehow hooked it around the cow's neck. He was pulling, and I was pulling and pleading with that doggone cow to help herself out the mud, but she was just doin' what a cow does. Then I slip off into the creek with the cow. She starts thrusting around. I lose my footing. I'm up to my neck in rising waters and my foot finds no purchase."

"What happened?"

"Bigger Frank told me to let go of the cow and give him my hand. I didn't want to. We didn't have money, and even fallow, that cow mattered. Plus, I respected my daddy. I wanted to save his cow."

"What did you do?"

"I slipped off into the mud and went under. I thought I was a goner, until daddy's hand snatched me by the collar and out the mud. Soon I'm on the side of the creek watching that cow drown. Bigger Frank stands me up, takes two whacks at my backside. Then he just grabbed me. He held me so tight. I couldn't hardly breathe, but I didn't want him to let me go, neither. Later on, when it was just me and him, I told him I was sorry I couldn't pull the cow out the creek."

"What'd he say?"

"He wasn't gonna lose his baby boy to save some fallow cow. Especially one without the sense to help herself out the damned mud."

Elliot smiled. "I'll be back later."

"Don't forget Uncle Buster's catfish."

Frank hopped out the car and walked into the house. Elliot silently resolved never to forget his uncle ever again.

CHAPTER 18

He passed through Riverdale, Illinois and into the far South side. There he crossed Lake Calumet. Blinded by the polluted rays of the industrial sun, Elliot pulled down the visor and found his mirrored sunglasses. He looked out at the marina, where the more well-off amongst the middle class enjoyed boating, plenty of Negroes amongst them. Underneath a pockmarked sky, boats headed out for afternoon fishing through the full-throated waterway. It was the type of fall day that made kids regret the end of summer. He had the windows down. The radio was up. Chicago was, for Elliot Caprice, a bad idea lit up real pretty.

Out to the west, just past the junction tracks, lay Old Man Pullman's railcar graveyard. Elliot remembered fetching Uncle Buster's colored newspapers from Southville station every Thursday, always delivered by one of Pullman's boys, uniformed and snazzy. Everything about Pullman's railcars once symbolized the powerful magic of Negroes aligned in yearning. To be good enough—to ride in style—was the brass ring. How would Randolph feel to see the old cars rusting underneath the massive company town clock, now dead? Elliot never forgot what Isadora Rabinowitz told Doc that fateful day. When white boys lose, they fight back, dirty.

Izzy's takeaway wounded him. He hated being spied on in any instance, but he felt especially distrusted by a man whose secrets caused him, and his entire town, daily harm. Izzy didn't have to live in unincorporated county with no services and no help, like he and his uncle. He didn't have to mind the low areas that were most harmed by his power, like Sugartown, or the outskirts, by Mamie's. Izzy didn't lift a finger against the Turk when it involved Duffy's Tavern, but kill one of his collection boys outside of Abe Saperstein's, and it meant blood.

Abe had a point. Who was Izzy to judge? Same as he'd light up over a dying man in a clinic, or pluck a teenager to be his bag man, or bring the short paper racket to a small town that had enough problems, Izzy had the natural gall to inflict the state's power on those who line the gutters. He debated the use of police force as if he were no criminal. He was passively relentless. He tapped Elliot's phone after giving it to him. The price, after the fact. That hurt. That wasn't business. That was personal distrust. Elliot considered the movement, and the angst and fervor it drew from Negroes in town, and how that could make Izzy afraid for his fortunes. It's rumored the Turk's entire crew was colored. Perhaps Izzy chose sides before Elliot had to.

Perhaps Izzy figured Elliot already had.

Bradshaw needed to prove to Mikey that each homeowner surrendering their land to the Neighborhood Improvement Association would achieve fair compensation for their property, plus guaranteed affordable housing in the new State Street Corridor project, or Mikey would be at his throat. That involved a checklist as long as both his arms and lots of paper. He made Bradshaw for the shady type back in Mikey's office and wanted to get out in front of whatever obvious con he was pulling.

Hungry, and disorganized to boot, Elliot needed a safe perch to lay low and strategize. He remembered Gladys Holcomb, proprietor of Gladys' Luncheonette, on 41st and Indiana, twenty blocks or so from the meet. She was good folks. Always appreciative of a Negro cop's patronage. There he could anchor down with a proper meal and wait out Bradshaw's appointment time, the pompous futz. The food was legendary, the service as good as could be expected, and everyone minded their own business.

The joint was located in the basement, so he'd be able to see anyone before they saw him.

Bronzeville was where enterprising colored folk took hoe to city, adapting the swinging survival first made in the rich soil of Mississippi until it found purchase in the Black Belt, that perfunctorily named stretch of the South Side where new arrivals to the Great Migration were relegated by law. Perhaps the City Hall ofays figured this was best, as they wouldn't want to sully Chicago for all its other immigrants, as if a few extra colored folks could do anything to make it worse.

He arrived just after the lunch rush and didn't wait to be seated, choosing a booth in the back next to the payphone. A young waitress walked over. She was smooth dark chocolate, with naturally red lips, and eyes of anthracite. She wore a frilly white apron around her torso. Damn if she didn't have big legs.

"Smart man, getting in here once the food is all gone." Her lips reminded Elliot of ripe plums. Her teeth were perfect. She was way too dark for Jack and Jill. Elliot took off his hat and winked at her.

"Classy, too. What will you have?"

Elliot pulled out a buck. "Dimes."

"Dimes, and a biscuit to start?"

"And chicory coffee."

The waitress left. Elliot looked around. The ornamental sheet metal ceiling and classy white-globe pendant lights were just as he remembered. The bars on the windows were more recent. He thought back to his brief dalliance as a crime fighter, before the whole madness with John Creamer, Wiggins, and Estes Kefauver. Places like Gladys's made a Negro policeman feel like a hero, rather than a pariah. Bronzeville had good folks who brought dignity to all their kind by refusing to believe white folks' ice was colder. They deserved real police, those who cared.

The waitress returned with the coffee and one of Gladys's famous biscuits, fresh and hot. She reached in her apron and slapped ten dimes on the table.

"Don't know who you're calling with all of those, but I hope it works out alright."

"See here, darlin'," Elliot said. "I've business with some colored muckety-mucks in a few. I'm trying to hang tight. Can you spot me the real estate in your section?"

"You should order something."

"How about whatever the lunch special was, if you have any left."

"Only if you eat it," she said. "I won't have you wasting away in my station."

Elliot watched her as she sauntered away. He bit into his perfect biscuit, washed it down with coffee, inserted a dime into the payphone and dialed a number from his pocket notebook.

A Negro answered. "Yeah."

"Elliot Caprice, for Marion Bradshaw. He's expecting me."

"Ay," the receptionist said. "One of y'all get the boss man on the phone."

It didn't sound professional, at all. More like an auto garage. In time, Bradshaw picked up the horn.

"Caprice," he said. "You still coming around?"

"I'm in Chicago now," he said. "I can be there within the half-hour."

"Make it an hour," he said. "After this, I won't have any more disruptions to my business."

"I get what I need, and we're clear."

Elliot hung up the phone. He noticed two young Negro girls in Catholic School uniforms sharing a pop and French fries with far too much ketchup. He remembered when he and Molly would sneak off to Mamie's together and have lime pie, back when all that was at risk was skinned knees and the tiny little chips in the black-lacquered finish of his boyish heart. He remained transfixed on them in their youthful joy.

He inserted another dime and dialed.

"Elliot Caprice, returning Jon Costas' call."

"I'm afraid we don't—"

"McAlpin," Elliot said. "Jonathan McAlpin."

He had forgotten to use the fat cat's government name. He was always calling, the lesser lord, offering Elliot little opportunities to mind his crazy family business for him. Once he took his money and friendship in exchange for giving Sam Giancana a black eye, the Greek stuck to him like he was rubber, and Elliot was glue. He hadn't the time to produce a light for the hand rolled he fished from his pocket before the wealthiest swell in the Midwest hopped on the phone, eager beaver.

"Lovely to hear from you, my friend."

Whenever Jon called Elliot his friend, it meant he had already found him something to do.

"Jon, some business of Attorney Rabinowitz has finally crossed yours. Real estate. Figured you should be aware."

"Why didn't the attorney call?"

"Well, he's taking a drubbing in the Negro press. Under siege, if you can figure it. I'm calling out of courtesy."

He cursed up a storm, in Greek, about his real estate woes. Elliot chuckled as his gorgeous sponsor served him smothered steak and potatoes with mustard greens. He put his hand over the receiver.

"Much obliged, Miss—"

"Mayretha," she said.

"Mayretha." Elliot grinned. "Thank you, kindly."

"You're welcome, Mr. Caprice, sir."

She pulled the offending copy of the Chicago Bee out her apron and sat it in front of him with her grease pencil. The girls at the table were giggling. A younger, bright-faced Negro lad with an apron and paper hat stood by the kitchen door, grinning.

"They're afraid to ask themselves."

"One moment please, Jon."

Elliot looked over at them, glared, took the pencil, and wrote his initials E, and C at the bottom of the photo. He next drew a smiley face over his own. Mayretha took it from him and laughed when she saw it. Elliot wondered whether he needed to get back to Southville so fast. She winked at him and nodded as she sauntered away, legs still big.

"This business of the firm's?" Jon Costas-McAlpin cleared his throat. "Is it the race kind?"

"It's being couched that way," Elliot said. "You ask me, it's just some ol' entitled mess, but I don't have the law degree."

The schoolgirls shrieked and laughed as Mayretha shared his mischief. As they openly stole glimpses and made private jokes, Elliot hoped he hadn't begun blushing.

"I'm free at four o'clock. The club?"

"I can make that."

"I'll tell my man," Costas said. "Go in the front."

"No thanks, Jon," Elliot said. "I don't want anyone confusing me for a big shot."

Jon Costas-McAlpin laughed as he hung up. Mayretha returned with more coffee.

"You're just too nice, aren't you." Elliot raised his cup.

"It's a ruse," she said.

She smiled again and turned from him to find something else to do.

"Miss Mayretha," he said.

She turned. He nodded.

"Fine, as May wine."

Mayretha winked and sauntered away. Elliot tore through his lunch happy it was something other than beans, or scrapple.

CHAPTER 19

Between a liquor outlet which clearly didn't discriminate, and a defunct furniture store offering easy credit in a past life, was the storefront office of the Near Westside Improvement Association, which wasn't on the West side at all, but where the South side Negro bourgeoise touched colored poverty, apparently for longer than it could stand. He walked into the crudely furnished office and could see all the way back to a loading dock, where scowling Negroes watched the doorway and each other, as they emptied trucks of pallets. No permits for wholesaling were posted, nor were any business licenses.

A few of the angry and bow-tied were holding post, taking orders from a taller, sleek-looking Negro with an athletic build, a military gait, and an obvious grudge. His bow tie wasn't a clip on. He wore glasses like their leader, Elijah Muhammad. The man was slick as an eel, with the tension of crime in his shoulders. He remembered the black Muslims were easier to deal with on the job than the other prosperity cult crazies. Elijah Muhammad was about his money, first and foremost, and knuckleheads messed with the money, hence rigid, conservative discipline.

All this made Bradshaw's own personal Muhammad that much more curious. His lips were dark, and his teeth discolored where he'd hold an unfiltered. He was a bit jittery. The sort Elliot would single out in a stop and frisk. None of his men were lighter than a bar of chocolate.

He made eyes with Elliot, then walked over.

"You're that cop, Caprice."

"Former cop. Keep that straight."

"Bradshaw's expecting you. Hang tight."

He stuck his hand out and touched Elliot's chest, his first slight. Elliot silently cataloged offenses. Bradshaw's community redevelopment office began to feel anything but. A door opened to a side office with two women who wore white gowns and head coverings. Bradshaw stepped out, looking slightly unnerved.

"Caprice," he said. "Saw you in the Defender today."

"Saw you in the Chicago Bee," Elliot said. "You're a regular man of the people, Bradshaw. T.R.M. Howard, Elijah Poole. The new colored congress."

"Caprice, you amaze me," Marion said. "You have the complexion for the protection and you're all nigger, man."

"I'm also susceptible to flattery."

"Come in."

The toughs covered Elliot until Bradshaw waved them off. They entered his opulent office. Everything else in the facility was made of cardboard, but he had the finest mahogany desk with tufted Italian leather upholstered chairs. An identical couch sat on a wall behind the seat he offered. It looked dirty. The room smelled like sex. Elliot made a back door that locked with a key from the inside. No one left the office from that door unless he let them out.

"I have to tell you, Caprice, I'm hoping you and I are able to discuss things with a bit more gentility than Michael Rabinowitz."

"Mikey's a white boy," Elliot said. "Feisty as hell, but that cuts both ways."

"I had to compete with guys like that in school," Bradshaw said. He cut his eyes. "Feels they need to be in the room each time Negroes get together and figure out their own problems. They don't let us in their rooms, do they?"

Elliot pondered the meet with Mattie Smith and Vernon Jarrett. He also remembered having never entered Izzy's house. Bradshaw sat behind his desk, like a big man. A bottle of Old Forester found its way out of his desk drawer with two rock glasses.

"What's your rank and file gonna say?"

"They're not all squares," Bradshaw said.

"They weren't when I'd arrest them in South Chicago, that's for sure."

Elliot accepted the gift of cheaper bourbon with a short sip.

"The Muslims aren't afraid of the rough stuff," Bradshaw said. He grabbed a pack of Fatimas from the desktop and slapped out a smoke. "You just have to keep them in the dark, much like your field help."

"My field hands don't look like they're off the prison bus."

"Just off the turnip truck." Bradshaw downed his bourbon and poured himself another, neglecting Elliot's glass. "That's a lot of land your family sits on. The bank had it for a while, no?"

Elliot took another sip. He relaxed in his seat. "I got it back. And it's my uncle's land."

"There's a lot of expansion to the outskirts. The notion is ofays are moving to communities like yours, not to get away from Negroes, but dagos, and organized crime. They'll start building there, soon."

"No one is running toward Southville to escape organized crime, Bradshaw."

"The point is," Bradshaw said, and he leaned forward across his desk. "This handful of Negro land holders your Jew represents—"

"My Jew?" Elliot frowned. "You're his college buddy."

"These eight families are in bed with Rabinowitz to stop Negroes from buying into the neighborhood before it prospers and Negro representation dwindles."

"It's their land value that's dwindling, so says the families, who are all colored, like me and you."

"Like me." Bradshaw sneered.

"Fuck you, stocking-cap," Elliot said.

"You think these barefoot niggers won't sell to the Jews next week? Once you're done busting me out, Rabinowitz's daddy comes in, and for less. Feels to me, that's the point."

"Mud that can drown a horse," Elliot said. "That's what Chicago had in Douglas, on the edge of the Black Belt. As soon as there's a tough rain, or snow, lower-class Negroes start dying, by the hundreds. Everything stops. Tensions mount. Knifings. Gunshots. Robberies. Grandmothers dying in their slum apartments from heat stroke, or the freezing weather sets in and no one in the city can spare colored folk heating fuel. You ever kick in the flat door to where no one has seen the family for a week?"

"I have," Bradshaw said.

"Yeah?" Elliot downed his pour of booze in one shot. "How long before you leased it to the next poor Negro, Bradshaw?"

Bradshaw poured himself a third shot without offering Elliot anything, then put the bottle away. Elliot watched his hand. It came back with a file folder.

"It's all here, he said. "It's yours to keep. I've filed this with the Planning Commission already, as well as filed a complaint with the Bar Association. I'm done with Michael Rabinowitz's harassment. Freeman talk to you?"

Elliot wouldn't say a word.

"I know she did," he said. "Stick with your own, Caprice. The Jews stuck together and got a nation out of it."

"When the movement to free Negroes needs a land-locked string bean farm, y'all can have it."

The black Muslim knocked twice before opening the door.

"Got a cop here," he said to Bradshaw. Elliot's guts went hot. "Some of the brothers were scrappin' in the alley."

"Goddamnit, Muhammad, what do I pay you for?"

"I took care of the brothers," he said. "You take care of the heat. White devil probably wants a payoff."

An exchange of loud shouting broke out outside the office. Bradshaw leapt from his desk and marched toward the door. Muhammad followed.

Elliot walked around Bradshaw's desk, poured himself another bourbon, and opened the file folder. A stack of perforated message slips lay atop the blotter near the telephone. Elliot rifled through them. One was from Mikey. Four were from Elaine, two of which predated the others.

Elliot grabbed the file folder. Underneath was a legal-sized ledger book bound in green cloth. Elliot opened the ledger and saw a list of names, some obviously obscured with symbols, and odd notes scratched into the margins. A codex lacking a codicil. The numbers spoke for themselves. It was a long list of monies either owed, or held, obviously in trust to Bradshaw.

Halfway down the third page, listed as having more than a few recent deposits, was the South Side Zionist Association, a defunct organization established to help Jewish folks turn Chicago into a homeland, at least until they got a homeland. As well-intentioned Jewish folks often wound up on the skids in the Windy City, same as anyone else, it ended up a collateralized asset of Izzy's, although he kept the community halls running and gave the kids a nice ice rink every winter. Elliot couldn't imagine Izzy being taken in by a slick head like Bradshaw, but a lot of money was at stake. He pondered whether Mikey would take on a Marion Bradshaw to strike a blow against his pap, with whom tensions increased. Mikey certainly would. He'd relish the chance.

It made his head hurt to think of it, so Elliot took the ledger book and placed it in the file folder. He marched out the door and made for the exit when he saw pandemonium on the loading dock. Elliot walked over to the locked door Bradshaw exited earlier. He knocked softly, opened the door, and entered the small room, no bigger than a pantry, where the two women in white counted short paper out by hand, stacking the bills and placing rubber bands around them. One worked from a pile of cash half as tall as a child. Another sorted through contraband; short paper, loose change, watches, rings, religious jewelry. Elliot blinked when he saw what could only be one of Abe Saperstein's pharmaceutical bags. He meant to walk in and grab it but was yanked out of the room by two Negroes in shop cloth. They held him to the wall.

"Caught this one on the move."

"Let him go," Muhammad said. He closed the counting room door.

"Sorry, boss," Elliot said. "Figured it for the head. Bradshaw's cheap liquor ran right through me."

"Sorry to manhandle you, brother." Muhammad sent off the goons. "Can't be too careful."

Elliot fixed his lapel. Muhammad slapped him on the shoulder.

"Now take a walk." Muhammad pointed toward the door. "Cop."

Elliot did so, to make the meet with Jon McAlpin, otherwise, regardless of the odds in favor of the Bowties, he'd have shown Muhammad what he could do with that hand.

CHAPTER 20

Elliot bundled his jacket as he stepped across the street and into Lucille's warm confines. Weather patterns in Chicago felt like Southville. Cold, mostly dry, until it rained too much, enough to drown field and farmer. He was worried over the string beans again when he parked at a meter on South State Street and walked west. At the corner was a young buck, no older than eleven or so, passing out handbills. The kid wore an old wool coat but no scarf. His gloves were missing fingers. Atop his head, a brim with a hole in it, at least two sizes too big. Through chattering teeth, he shouted toward Elliot.

"Hey, pally! Free information!"

The kid ran over holding up a handbill.

"What information, Moon Mullins?"

"On how the good white race can protect ourselves from the evil of mon...mon..."

Moon obviously hadn't rehearsed enough before he took to the street. Elliot snatched a handbill and read the headline, in all caps: WHITE WOMAN PAYS THE UNBEARABLE COST OF MONGRELIZATION, complete with underlines and exclamation points. Underneath, the subheading: NEGRO MONGRELS KILL WHITE NURSE ON SOUTH SIDE.

"Imagine that," Elliot said, and he kept reading. Center page, crudely typewritten: "THE WHITE CIRCLE LEAGUE OF AMERICA is the only articulate white voice raised in protest against negro aggressions and infiltrations. If persuasion and the need to prevent the white race from becoming mongrelized by the negro will not unite us, then the aggressions…rapes, robberies, knives, guns and marijuana of the negro, SURELY WILL."

"Don't forget to look on the back," the kid said.

Elliot flipped it over. It went on.

"WE ARE NOT AGAINST THE NEGRO! WE ARE FOR THE WHITE PEOPLE!"

"Oh, well, that's good to know." Elliot shook his head.

Underneath all the proselytizing was a dashed line and, in large block letters: "NO WOMAN SHOULD BE WITHOUT DEFENSIVE PROTECTION!" At the bottom of the leaflet were clip-and-mail ads for brass knuckles, a switchblade billed as deadly yet short enough to be "unprosecutable," and something called The Magic Wand Defense Chain, which seemed like tacky costumery but, according to the League, was enough for a snowflake to save her life from the hordes of coloreds out for her blood. All two dollars each, postpaid to THE WHITE CIRCLE LEAGUE, located at a suburban P.O. Box. ENCLOSE CASH WITH ORDER, it read, again, underlined. Even the lost cause segregationists of Chicago, USA were running a short paper hustle.

Elliot stood over the freezing cold propagandist.

"How much you get paid to pass these around, shorty?"

"Four bits."

Elliot reached into his pocket, pulled out his billfold and peeled off two Washingtons. Baby Goebbels looked around to see if he'd be spotted.

"C'man. Hand 'em over."

The frigid little guy shoved them into Elliot's hand and was set to take off.

"Hang on," he said. "You don't really believe all this meshegas, do ya?"

"Nah. I just needed the scratch."

Moon Mullins ran down the block where he met up with two other young solicitors for The White Circle League, which was likely just some asshole sitting in the basement of his shitty suburban bungalow so far away from Chicago he'd have to travel on a commuter train for two hours before he saw one Negro. Elliot continued to his meet.

At the first city ashcan he came across, he put one of the handbills in his pocket, ripped the rest in half, and stuffed them inside.

If he wasn't already uncomfortable, the private elevator man at the Chicago Athletic Club wouldn't stop staring, and smiling. Elliot tried avoiding eye contact, but the poor man wouldn't pull the gear and close the doors. He had a stack of Negro weeklies in a small box near his stool.

"Yeah, it's me."

"I knew it," he said.

"Don't ask me to autograph anything."

"I ain't gonna bug you, Mister Caprice," he said. "I see you moving and shaking with the white folks. Figure you on some detective business."

He threw the switch, beginning their flight to power.

"Say, you work for Mister McAlpin or sum'n?"

"Sum'n."

"He good folks, Mr. Costas. Or Costas-McAlpin. These ofays change their name however they want. Always has a kind word for us colored fellas. Gave us bonuses out his pocket when the other members turned cheap."

"Government money is drying up."

"They're sore that the movement for civil rights is on, these white folks here. I took some days off for family. My mama got sick. When they found out I go to meetings, they docked the pay I had coming. We lost our place, my wife and me. We got a little girl. Now we all staying with my sister."

"Meetings?"

"At the RNCL office. Last time, it was that lawyer, Thurgood Marshall.

Time before that, Medgar Evers. Know him?"

"Not personally," Elliot said, with a wink. "Hit me with this RCNL."

"Negroes got an improvement association—"

"Aw, Jeez."

"The Regional Council of Negro Leadership. It's run by this rich swell. A Negro surgeon, Dr. Howard."

"T.R.M. Howard? That fella?"

"The same. Rich Negroes like Dr. Howard, who walk it how they talk it, aren't preferred by Mr. McAlpin's fellow members. They got the same money, but they won't be taking this elevator, no sir."

"Don't outspend them," Elliot said. "It's sacrilege."

"He has colored-only banks. My wife's cousin got a home loan from one, just off his personal writ. A Negro, walking in a Negro bank, getting money, while crackers are walking the bread line."

Elliot remembered Frankie Freeman's citation of the Bee, and Howard's presence in the article. He was a surgeon, and a polymath, who made his fortune on his own terms and advocated economic insistence of the black existence. Elliot was struggling through his first bean season back and his money pool came from gumshoeing for rich no-goodniks and chasing down philanderers. Maybe Freeman was right. He may have been wrong about things.

"Be well, Mr. Caprice," the operator said. "We need you out here."

"Christ on the cross," he said, to himself. "I'm a celebrity."

The boatman threw the gear. The elevator car coasted to a stop. The operator pulled open the door, smiled, and pointed the way.

CHAPTER 21

The Venetian Gothic atmosphere of the Chicago Athletic Association reeked the same to Elliot as the tavern back rooms he stumbled into his whole life, following around slobs demanding Izzy's coin. He made Jon's body man, the lanky Grecian bruiser, Leonidas, out by the service entrance. His hand was in his jacket where one would keep a piece. His neck was tense as he gave Elliot the Chitown nod. He seemed stiff, not like their first occasion, in Jon Costas's office. It was familiar to Elliot. It felt racial.

Jon walked over to the cathedral windows, happy hour brandy in hand, looking out upon the city his family helped carve into forty thousand parcels of death. Elliot watched him for a moment, dressed in the trappings of cigar-chewers, standing against the Venetian Gothic atmosphere in his burgundy velour smoking jacket cinched at the waist. His salt and pepper was more salty, but the Greek seemed a bit more fit since they last shared a drink, and a problem. Elliot recognized it in himself. Waking up daily, standing in the mirror as he catalogued his hurts before each sunrise. Stretching and priming his muscles and sinew for the day's toil, ripping open his recovering tissues with each pull of green from the earth, silently loving the hurt, even as it broke his deepest heart to accept he was bred to love the pain of labor, and in that way, he may never be truly free.

"Elliot," Jon said. He pushed his glass out toward him and approached.

He had a slight stammer. Leonidas moved to cover him. Jon pointed at him and kept stumbling forward.

"*Chalaróste ídi gia, chári tou Christoú.*"

Elliot reached out and caught him by the shoulders.

"It's the goddamned slippers," Costas-McAlpin said, laughing, kicking them off. "They make me wear them. How's the farm?"

"Keeping me broke," Elliot said. "And those nice cases we were landing have dried up now that the attorney has shitted where he ate with the movement Negroes."

"If you need money, we could use a new man, especially since Monk passed." Leo's jaw tightened.

"Shame to hear about Monk, Leo. Your brother was a solid man."

"We've gotten death threats," Jon said.

"That's what has you both buttoned up so tight?"

"The Delta gave him grief," Leo said. "From the day they convinced him to serve on the planning commission."

Jon and Leo carried on in Greek, like the first cousins they were. Elliot waved his hands.

"What's all this now?"

"I'm handed all this land. I realize, I'm doing quite well—"

"He helped," Leo said. "He started helping."

"Ah, jeez," Elliot said.

"Soon, a few of my fellow Sea People decided I owed the Greeks."

"Owed them what?"

"Assurances that Greeks would be represented in the spoils of the new university project."

"The Outfit somehow wrenched enough land for a Little Italy," Leo said. "Since then, each ethnic group has to carve their space. Same as it ever was."

"How much real estate did your pap leave you?"

"Maxwell Street, out into the corridor where the campus would go."

"All of that?"

"Key parcels, some residential, mostly commercial. Farmland that was nearby."

"Izzy Rabinowitz's crew ran dog races out that way." Elliot looked out the window. Raindrops fell. "They pave it yet?"

"Perhaps this is the first shovel of concrete."

Elliot shook his head. "Well we can't have you hiding out. Who put the contract out on you?"

Elliot produced his notebook and pencil.

"The Insane Popes," Leo said.

"All of them?" Elliot put away the notebook. "Jon, Christ on the cross."

"A gang of Greek greaser kids, something or another."

"It's the biggest gang of non-Italians within the city. If you're white, and you're afraid to let your kid walk herself to school, it's due to the Popes."

"The newest members of the McAlpin Family fan club," Leo said.

"They've gone after poor Margaret," Jon said.

"Your wicked stepmother, poor Margaret?"

"And she gets harassed by your old foes in the Black Belt. Her annual mixer for the International Policewoman's Association was ruined with a bomb threat."

"Pity the rich," Elliot said, holding up the file folder. "Here's the source of our trouble."

Jon girded himself, stood up, and walked to a desk where he cut on the light and donned reading glasses. Elliot handed him the paperwork from Bradshaw's office.

"Your Near West Side Improvement Association is in that file."

"Marion Bradshaw? That asshole?"

"The same," Elliot said. "Mikey is suing him to block the transfer of those assets to him."

"He's somehow talked his way onto the planning committee despite not possessing a single deed of land in his name."

"That's the next eight families on his list. Bet they loved the knock on the door they got from the Bowties."

"We've had run-ins with them, same as the Popes," Leo said. "Maybe talk to your brothers out there, get 'em to relax."

Elliot reached into his pocket and produced the White Circle League handbill.

"You wanna discuss who's brothers, now?"

"Don't link me with those crazies," Leo said.

"Well, then, don't take Marion Bradshaw as my first cousin. I work for a living."

"Slick Willie Sutton, that Bradshaw," Leo said.

"He's convinced land holders in the area to sell to him, on contingency, as some sort of colored-only real estate investment cabal. Those who haven't gone over to him are labeled race traitors."

"Between me, you, and the wall," Elliot said. "Bradshaw has Negroes turned against Michael Rabinowitz and Associates."

"He's changed the name of the firm, has he?" Jon finished the brandy in his glass. "Why would Attorney Robin—"

"Rabinowitz."

"—come all the way to Chicago to push against Marion Bradshaw, much less oppose his place on the Planning Commission? Not that I'd argue with him."

"The Chicago Bee outed him as a Rabinowitz, at Bradshaw's behest. Played up changing his name in college as some ruse to fool Negroes. They're fighting real dirty, but Michael fights back. You know the attorney."

"Bradshaw drives a wedge between people," Jon said. "We've watched him do it on the commission. He uses rhetoric to isolate his opposers. Once they fall out of favor, the factions do the rest."

"I just can't figure why Mikey got himself mixed up with this mess, unless he knows Izzy's money is in with Bradshaw. Otherwise, it makes no sense."

"Are they quarreling?"

"Izzy turned up the heat on the competition for short-term loans out in farm country. It's bad enough where, had Bradshaw not outed him, the short paper war would. I just don't get what it is about Illinoisans, and owning land. Lusting enough to kill for it. Anyhow, we're radioactive. You have the right to know."

Jon Costas-McAlpin stood, filled up his glass with brandy, and handed it to Elliot. He then poured Leo one. With the bottle he enjoined them. Elliot stood.

"*Philia*," he said. *"eis toùs aionas ton aiōnōn."*

Leo and Jon touched glasses. Elliot felt itchy in his legs, but from the inside, as if he was stepping on lightning.

"Hold firm against the bastards, Elliot," Jon said. "Let us know what we may do to help."

They toasted. The private elevator bell rang on cue. Elliot handed Jon his glass and quickly fled. As the doors closed, he noticed an eerie feeling inside him. How far he had come, in such a short time, with his network of powerful white folks. After his descent, he tugged his hat at the giddy elevator man and darted away.

CHAPTER 22

As he stepped into the lobby, he smelled wealth. There he stood, toe to toe, with Lady Margaret Thorne-McAlpin, Duchess of Kenilworth, Illinois, the Midwest's first butter-and-egg woman. She wore a fine silver gown made of satin, with tiny pearls sewn along the skirt seams and pleats. They reached from the bottom, all the way to the top of her neckline. She was as tall as him without the cream-white low heels. Her hair was flaxen curls. She smelled wealthy. She still had that scar on her nose.

"Elliot Caprice," she said. "Fancy seeing you here."

"Likewise," Elliot said, squeezing the words past the lump in his throat. "Lincoln Park becomes you."

"Ah, yes. The trappings. I have to meet my stepson here to negotiate my end of these real estate holdings. You should come up and see me over at the new flat. I have the penthouse floor."

She reached in her clutch purse and pulled out a Gitanes-Brutes. Elliot found a hand-rolled and offered her a light with his Zippo. He lit up himself. She exhaled at him.

"Never mind me. How are your lima beans? Or was it pintos? I can't recall the varietal."

Elliot smiled tightly. "Heard you're having some trouble with a few mutual friends."

"You have no friends in Bronzeville, Elliot Caprice, I assure you. The Negro press has seen to that. My, my, you are riding the lightning. That whole Kefauver mess will be the death of you."

"Ah, the full-bloods are always mad about something or other. How'd you piss them off?"

"With your help, I'm afraid. As you retrieved my stepson's shipping concern, you displaced more than a few establishments in the Black Belt that enjoyed my services."

"The Black Belt," Elliot said. "Where you hold events for lady cops in the neighborhoods you sold reefer. Even for a limey, honey, that's cheeky."

"More than a few policewomen seem to recall you," Margaret said, with a smile. "Nice photo in the Chicago Daily Defender. Good to see your name spelled correctly in the caption."

"Be careful how much you go asking about me, Margaret. You don't want to be colluded."

"Oh, I think I know better than you how we're colluded."

"You mean Kefauver? I tried to tell you, in your garden that day, you didn't want me."

"What I didn't want was for you to find yourself feeling guilty and inadvertently disrupt my life."

"I told you I'd find Alistair. I found him. You got what you got."

"You were to contact me as soon as you had leads. Not hand him over to the son of the man who kept me as a whore."

"Maybe the Black Belt is mad at you for using your power, influence, and reefer to take over the black-and-tan party scene, just to go Miss Ann on 'em afterward. You know that's the Negro underworld's game, Margaret."

"As white bitches are the Negro's du jour, I beg to differ."

"Willow Ellison wound up dead in my barn after she refused to deal aitch for Chauncey Ballard, like how she dealt marijuana for you, which is how you became the North side's race party queen."

Elliot could tell it was true, because Margaret stopped breathing, her cigarette just burned in her vacant mouth.

"You left out some things," Margaret said. "I left out some things."

"Those are heavy things, Margaret."

"Oh, what were you going to do, lawman? Deliver a stern lecture? Save her from herself?"

"Chauncey Ballard is never getting out of Stateville pen. Alistair, neither."

"I was as shocked as anyone Alistair degenerated to a heroin dealing murderer."

"None of this starts until you pulled the first con, lady. You're the snowflake what started the avalanche."

"Everyone is obligated to take care of themselves. I trusted you to know that, my error."

"It's hard, Margaret, holding the con. Being respectable. Finding favor with them after crawling out of the gutter they force you into. You may be able to steal old white money and spend it right in front of them, but if you owe the Black Belt anything, you better square it. Fast. They don't owe you a damned thing."

He turned from her and angled toward the door.

"More crusading to do?"

Elliot turned around.

"I have to go home and tell my uncle we lost the farm again."

She walked over to him and grabbed him by his lapels, with both hands.

"Take the goddamned money I owe you, blasted hero."

"It's got blood on it," he said.

"What doesn't?"

Elliot grabbed her around her waist, pulled himself nose to nose, and pressed his lips upon hers. It wasn't a kiss, more like, better out than in. He let her go. She clutched herself and gasped.

"Leave me be, Margaret. You scare me."

He pushed the door open, and pushed pavement, all the way to Lucille.

He arrived at Mamie's thankful she had set his typical catfish order aside. More than a few of his own field workers were enjoying their fill at the front counter. Other Southville notables, those who find the Caprices less than savory, side-eyed him as he moved up in the line that stretched out the door to the crudely paved street. Mamie saw Elliot, waved to him, and called to the kitchen for his carry out.

"I'll get you on your way," Mamie said.

She received a paper sack from her husband, far larger than expected, and passed it to Elliot.

"Miss Mamie," he said, keeping his voice down. "Please, don't—"

"I threw some extra in there for you," she said, adding in a hushed breath, "Half these fellas in here eating with your money."

"They work for their money."

"They work to live."

Elliot nodded, reached into his pocket to tip her, but he forgot the fill-up in Chitown ate into his short paper. He remembered the money Margaret owed him, a windfall, by any standard. He cursed himself for being uppity, same as back when he told the papists to kiss his ass at breakfast, when he was also hungry and without means, but shot his proud fool mouth off anyhow.

"It'll be alright, young fella," she said. "Tell your uncle I said, 'hey.'"

Elliot pulled his hat down, nodded, and turned away, all misty. That was the last, best tell. He was eating off charity. It was time to pull up stakes. The Caprice Family Farm had been busted out.

He stepped outside and made Ned Reilly ticketing the cars parked outside Mamie's.

"You're ruining the dinner special, you know that?"

"They're turning up the heat on everyone," Ned said.

"Everyone colored," Elliot said. "Seen Georgie?"

"Preaching tonight," Ned said. "Every night."

He tore off a ticket and shoved it in the windshield of a red Ford pickup.

"What's the word on Mose?"

"No suspects."

"What do you mean? I made Chester leaving the scene."

"You sure?"

"Stupid bowler hat. Green Buick. I told George."

"Elliot, you've got to support the ordinance. This town needs law."

"George asked me to get Izzy to kill it at the county board meeting."

"George spends all his time with the movement. How would he know what Southville needs?"

"Maybe he thinks you've got me." He smiled.

"Elliot, c'mon. You know I'm right."

Elliot chuckled and turned toward Lucille, then turned back.

"Ned," Elliot said. "A favor?"

"Sure."

Elliot took the ledger book out of his coat and handed it to him.

"Maybe put this in the gun safe for me? It's sensitive, legal business and I can't trust it up at the house."

"Sure," Ned said. "No problem."

CHAPTER 23

The Caprice men ate on the porch to not be rude to the field workers. For the transient, as sad as they walk, their walk continues.

"String beans," Elliot said. "She threw in string beans."

Buster took the paper container from Elliot and looked inside. He dug in his fork, pulled out a mouthful, and chewed.

"The competition's moved in."

Everyone fell silent, Frank for three seconds, until he reached for the container of string beans.

"Unk." Elliot couldn't look at him. "I think we should maybe think on what comes after."

Buster looked out at the horizon line from his porch. Elliot reached out and grabbed his hand.

The Big Fella stood, solemn. "I'll go to my room."

"Stay, Frank," Elliot said "Unk, I'm sorry. It's time. We're not the only ones. They're coming for Negro's land everywhere."

Uncle Buster pushed Elliot's hand away, stood up, and walked to the porch rail. Elliot rose and followed him.

"You'd get great money for it, Unk. The longer you wait, the more folks sell out around us, they'll make us like the dead bean farm between our place and Miss Betty's."

Buster's head fell.

"I'm sorry. We were just one good harvest shy." Elliot looked down at the porch floorboards.

"I'll clean up," Frank said.

"I'm going to Duffy's to tell Molly," Elliot said.

"Your girlfriend."

"She's not my girlfriend, Unk."

"It's his girlfriend," Frank said.

"Nope." Elliot lit a smoke as he walked away.

They managed to sneak a date here and there, nothing too fancy, as she had the best food for the dollar and heartiest pours anyhow, which they'd enjoy between pours for the ofays and Negroes who slapped the rickety bar demanding their current cultural discount.

"Molly, buy a round for an old veteran."

"I'm tight, Miss Molly. You know how these ofays do us dirty."

"Three cheers for Sean Duffy's wee lass," which was the Irish-American kinfolk special.

The Jews what drank in Molly's presence were Abe and Doc, when they'd hang with Uncle Buster near the crappy Magnavox watching baseball. No other Jews hung out in Duffy's, including Izzy, who couldn't darken Molly's front door for all he brought through Sean Duffy's back door through the years. Half the folks in the bar didn't like Elliot, the other half couldn't stand him, but there he'd sit, into the wee hours, enjoying the tiny moments they'd meet eyes. She had smile lines at the creases of her mouth and eyelids, despite it all. He watched her move with a sea bird's grace, darting about the ungraceful, dispensing beer nuts along with tiny little blessings.

He resolved to leave the firm for good in the morning, penance for allowing his gumshoeing to ruin his focus. Besides, he couldn't live with the doubt Mikey and Elaine caused within him. Mikey's business was ever a tangle, and always about his daddy's mess. He felt like a pawn, even more since being bailed out of jail in St. Louis. He felt caught in the middle. Between Mikey and now the rest of the world, including the Negro one, and Bradshaw, who was proving his ability to whip his ass.

Molly wandered over. She smiled that same smile, as if everything would be alright. She found a glass, and his Blanton's Reserve, and made him a pour as he sussed it with pencil and notepad. Not as if he was writing anything worth sussing. Marion Bradshaw had Elliot Caprice in his sights and he operated, through power and influence, in Elliot's blind spot, which lay firmly behind his acceptance that he was, too, a son of great privilege. Bradshaw's ability to thwart and throttle him proved he was ill equipped for the fight ahead. He kicked the bronze rail underneath the bar. It fell off on one side with a loud clang.

"Elliot Caprice," Molly said, in a sing-songy tone she used when she was set to tell him his own business. "You know everything in Duffy's is held together with spit, and bubble gum, and I bet you didn't bring me any bubble gum, did you?"

"Aw, lay off me, Molly Duffy."

"Lay off my bar, Jackson." Molly wiped his station with the bar rag. The soapstone bar top shook. The rail rattled. "You know Sean isn't fixing anything around here anymore."

"I'll fix the frickin' rail."

"I know you will," Molly said. "You've been saying you would since growing season."

Elliot placed his hand atop Molly's, stopping her wiping. He looked into her eyes, which was always so hard to do when he had truths to tell.

"Molly, I may be rambling on again."

"Oh?" She snatched away. "Well, at least you're saying so this time."

"It's nothing like that."

"I have to run the empties out." Molly tossed the rag in the sink, snatched off her bar keep's smock, and ran away. Elliot walked around the bar.

"Get me another when you're back there, Lightskin," someone said, to laughter from the crowd. Elliot followed her to the supply room, where wooden crates of Pabst and Schlitz long necks piled up.

"Where's Sean?"

"Unwell," Molly said.

Elliot knew that meant he was on a bender. He grabbed a crate, except Molly snatched it away from him.

"I didn't ask you to do that." The crates slipped from her grasp and fell to the floor. "You're always stuck between doing nothing and doing everything, damn you."

Elliot stood stiffly as she walked over, finger waving.

"Not once, Elliot Caprice," she said. "You disappeared on me, and you couldn't reach out to me, not once?"

"Molly." Elliot reached for her. "I disappeared on everyone. On myself."

Molly punched him on his bad arm. Elliot winced.

"What is that?"

"Nothing," Elliot said.

"Your shoulder."

"It's old. Gunshot wound."

"You've been shot?" Molly's eyes moistened and reddened.

"Twice."

Molly shook her head. "Why don't I know that?"

"Molly."

"Why wouldn't I know you've ever been through that, Elliot?"

"You not supposed to know, Molly." Elliot looked at the floor. "You're not supposed to know any of it."

"Don't you dare treat me like some precious white girl of yours, Elliot Caprice."

"How about I've already delivered too much to your back door already?"

Elliot ripped his hat off his head and clutched it.

"You left, Elliot. If you were concerned about all that, you would've stayed."

"I ran, Molly."

"You ran right back."

"My uncle needed me, fat lot of good it did." Elliot's jaw and neck stiffened. His countenance fell. "That's what I mean to say. Seems like we're selling."

"What?"

Elliot nodded. "They pressured us from all sides. We tried coming to terms with it tonight."

Molly fidgeted with her dress. "Where will you go?"

"I'm going to get my uncle set up however he wants, and help Frank move on. Otherwise, I haven't decided. But they've been coming for that old man's land for decades. They finally got some help from the drought. Our crop won't make it."

"Oh, Elliot," Molly said. She went to him and clutched his hands.

"I just wanted to tell you, you know, before you saw some sign out front." Elliot shoved his hands in his pockets. "Before I came along, that old man owned two thriving plots of land and prolly a piece of Betty's road house. He takes in his brother's bastard—"

"Now, hold it right there," Molly said.

"He loses everything. Colored folks' land, just gone."

Elliot put his hand over his face. Molly pulled his hand away and wiped his tears.

"Listen, they cooked up this shit," Molly said. "State cops walking around. The rhetoric on the radio. Fucking pamphlets. You didn't do all that, you jackass."

Elliot wiped his face, walked over to the sink counter, where there was a bottle of corn. He pulled the cork and took a swig, wincing. He passed it to Molly, who did the same.

"That's enough," she said, holding out her hand. "You and cheap liquor is dangerous, and you're in enough shit."

"With everyone else, or just you?" Elliot looked up, into Molly's beautiful blues, and smiled as he tendered the cork.

"They're coming around here, same as the farm," Molly said, corking the bottle. "Bastards knew Sean Duffy was off the wagon. Asked me if I ever considered selling once he's gone. They're playing nasty. You know this ordinance?"

"Yeah," Elliot said. "George and Ned are split on it."

"All the blood the Outfit spilled to pave this shithole, now they want to come around with their sobriety laws."

"I think I'm going to talk, Molly." He couldn't believe he said it. "I'm going to give Izzy up."

"Is that what you want to do?"

"I want the FBI to stop following me. I want the short paper war to be over."

"Do you have to be the one to stop it?" Molly shook her head. "See? This is what you do. Same as with Mose."

"What about Mose?"

"I had it."

"You had it," Elliot said.

"I had it," Molly said. "You turned it into a fight."

"He was terrible to you," Elliot said.

"Boys are terrible, Elliot." Molly grabbed another crate and stacked it out the door. "Whites are terrible. Negroes are terrible. They'll always be. What's that got to do with you?"

Molly touched Elliot on the face.

"You beat yourself to hell. You make too much out of nothing. Christ on the cross, Elliot Caprice, would you just do what you have to do for yourself? The rest of us have to deal with it anyhow."

She put a new kiss on him. One that was totally unfamiliar.

"Now, go out the back. I can't have them see you breaking the rules around here."

She was serious. Folks could get their booze from anywhere. Duffy's is where one went for order. As he crossed the doorway, he turned back.

"I love you, Molly."

She cackled and shook her head. "No, Elliot Caprice. I love you. You love…death, maybe."

"Will you ever forgive me?"

"If you finally keep your promises." Molly raised her thumb and pointed it behind her. "About fixing the bar."

Molly was the kind of smart that made a man lose his lust to flights of imagination. She freed him from his enchantment when she pointed out the door. Elliot nodded, put on his cap, and dipped out. He hoofed it to Lucille, content to call Frankie Freeman in the morning and make an appointment to spill his guts. After that, if the movement to give Negroes every right to be just as bad as white folks needed anything else, they'd have to pick his bones for it.

CHAPTER 24

Roseland was quiet. He didn't remember what night of the week it was. Where he should have been, or shouldn't have been, as a manner of saying he was mad enough to forget his Shabbos goy training. He stood in that backyard, in his bloody debate team blazer, staring at the swing set he and Amos built. He didn't know what he was thinking ringing the bell and waiting. Rebecca, or who he thought was Izzy's wife, as he was never allowed in the house to see for himself, looked out the kitchen window.

"Boychik," she said.

Elliot shuffled to the window, using his hand to conceal the cuts and bruises on his face.

"Miss Rebecca," he said. "I'm very sorry to disturb—"

She shut the shades. Elliot backed away from the window. Common sense took over and he turned to split. He was halfway to the gate when the screen door opened.

"Hey," came the loud whisper. Elliot stopped. "The hell's your deal, kid?"

He could hear Izzy walk up to him in the grass.

"I'm talking to you," he said. He grabbed Elliot on the shoulder and spun him around. "Fuck me, in the face."

"Iz," Elliot said. He couldn't look at him.

Izzy Rabinowitz was at the height of his powers in the rackets in the

Midwest. In a few short years, he had come on strong enough to subdue the Quad Cities and Chicagoland farm country. He had grown more ruthless as sides switched along racial lines when it came to organized crime. The Irish were enjoying a new use for their proximity to crime in law enforcement, go figure, and Jews had enough problems, worldwide. As Elliot was away at Bradly Poly, getting himself beat to hell by the police and adulthood, it had gotten a lot more dangerous to be the short paper king of the Chitown boondocks.

"What happened to you?"

"Izzy, you were right."

"Who did this?"

"Urbana cops," Elliot said. "Debating, while colored."

"Come sit down with me." Izzy grabbed him by the arm. "C'man, kid. You're not making sense."

Elliot snatched away.

"No, goddamnit!" Everything within him hurt. "I'm tired of everyone telling me what to do with myself. Will you listen to me?"

Izzy's eyes went wide. Elliot was standing, fists balled, nose bloodied, face bruised, knuckles red, as if he wanted to fight the world, and he brought it to Isadora Rabinowitz's family home. On Shabbos. Rebecca Rabinowitz stood in the door. A young kid, somewhere around eight to ten years old, walked up behind her. Elliot found the sense to lower his voice.

"I'm sorry, Iz." He looked jittery and nervous, in his dirtied and bloodied Bradley Poly debate club blazer. "I know I'm out of pocket."

Izzy said nothing.

"I should've listened to you when you told me about playing it straight. It's just a different kind of crooked."

Izzy folded his arms in front of him. His face softened as Elliot held back tears.

"Kid, you're not making any sense. Go home to your uncle."

"Fuck my uncle."

Izzy slapped him across the face, getting him right in the yap.

"That mouth," he said. "Always that mouth."

"Him. You. Fucking cops. Professors. This whole town."

"Go home, kid," Izzy said.

"I got no home. Why you think I'm here?"

"You're no good to yourself right now."

"Use 'em up, on to the next colored skin boy, huh?"

Izzy one-two'd Elliot in his mouth. He fell back on his ass in the grass. Izzy stepped over him, grabbed him by the collar, and pulled him onto his feet.

"You little piece of shit," he said. "I got the Outfit on top of me, New York muscling in. You bring this to my backyard, on Shabbos?"

Izzy tussled with Elliot, who didn't struggle. He was heartbroken.

"Isadora." Rebecca reached out to him from the doorway.

"Daddy!" The boy was by the back door. "Don't hit him anymore."

Elliot stared silently at him. He raised his hands.

"Very sorry to bother you," Elliot said. "I'll leave."

"Listen, kid," Izzy let go. "I'm sorry I hit you. Just, come sit down. Please."

Elliot buttoned up his jacket. "I won, see?" He pointed to the ribbons.

"Yeah, kid. You finally talked ' em down, huh?" Izzy awkwardly smiled.

"Tired of talkin' tho, Izzy." Elliot dried his face with his hands but only smeared the blood across it. "And I'm tired of waiting outside."

"Go home, Elliot," Rebecca said. "Go to your uncle."

Elliot looked at the boy. "I'm sorry the kid had to see me messed up. That Sidney?"

"Mikey," Izzy said.

"He's gettin' big."

"He's fat," Izzy said. "Likes his sweets too much."

"Please don't tell Doc I left school," Elliot said, as he turned and started walking toward the gate.

"Elliot," Izzy said. "Wait."

Elliot began running as fast as he could, which was pretty damned fast when he wanted, until he encountered the state police haranguing a group of colored men on the side of the road leading through Sugartown.

"You niggers got jobs?"

"Work or fight," another cop said, shoving a baton in the face of one. "You boys farmers?"

"Yessuh," one said.

"Show me some work papers, boy."

There were a phalanx of MPs standing near green transport trucks Elliot had seen in the newsreels before the movies. Men were led into them, two by two, mostly Negro, all poor, all conscripted right on the spot.

Elliot walked west until he came to rest at the Southville train station. Asking around, he learned soldiers were out for deployment to Fort Lexington. He saw them with their rucksacks and field cottons, looking desperate. He noticed Negroes lined up to be loaded into boxcars. It offended him deep down into his bowels. White conscripts pointed and shouted epithets of unworthiness. One threw a rock. A colored caught it and threw it back.

"Crecy," a Negro officer shouted. It was the damnedest thing Elliot had ever seen. Crecy, the rock thrower, straightened his back and took his lumps from another colored man. Regimented men—white regimented—responded to his command. Elliot rummaged through his pockets for a handkerchief, finding a dirty one in his inside pocket. He wet it in the water fountain against the wall and employed a station window as a mirror to clean himself up. As he approached the most sharply dressed and powerful colored man he had ever seen in his life, he ducked at the sound of gunfire. He ducked again, but realized it was the pick-up's engine.

***

Elliot lifted himself out of his uncle's bed and walked to the window. The morning sun hurt his eyes. He looked down to the porch to see Frank Fuquay backing up the pickup. He had an army of field workers with him, all colored. As they stepped out of the cab and onto the porch, Uncle Buster walked over and distributed canvas bags. Most men had their own gloves and such. All were excited to work.

Elliot left the room, ran down the stairs, and onto the porch. He still had on his pajama pants.

"Unk," he said. "What's going on?"

Uncle Buster walked up, reached into the front pocket of his coveralls and put something in Elliot's hand. His grip was full of string beans, perfectly green, as if they weren't three weeks late.

Elliot shook his head.

"I'll be damned."

"We gotta work fast," Buster said. "There're still markets to make."

Buster patted Elliot on the face and went back to work. The phone rang. Elliot walked back inside and into the kitchen.

"Caprice Family—"

"Elliot," Mikey said. "I don't know what you've done, and I don't want to know."

"Mikey, wait a minute."

"Whatever you stole from Bradshaw's office, get it here, now."

"Will you let me explain?"

"I'll let you explain how Jon Costas-McAlpin called me today to discuss the complaint."

Mikey hung up on him.

CHAPTER 25

As the land grant campus expanded South toward Maxwell Street, and west toward Taylor Street and Racine Avenue, adjacent neighborhoods would improve. With the races all lined-up with their knives out, Bradshaw was set to flush the floor and profit. The city clears out Negroes. The university gets their campus, and a fat endowment.

Bradshaw represented Negro money through his area investment firm, which wasn't nearly enough to challenge the Jon McAlpins of the world. His organization was insinuated with Black Muslim toughs, perhaps as counterbalance to the Negro underworld elites and their dwindling, yet remaining, power. How he managed to bring rival Negro factions together in spirit, much less fortune, was a mystery. He was proving formidable. Frankie Freeman, terse as she was, had it cold. Bradshaw had the goods on Elliot, Mikey, and the firm from the get-go. He built his con on it.

Negro enterprise in the Midwest reached a fever pitch. Whites demanded broader boundaries, cruelly moving the herd of poor from the West side of the city out South, into cinder block oblivion. It was as close to paying for one's nut with their labor as you could get without calling it slavery. Elliot understood why Mike would go after a Talented Tenth who appeased the State University Commission on behalf of Negroes who didn't have enough sense to feel oppressed. He just didn't know what Elaine had to do with it. Freeman intimated they were socially active together, often with other professional Negroes. The date of the messages suggest Elaine called Bradshaw even before the case began.

"Elliot," Charles said. "Just get out of here now."

"No," Elliot said. "He's going to take his medicine."

"Is that him?"

Mikey came out of his office fuming.

"Where's the book from Bradshaw's office?"

"I told you, it's best not to muck around in any of it, but you don't listen. Now they're ruining me, same as you let them ruin you."

"Give me the ledger," Mikey said. He shoved out his hand.

"I don't have it," Elliot said. "You don't want it anyhow."

"Why not?"

"Why do you think?" Elliot kicked the ashcan. "Enough with this protracted battle between you and your father. You are who you are. Deal with it, like the rest of us."

"What are you talking about?"

Elliot lowered his voice. "Your pap's money is in Bradshaw's fund, along with most of the short paper he collected from Southville in the growing season. And I know you know that."

"I didn't know that."

"Same as you didn't know Mattie Smith would ask me about Teddy Roe?"

Mikey eased off. "I'm sorry, Elliot. You should've kept your nose clean."

Elliot grabbed Mikey by his lapels.

"I'm taking my break," Charles said, and he stood up, grabbed his hat, and dipped out the door.

"And when was the Rabinowitz family ever going to let me?"

"Let me go."

Elaine's door opened. Elliot could hear her hard heels against the floor.

"This Frankie Freeman you're so impressed with," Elliot said. "She says you're poison to the movement. Says I enable you, as your token nigger."

"Elliot, you will not use that word in this office."

"You've got a lot of nerve, Elaine. You're just as colluded in the whole, rotten, uppity mess."

Elliot let go of Mikey's jacket.

"Give me what you took away from Bradshaw's office or you're fired."

"I'm an independent contractor," Elliot said.

"Make today your last day."

"It's good the string beans came in."

Mikey stormed away to his office.

"Elliot, you're not quitting."

She followed Elliot out to the hall.

"What exactly do you and Marion Bradshaw have to talk about so often? You left him several messages over the past few weeks. What's going on?"

Elaine unconvincingly waved it off. "Of course, it's for the case."

"Uh huh. Everyone's got their gob going about making the world a better place. Seems like no one wants to do shit about it but insist I be a better person, so I can make it a better place, and I'm sick of it."

Down the hall he went, angrily pounding his heels across the marble floor toward the men's room. Dirty money plays for new money Negroes. Civil rights; humanity, bestowed in bite-sized increments. He patted his face with water, dried it with a hand towel, and leaned against the sink. He felt betrayed, by Mikey and Negroes like Freeman, who held respectability over his head, and Bradshaw, who courted respectability to leverage against other Negroes. That was always the rub, what other colored folks thought of him. The ofays he could take. They were always the same, but Bradshaw was a new kind of Negro, one foreign to him, and dangerous.

As he opened the restroom door, he heard the sound of breaking glass and a vehicle peeling off. He ran back inside the office. Mikey, fuming mad, marched down the hall.

"That's the last window these assholes are getting out of me."

"Mikey, slow down."

Elliot followed until he saw fierce smoke billowing from Elaine's office door.

"Bomb, Elliot! Get out!"

Elaine ran up behind him. "Michael!"

"Elaine, run!"

Elliot ran toward her as fast as he could, grabbed her around the waist, and darted to the main office.

Clouds slapped together behind them. The force of the blast carried their bodies out into the hall. Searing heat passed through them as the two, intertwined and tumbling, fell down onto the foundation of the building that once held their hopes and dreams. They hit the floor hard. Elliot lost his grip on her. He was buried in debris. Blood and soot clouded his vision. Something heavy was atop him. He could barely breathe.

"Elaine," he cried.

He pushed himself up through the debris. The street outside was on fire. Lucille was buried in her parking space. He saw Elaine, limp, listless, on the tile outside the place where the front door to the building would have been. He staggered to her, found her arm and pulled her clear out into the street where he laid her on the pavement. Hoping against the obvious, Elliot walked back inside. The remainder of the roof began to quake before there was a secondary explosion.

CHAPTER 26

While he hated to do it to any Negro, especially a young one who worked for the Caprice family, Ned Reilly had little choice in the matter when he hauled young Eugene Brophy into the jail for battery. The troubles over labor amongst the races reached ferocity, and Eugene, as eager as he was to give some hell back, was courting disaster with a baseball bat and his uncompromising mouth. He reminded Ned of Elliot. The anger. The restlessness. While time and forgiveness entered their relationship, the Deputy didn't exactly want to be obligated with minding a younger, angrier version of the kid who picked on him.

"Christ, what were you thinking?" Ned slammed Eugene into the seat across from his desk. "Eugene, you're lucky you didn't die today the way the state police are behaving."

"You're lucky, ofay," Eugene said.

Ned put his face in his hands.

"You white boys always telling us to wait, while you take. We tired of you making the rules all the time when you don't pull your own damned food from the ground."

"Sit there and shaddup while I figure out exactly what to do with you."

Eugene huffed and slumped in his chair. George walked in dressed fancy, and thus for something other than law enforcement.

"Not again," Ned said.

"What's his story?" George rummaged through his desk. "Have you seen my formal badge?"

"George," Ned said. "Damn it, enough with the speeches, already. I just pulled Eugene out of a scrum of fifteen drunks outside the Seed and Supply."

"Some guys came around saying us Negroes are scabs to the working man," Eugene said.

"What guys?"

Eugene took a crudely printed handbill from his hip pocket and handed it to George.

"The White Circle League," he said. "Talkin' 'bout Negroes drive wages down, and prices up, and that's why the bank is pressuring everyone to sell. The white boys threw bottles. Glad I had that bat."

"Have you seen these?" George handed the handbill to Ned.

"No," Ned said, as he read, noticing the remarks sounded a lot like the Stateys. "It doesn't matter. They're not breaking the law. Eugene did."

"What law?"

"Disorderly conduct, inciting a riot."

"I told you, the fight broke out and I had to defend myself."

"Call the law," Ned said. "Otherwise, you're part of the problem."

"That's what y'all ofays don't get," Eugene said. "We know your laws only protect you."

"It's been protecting you all afternoon, you little jerkoff."

"Ned!"

"I blame you," Ned said.

"Me?"

"It's the harvest, George. You've lived here your whole life. You know what happens when the Negroes and the whites meet in the middle. Chaos, always. And now, of all times, you allow yourself to be distracted."

"I am not distracted."

"Mose Boysaw, George!" Ned kicked the desk. "Elliot Fucking Caprice and I are investigating the death of a guy we all went to high school with, goddamn you. Where are you? Out running around, fulfilling your daddy's promise."

"My father served his community."

"And my father ran out on me and my Irish mother when the Depression was on. We don't have to do what our daddies do, George."

"I didn't do anything wrong." Eugene turned around in his chair.

"What in the hell did I tell you?" Ned swiped at Eugene's head, who was startled, as was George. He grabbed Eugene by the lapel, drug him to the holding cell and pushed him inside, shutting the bars without locking them.

"One more frickin' word out of you, Eugene, and I swear on my ancient mother, you're going to Menard Federal Pen."

Ned went for the key ring.

"Just what a white man would do."

Ned Reilly, having about as much as he could take, locked the cell door.

"Hey!"

"That's what a white man would do."

"I fucking hate you ofays," Eugene screamed.

"You Negroes are no prize."

Ned pulled a bottle of Blanton's Reserve from his desk drawer.

"Process him. Make Elliot pay the fine."

"You don't know what I arrested him for, George."

"He's a delinquent."

"He's a citizen," Ned said. "Perhaps not the kind you'd prefer."

George turned toward the door and nearly put on his hat when the windows over the desks shattered. Instinctively, Ned hit the deck. George drew his service revolver and covered him.

"Anyone hit?"

"No," Ned said. "Eugene?"

"I'm okay."

A crash of glass, followed by a blast of heat, and the bed in the cell went up from a Molotov through the window. Eugene batted the bed with the pillow, but he only spread the fire. He collapsed to the floor and pushed himself against the bars to get away from the flames. Ned belly-crawled to the cell door to let him out. He tried standing, but machine gun fire filled the jailhouse. The inferno grew. Eugene began to panic. His mouth neared a scream.

George Stingley threw open the door and fired in the direction of their attackers. He took two in the belly and collapsed inside the doorway. Eugene's mortal fear rose through his throat and out his mouth. Ned got the cell door open and yanked Eugene out and onto the floor before ducking and covering himself.

"Get the sheriff in here."

Eugene ran to the doorway and dived underneath a new hail of bullets before pulling all of George's body back inside the jailhouse. George slammed the big oak door with his foot as they took cover behind it.

"Is he bad?" Ned returned carrying a shotgun. He tossed Eugene his service revolver.

"He's bleeding," Eugene said.

Ned cocked a shell into the barrel. The phone in the jail began to ring. Eugene kept casing the windows.

"I think they gone."

"Stay low anyhow." Ned answered. "Reilly. Be advised, the Southville Jailhouse is under attack."

"Deputy."

"Miss Betty?"

"Come quick," she said, her voice breaking. "Send the fire department."

CHAPTER 27

Frank Fuquay whacked at the rusted bolts where the harvester's camber met the hopper. Uncle Buster stood over him as if it helped. Frank wiped off his face and neck with his red bandana.

"You smell that," Buster said. He sniffed and turned his head. "There."

Across from the abandoned string bean field, above Miss Betty's SRO, black smoke billowed into the sky. Frank flew from the harvester, ran inside the house, grabbed the keys to the Ford pickup, and took the access road to Main Street. He banked a right at the abandoned farm and hauled to Lincoln Drive, where he would swing a left and access Betty's from the rear. He considered cutting through the abandoned field but couldn't risk the axles of the only working machine left during harvest. That morning it almost didn't make it back with the load of migrant workers they picked up in front of the Seed and Supply, where Negroes openly traded their own labor in front of the increasingly angry, white unemployed who openly questioned the Negro's dominance in the agricultural day labor market.

From Lincoln Drive, Frank made three white men, all wearing balaclavas, cutting through the trees that separated the clearing from state land. He ground to a stop in the gravel parking lot. Miss Betty's was an inferno. Frank hopped out of the pickup and watched as fleeing Negroes crawled over themselves stampeding out the back. Many, burning in fire, leaped from the windows on the second and third floors. Frank left the hellish pandemonium, ran to the front door to the common room, and found it held shut by a railroad lock and chain. As he tried muscling the door, he heard panicked screaming. The few small windows began breaking from the inside. Black bodies reached out, clutching for freedom.

Frank ran to the pickup, put her in gear, pushed the hammer down, and leaned on the horn. He hit the brakes, imparting a skid, and crashed through the flimsy wall of the SRO. Woozy, after braining himself on the steering wheel, he watched tenants flee through the gaping hole he made. The Ford was dead.

He turned to leave the cab, only to be met by another man wearing a balaclava who held a shotgun. Frank kicked the driver's side door out, sending him flying. He hopped out the truck, turned, and found a second masked man swinging a burning board. It caught Frank flush on the left arm, searing his flesh as it tore into it. Frank slapped the board away, grabbed the balaclava by the back of his head, and sent him, nose first, into the side of the pickup. Shotgun returned as Frank fell to his knees, dizzy and hurting. Shotgun was opened up with Ned Reilly's service revolver.

"C'mon, Frank."

With the Deputy's help, the Big Man rose to his wobbly legs and leaned on the truck to stabilize himself. Frank watched as Ned ripped off the mask of the arsonist.

"Oh, Christ," Ned said.

"What?"

"He's a state cop. Patrols Sugartown. He detained Eugene on a lie before Elliot and I showed up. How do you feel now, mouth?"

"You're a traitor—" The cop coughed up blood on himself. "—to your kind, Reilly."

"Die quietly, asshole." Ned checked Frank's wound. "We have to get help."

The common room caught fire. Outside, the county's well-apportioned fire department finally arrived, ambulances with them. Inside, an arsonist lay in his own blood, his sinister face scowling. The fool had the nerve to look tough.

"You'll burn with this nigger, Reilly," he said, defiantly. "You'll burn with all of them."

"As will you," Ned said.

Frank Fuquay shook his head as they walked away, leaving the man screaming epithets on the floor.

Frank followed Ned out to the gravel lot. Residents working in neighboring fields returned, witnessing the flames and the carnage. Brave souls tackled the burning and panicking, furiously patting them out with their hats and their canvas field bags. Others wandered across the gravel lot, screaming in horror. Some wondered aloud about where they would go, what they would do, and why God would white on them so badly. Black-sooted faces cried out in despair, the proprietor's own anguished face amongst them. Miss Betty couldn't stop screaming as she witnessed all she worked for burn away. Percy Bridges went to his big sister and cradled her in his arms.

"It's alright, Betty," Percy said. "We'll figure out what to do next."

"They couldn't take me, fair and square," she said. "Goddamn them. They always change the rules."

Buster Caprice walked up through the abandoned string bean farm. He made a beeline for Betty, arms outstretched.

"They finally got me, Nathan," she said.

They embraced as Eugene rode up in a cruiser.

"Deputy," he said, rolling down the window. "Doc Shapiro took Sheriff George to a hospital in the next county. He wouldn't stop bleeding."

Ned took off his badge, walked over, and pinned it on Eugene's shirt.

"Get as many folks as you can away from the fire."

Eugene nodded and galloped over to assist.

"Frank!"

The blood-curdling scream came from the cab of Sean Duffy's pickup, which rode up wildly. Molly hit the brakes and stepped out crying. Frank ran to her.

"He's dead, Frank."

"Who, Molly?"

"Elliot," she said. "It came over the radio. There was an explosion at their office. The news says they're all dead."

In the distance, Frank made activity on the Caprice front porch, followed by sustained shouting from the workers in the fields. Frank watched them scurry about, until one fell in the dirt, followed by the delayed sound of a distant gunshot. He left Molly with Ned and ran until he reached the front door of the farmhouse, which was wide open. The living room had been ransacked. Frank heard footsteps past the kitchen and followed the sound. He made a balaclava-faced goon running out past where the covered porch back door meets the field. Elliot's stuff was tossed. Frank almost got the goon by the collar, but he stumbled, fell out the door, and into the backyard. Frank held his mask as he ran way.

He didn't seem white at all.

The Caprice Family barn burned wildly, casting angry reds and oranges across the field. A large circle with a cross at its center was painted in white over the doors. Gunfire rang out. Another field hand tumbled into the dirt. The remainder scattered and ran for their lives.

Buster stepped out.

"They cut the phone line," he said.

Molly walked over to Frank, who was on his knees. He dug his hands in the dirt and grass, gritted his teeth, and screamed inside himself.

"Come, Frank," Molly said. She pulled him at his shoulder. "Let's get to the tavern."

Frank rose to his feet and walked away, looking back at the barn as it crackled and roared.

"It feels like the end of the world," he said.

Buster Caprice, whose barn burned in the approaching night, walked with them, expressionless.

"It's what they do."

CHAPTER 28

Frank turned the dial on the Victrola behind the bar at Duffy's until he picked up WKEI, serving Negroes in the Quad Cities.

"I listen to them sometimes," he said. "Negroes own the station. They'll report something."

Ned hung up the phone. Molly Duffy walked over.

"Springfield PD says Michael Rabinowitz is dead. They have remains."

"What about Elliot?"

"All they'd tell me is Elliot was made at the scene pulling someone clear before going back inside."

"Where is he?"

"I don't know," Ned said. "They said they couldn't talk about it and hung up."

Frank looked over at Uncle Buster, sitting with Miss Betty, each consoling the other.

"They hit the jail," Ned said. "The SRO, and the Caprice place."

"Eugene," Frank said. "Come here a sec."

Eugene walked over from covering the door.

"Yeah, Fuquay?"

"You were at the Seed and Supply today. You felt it, right?"

"Since first thing in the morning. Crazy folk getting riled up over race nonsense."

"The fella I put down at Miss Betty's is a state cop," Ned said. "No telling how many of them are. We can't trust them."

"Now, we can't trust them?" Molly threw her bar rag at Ned. "You asshole, they're set to patrol Southville with an army once this ordinance passes."

"I'm not going to defend the need for law enforcement, Molly. Southville deserves peacekeeping."

"In thirty-four years, I haven't seen peace inside or outside this tavern, but you figure the Illinois State Police is bringing it with them. Damn you, Ned."

The Big Man walked over to the phone, took out his wallet, found a business card inside and flipped it over. After dialing, it rang for what seemed like forever.

"Yes." A white man answered.

"Jon Costas, please. Frank Fuquay calling."

Frank waited as an hourly news report on the attack was available from the radio station. Michael Rabinowitz, crusading civil rights attorney and son of crime lord Izzy Rabinowitz, perished in an explosion that destroyed his small, scrappy, law firm. His colleagues, Elaine Critchlow, paralegal, and Elliot Caprice, former Detective of the Chicago Police Department, perished as well. Several area businesses were damaged. The entire legal sector of the state capital, as well as the burgeoning civil rights movement in the Midwest, mourned the loss. It included a recorded statement from Frankie Freeman, a crusading Negro attorney from St. Louis and, up until that point, an outspoken opponent of Attorney Rabinowitz's methods. She expressed sadness and remorse for the families affected in the tragedy and praised his legal savvy and commitment to Negro suffrage.

"That's who the boss went to see in St. Louis," Frank said. "He mentioned she was a hard case."

The report continued with related news on the case of Chauncey Ballard, convicted of murder in the first degree of both Willow Ellison, of Madison, Wisconsin, and suspected of murdering Esme McAlpin, wife of Jonathan McAlpin, murdered scion of the wealthy McAlpin Family fortune. His accomplice, Alistair Williams, himself the murderer of the late Mr. McAlpin, awaited trial in Menard Federal Pen. They were the Negro press's Leopold and Loeb.

"Frank," Jon said.

"Mr. Costas," Frank said, clearing his throat. "I know the boss is a friend to you, which is why I'm calling. There's been an incident, sir. The office—"

Frank choked up.

"Young man, are you alright?"

He cupped the phone, breathed deeply, and collected himself.

"The law office, sir," Frank said. "It was bombed. It's feared everyone is dead. We can't get any information."

He began to cry, but sucked it up. The phone shook in his hands.

"Oh, dear," Jon said. "This is madness. I'll help however I'm able."

"Thank you, sir," Frank said. "Right now, we can't get a word from the law one way or the other."

"It's best you stay by a phone. I'll seek out answers and get back to you."

"Please find me at the farmhouse, sir. I have his uncle with me. He's quite worried."

"I understand," Jon said. "Help is on the way."

As they walked into the house, Frank debated what to wear. He was going to Springfield alone, doing whatever he could to help the boss. He dressed in his rambling clothes: charcoal porkpie hat, black pea coat, tan shirt, black tie, field jeans, black boots. Ned and Eugene came in from holding post on the porch. There was a lot to do, getting the hands situated, making certain everyone was safe. Balancing everyone's needs diminished Frank's resolve, but not his desire.

"We're clear," Ned said.

"Thanks for checking one last time."

"I feel bad," Ned said. "I didn't see through those guys. Now we're getting this madness passed out on the street."

Ned showed Frank the handbill.

"White Circle League," Frank said. "They're from where I'm from, in the South. I'll be damned."

Buster came downstairs with a pack. He wore his canvas jacket and field jeans. Miss Betty walked over to him.

"Nathan, where are you going?"

"With Frank," Buster said.

"They're taking bodies," Betty said. "You cannot leave this house."

"Uncle Buster, Elliot would want you to stay here," Frank said.

The sound of tires on gravel grew. Ned and Eugene grabbed their shotguns and covered the door. Buster trotted into the kitchen and returned with his shotgun. Frank had his sidearm in hand. Betty had hers. Frank threw open the door and drew on the vehicle fast approaching the house. Ned and Eugene took position, locked and ready. The black and teal Lincoln Town Car hit the brakes, hard, skidding to a stop at a good distance. The driver's side window opened. A hand waved out the window.

"Hang on," the driver said. "We're friendly."

Leonidas, dressed in black coat and fedora, stepped out. He nodded toward Frank, who hadn't seen him since the days when he held guard against him during the Costas Cartage Affair.

"Remember me? Leo."

"From Jon Costas's office," Frank said.

"The Greek has the skinny on your boss," Leo said. "You should come with us."

"Us?"

The rear passenger door opened. Out stepped a long-legged blonde in a white mink who looked like she had been crying and chain-smoking the entire car ride.

"Hello, Francis," Margaret said.

Frank climbed in with her as Leo helped Uncle Buster into the seat next to him. She was gorgeous, just like the ladies in the magazine ads.

Frank remembered her from the Alistair Williams case, the night they barnstormed through Chicago at a breakneck pace and saved a killer's bacon, giving the mob a black eye in the process. She seemed different than before. In her stepson's office she was playing against time, holding steady as the walls were closing in. Now he could feel a different clock ticking away. Regret.

"Ma'am," Frank said.

Leo sped away. Frank looked out the back window.

"Jonathan has learned Elliot is alive," she said.

"He's alive," Frank said, slapping Buster lightly on the arm.

"And in custody of the FBI," Leo said. "His old friend, John Creamer."

"Oh, no," Frank said.

"Nabbed him for the Top Hoodlum Program, which sounds like something a child made up. They believe he's been informing the Negro press of his old travails as a means of covering his tracks. Kefauver wants a second go-round one day, and Elliot can't go giving every Negro newspaper the golden goose before he squeezes out a few eggs for himself. They'll charge him, if they have to, to get him to talk."

"Get him to talk about you?"

Frank held his stare, and his quiet. He kept his face soft, yet firm, even if his stomach was queasy speaking strong to a grown, powerful person.

"He's in hospital at Michael Reese, in Bronzeville, where Elliot and I have both collected a bit of trouble for ourselves."

"This real estate madness is giving us hell," Leo said.

The highway lights hit Frank's face.

"Good Lord," Margaret said. "You're just a baby."

"Twenty-two, ma'am."

"You're a long way from home, aren't you?"

"I thought so," Frank said. "Then I see the way you white folks do us, and I realize Mississippi follows me wherever I go."

Margaret sighed. Frank shook his head.

"You didn't deserve that, ma'am. I know you mean to help."

"I'm not sure what I mean to do."

Uncle Buster dozed off in his seat. Margaret McAlpin was quiet, staring out the window, watching the stalks go by. In time, Chicago's lights were visible in the far distance. The Town Car hi-fi played static. Leo turned the dial until Frank stopped him.

"Wait," he said.

In a very narrow band, with barely a signal, was a white man's voice. He sounded official. He called himself, "The Cardinal." "Now, you can trust your cardinal," this, and "You're hearing it from the cardinal," and so forth. He had something of a lilt. He sounded like good white folks, speaking calmly, and apologetically, about things best not uttered, but he had no choice but to tell the truth, so help him God, and the Vatican, who made him their messenger.

Through white folks' weakness for colored entertainers—for all things colored, really—jazz brought marijuana, and therefore the new American civil rights movement, which was designed by the Jews to replace white men with Negro savages under their control. Soon our cities and towns will be overrun with violent, revenge-minded niggers, as evidenced by Chicago, Detroit, Baltimore, and anywhere Negroes dared stand free, and dare to have personal lives.

"But fear not, white race," the Cardinal said. "Good, white, God-fearing Americans are standing up and drawing a line between Negro migrants and their Jewish shepherds."

The signal grew scratchy.

"Sponsors to this very program, such as the National Association for the Advancement of White People, The National Vanguard, and the White Circle League. Call now and join the fight to keep America white."

Leo switched it off.

"You'd be surprised how many radios at the club are tuned to this guy. We're all fighting each other on the streets, but the big shots are just telling us, to our faces, what they're doing to us all."

Frank leaned back in his seat.

"You'll stay with me in Lincoln Park," Margaret said. "Until we sort all this out. I'll make you comfortable."

Frank held his tongue as the Town Car crossed into Cook County and up the highway into Chicago.

CHAPTER 29

He wasn't particularly tough, unlike Jefferson. Sure, he could hold his own if tested, but he kept to himself. If he fought, it was to end confrontation, again unlike Jefferson, for whom conflict was only resolved with blood, and plenty of it. Buster Caprice learned to swiftly take a man down, before Jefferson could get involved, because then someone could die, same as back in Yazoo, which was why they were in that boxcar headed to Chicago in the first place.

He earned the nickname 'Buster,' as it was what he learned to do at the slightest sign of trouble when Jefferson Caprice was near. He busted up conflicts between men and busted up men who didn't understand when their lives were in danger for messing with, around, or about Jefferson Caprice. What Buster knew best was how to put part of his life into the ground and make it grow. He thought of doing that, but Jefferson beat lives into the ground back in the Delta, and so they rambled.

The train stopped at one of those small farming towns somewhere between St. Louis and Chicago, where good work could be had by a colored, as the government restricted European immigrants after *Casus belli* in 1917. He had also been warned not to step off the train in Southville for fear of the gangsters from Chicago who hid money there. Sure, Buster was afraid, except he had to pee so badly, and he figured if it were true they wouldn't care about him.

"Imma go lose my water."

"Bring back smokes," Jefferson said.

He rolled back on his bindle to sleep off the moonshine he sipped to pass the time. If he wasn't fighting and wasn't banging out a Ragtime number for tips, Jefferson sipped hooch, which, sadly, was how Buster preferred him, as he was a happy drunk. He was also an unholy terror when hungover.

Very little in Southville County was developed, but the train station was classy enough. It also afforded no opportunities to go behind a bush, or a tree, or a barn. Instead, Buster searched for a colored-only toilet until a trainman mentioned he was North, where none were there to help you stay alive. He let him in the porter's washroom. After he relieved himself, Buster remembered his brother's cigarettes.

As he stood in line in the convenience shop, he heard the train whistle blow and asked those ahead of him to let him pass. Colored, poor, voiceless, he went ignored. He couldn't go back without the smokes as Jefferson would be in such a foul mood and anything could happen, what with so many bodies packed inside that railcar. He couldn't just run out the door with them either.

The whistle blew twice, the signal for all aboard. One more whistle and the train would pull off with him or without. The former meant a life running after his only kin in the most dangerous city in America. The latter left him all alone, no family, no friends, no protectors, no work.

No fear.

He pondered, if only for a moment, the possibility of life, which was enough time for the third whistle. Billowing steam howled. The rhythmic churn of running gear kept time. Too many colored folks were trapped in those boxcars to allow the train to remain five more minutes.

Buster stepped out of line and slapped the package of cigarettes atop the counter. Leaving white folks' taunts behind him, he bolted out the convenience shop door. Down the track he ran as fast as he could. If he didn't catch the train, his only brother would wake up in Chicago and he'd be nowhere in sight. They didn't have a plan beyond a flophouse off Maxwell Street, in the Black Belt, which he read about in the pages of The Daily Defender. The newspaper kept giant bulletin boards in their publication offices for folks to leave information for friends and relatives lost through time and tyranny. Perhaps he could find him there. But if he couldn't, what then?

Chamber music filled his ears.

The train went further down the tracks. He couldn't bear to turn away until it vanished in the distance. He tried telling himself it was for the best. He was a farmer. He had no place in that teeming mess of corruption known as The Windy City. The only reason why it was in his plans was because Jefferson craved northern city lights. Truth be told, he felt less guilty about losing him than setting Jefferson loose upon Chicago without supervision.

"You're listening to WFMT—"

***

"—Chicago's classical radio."

Uncle Buster opened his eyes to the most beautiful thing ever, in front of the largest picture windows he'd seen, ever. She was strong, with long legs. She stood like she knew how to fight if she had to. He figured she was his boy's woman maybe, tough stance like that, although he wouldn't really know. He never said anything about his comings and goings since they fought about why he left Bradley Polytechnic, on account of him being light-skinned, full of himself, and angry enough to burn down the world. The mystery woman hummed along in time to the tune Buster didn't recognize. She sounded so beautiful, Buster worried the other shoe would drop and she'd tell him his boy was dead.

Buster sat up on the sofa. He felt dizzy. He'd never been off the ground so high before. Out the window, birds flew between the buildings, eventually reaching a fresh water body as big as an ocean.

"Ma'am," he said. She turned to him.

"You would have been more comfortable in a bed, sir."

"I got lost," he said with a wink.

Margaret frowned. Buster stood and put his hand over his eyes.

"Oh, very well," Margaret said, and she reached for a hand crank on the east wall. She turned it quickly, lowering the bamboo shades held on spools over the windows, ending the glare. "I'm sorry my cavernous sky palace is not comfortable enough for you."

She smirked. Buster wondered if she was cross.

He sat in the kitchen at her melamine table. Margaret put out bright red Bakelite coffee mugs. Buster wondered why everything in her house looked like candy with stars painted on it. As she poured out coffee for them, he remembered his nephew's story about the client who started as the mark and wound up a major player.

"I do wish you'd have slept in one of the bedrooms."

"They're too big," Buster said. "Has Frank called?"

"Not yet, I'm afraid. I asked my stepson to reach out through his people. These Federales scurry about with their secrets. Francis' direct approach may be best."

Buster's hands shook. A dribble of his coffee fell to the table. Margaret took a paper napkin from a holder and dabbed it.

"Imagine you know my nephew alright."

Margaret smiled a tiny bit, perhaps just to let him know a little more than he wanted.

"We are acquainted."

"He worked for you once," Buster said.

Margaret stared off. "More's the pity."

Buster sipped slowly, mainly because he was transfixed upon her shoulders and how perfectly they supported her swan's neck. Her angry swan's neck. He also noticed she had rough hands for a woman of her station. She opened a cigarette case and offered, but Buster pulled a perfect hand rolled from his flannel shirt pocket.

"Plain where he gets it."

"Miss Margaret," Buster said. "I can't begin to ask about you and my boy, but I thank you for your hospitality."

"My pleasure, Mr. Caprice."

"How long am I supposed to stick around here?"

"Frank Fuquay will call with any word."

Buster sipped again, slowly.

"Is this all your building, if you don't mind me asking?"

"Oh, no. I have another house across town," she said. "Several, I'm afraid."

"That's a lot of land."

"My late husband has handlers who meddle. I bought this place to actually have a life. Lots of guards. Lots of privacy."

"Ah," Buster said. "You and my nephew."

"No, though not for lack of trying," Margaret said, and she raised her coffee to him. "Likely as I have no mule."

She winked. Buster raised his cup to her.

"Is there anything about him…." Buster put his coffee cup down. "I wouldn't want to know?"

"Mr. Caprice, I'm not certain I'm the person to discuss this with you."

He placed both his shaky, black hands on the table, as if he laid his cards bare.

"You see, Miss Margaret," he said. "I drove that boy from me. He may not see it as such, but I did it. I didn't know what else to do. How he looks made it hard to discipline him, on account of how I look, you follow?"

She nodded.

"My Jew friend, Shapiro, had him for a while. Shapiro is true blue. Helped me teach him right. He fell in with his cousin."

"Rabinowitz," Margaret said.

"You know him?"

"I know what he meant to Elliot."

"Elliot looked like Shapiro some. Big nose. Curly hair. Skinny. I figured he could discipline him, help him stay straight, but the boy loses his North, you follow? He behaves so much like my brother. I lost my brother, you understand. To this city."

"I did not know that."

"The riots, in 1919. Red Summer, they called it."

Buster wrung his hands. They were cold. He was old. His weathered black face quivered around the eyes before they moistened in the corners. He remembered the train pulling off and learning how to despise himself.

"I'm responsible for him. I drove him from me. Now he might could die."

Margaret McAlpin took Buster Caprice by both his old, black hands and put her perfect aquamarine eyes onto his old red and brown ones.

"I've watched your nephew sacrifice himself to save you, your farm, and an enemy in the process, because it was right, although I did not see it so at the time, I assure you."

Margaret let go, took a sip of coffee and a drag of her cigarette. She studied Buster's face as she held the smoke, exhaling only as she made her point.

"Elliot Caprice is a full measure of a man, but until he believes so, we're all the poorer."

Margaret patted Buster on the knee.

"More coffee?"

"A light, please?"

Margaret leaned forward and silently offered Buster the lit end from the cigarette in her mouth. As she winked, and smiled, Buster knew exactly what the boy feared about her.

CHAPTER 30

Michael Reese Hospital was in Bronzeville, the polished end of the Black Belt, where most of Elliot Caprice's old cop stories were situated. It was always, "One night in Bronzeville," this. "This time, in the Black Belt," that. Frank sat ever riveted through the stories about the city, its attitudes and injustices. Now he rode in the back of Jon Costas's Lincoln, like a big shot, freely interacting with the stuff of the boss's nightmares. As they approached the main hospital building on South Ellis Avenue he wondered what his pap, Bigger Frank, would think seeing him that way, mired in the world's evil.

"Costas says Kefauver is putting together a new committee, bigger than before," Leo said. "Could be that's why they're holding Elliot."

Two black sedans with government plates were parked out front. Two men with black trench coats and black hats eyed every car that passed. Leo rolled down the window. An agent approached.

"I'm Jon Costas's man," he said. "This is—"

"Fuquay, Francis, M.," the stiff agent said. "Go inside, ask for the bridge to Meyer House."

Frank stepped from the car. Leonidas tried to, but Agent Stiff put a hand on his door.

"Alone."

Frank was led through the public lobby to a private hall befitting a fancy hotel. A black hatted guard waved them through to a private elevator manned by a Negro attendant. The elevator stopped. The attendant opened the gates. As Frank stepped from the elevator, he made at least three more guards, likely government types, standing in front of a room. One man walked forward. He was slim, with dark hair, and a scar across the bottom right of his chin. Black suit, black tie, white shirt. His shoes were expensive, unlike everyone else in the hall.

"Fuquay," he said. "John Creamer. We spoke on the phone."

"How is he?"

"Severe concussion," Creamer said. "Five broken ribs. Collapsed lung, left side."

Creamer opened the door. Elliot was bandaged across his chest. He was bruised and cut on his arms and face. An oxygen mask was strapped to his mouth and nose. He was also handcuffed by his left wrist to the bed rail. He seemed broken. Frank's heart ached.

"Is that necessary?"

"We both know how Elliot can be."

A wiry man, short, curly hair, tortoise-rim glasses, walked in the room. He carried a manila file folder.

"This is Special Agent in Charge Wiggins," Creamer said. "Fuquay works for Elliot Caprice on the farm. They met in St. Louis County jail, in the Meat Locker."

"The one the McAlpins have staying in the big house, hm?" Wiggins looked over the top of his glasses at Frank, who was unbothered. "My, how Caprice loves his associations with recreational criminals."

"The boss says the McAlpins are friends of the Creamers, if I recollect."

"Jon Costas-McAlpin is a rich Greek with a hang up," Creamer said.

"That stepmother of his," Wiggins said. "Margaret McAlpin? Lots of hostile chatter in the Black Belt about the queen of the race party set and your man Caprice. Are the guest rooms in Lincoln Park comfy?"

Wiggins made with the eyes again. Frank's guts turned.

"We want them all, Fuquay," Creamer said. "Accardo, Giancana."

"Rabinowitz." Wiggins pushed his glasses back to the bridge of his nose and produced a photo of Elliot smiling with Izzy at Mose Boysaw's funeral.

"Old buddies," Wiggins said. "What's that cute thing Caprice says about his white friends? Calls them his ace boon coons?"

"It was a man's funeral," Frank said.

"That's generally where the Director likes to arrest Outfit thugs." Wiggins put away the photo. Frank felt the squeeze begin.

"We don't have anything on the bombing," Creamer said. His tone had softened, but only a bit.

"As it could be anyone," Wiggins said. "Even Rabinowitz, who, friends or no, is sleeping easier thinking Elliot is dead."

"He's a sitting duck here."

"This is a private wing," Creamer said. "And these men are hand-picked."

"Rather than Margaret Thorne McAlpin's place, when the Negroes want him dead and he's all the way up in the sky, in her bed. At this point, if she gave them your boss, she'd be doing herself a favor."

"The waters are rising, Fuquay," Creamer said. "If Elliot makes it out of that bed, you're going to be surrounded by factions who all want you silenced. The time is now. Help us."

Never before had Frank Fuquay felt so sheltered, even beyond Mother Fuquay's smothering. For the longest time, he felt it noble to be kept out of Elliot's brushes with crime and criminality, but now he was in the center of a maze, and with no clear starting direction. It felt worse than being lost in the Mississippi backwoods in the dark.

"I need to bring his kin to see him," Frank said. "He's an old man. He's worried for him."

"My card," John Creamer said, handing it to Frank. "Tell them you're with me, and a witness."

"To what?"

"Whatever you'll give us," Wiggins said, expressionless. "Big guy."

Frank doffed his cap, turned, and stormed down the hall.

"Do jot down notes over at the Lincoln Park penthouse, Francis."

"That's quite enough about Lincoln Park," Creamer said to Wiggins.

Frank walked out to the car where Leonidas opened the door for him. The Big Man yanked the passenger door open instead and got in, red hot.

"What'd they say?"

"All of Chicago wants Elliot Caprice dead." Frank took off his hat.

"We knew that already."

Leo pulled off. Frank watched the road.

"They had a lot to say about your boss, as well as Miss Margaret. What is it with her, Leo?"

"I drive Jon to Pops McAlpin's place for a dinner, she's the maid. I bring him back after the funeral, she's holding the McAlpin family stake. I don't trust her, but I don't have to. I just drive the car, and carry the gun."

Frank watched the road, feeling dumb down in his guts how he trusted Uncle Buster with Margaret. What would the boss think?

"Leo," Frank said. "If I asked you to take me someplace without telling everyone else, you'd be square?"

"As long as you don't give me a reason to lie," Leonidas said. "Where to?"

CHAPTER 31

The security booth was foreboding, staffed with Sheriff's Deputies who all seemed too comfortable in their positions. They looked tired and out of shape. Not the sort you'd want at the front door if you cared for the contents inside. There were two halls, one with green walls, one blue. The blue went to the right. Green went straight back. He didn't quite have papers, so he produced his latest test results from the general equivalency exam with his name and address. He also had an envelope from his sister, Francine. They wrote letters to each other.

There was a gun rack behind the jailer with an entire wall of rifles. A mean-faced guard with pitted skin looked him up and down as he rifled through Frank's already faint privacy. Behind him, other guards drank coffee and chatted. Angry sounds bounced off the cinderblock walls. Shouts, screams. Epithets. Inmates seemed unruly and restless. In fact, most didn't seem like prisoners at all. The guards seemed to hate the place more.

An alarm went off. Coffee cups down. Guards fell into formation and grabbed weapons. Frank watched as a team of three ascended iron stairs that ran above him and took position upon a trellis. He wanted to run, but to where? His journey with Elliot Caprice steadily darkened his thoughts of the world, which for a Negro is already pretty bad. Now he was wandering through hell, where he once was a prisoner, but pulled himself up from the underground as a man. He did so by following Elliot, who lay at death's door, it seemed, and the County was so scary.

A nice old white fella, may have been Polish, wore a badge which read 'Miller.'

"You're who?"

"Frank Fuquay, private investigator."

"In which county?"

Frank thought for a moment. "Springfield, and Southville."

"Southville? Where's that?"

"Bean country, sir."

"And you have to speak with—?"

"Chauncey Ballard. I'm the one caught him," Frank said, tucking his balls in.

The white man scratched his head underneath his hat with a pencil, eraser end. "They don't let him have visitors."

"I'm not a visitor," Frank said. "I'm working a case."

"What case, Sherlock?" The guard chuckled.

Frank pulled the latest edition of the Chicago Daily Defender. In the dominant top-half of the newsprint was a photo of Mikey Rabinowitz from his college days. He had a baby face, with a suit and tie, looking out into the world, perhaps wondering what he'd make of it, or how he'd fix it. To the right, another snap of Elliot from his days on da job, baton in hand, holding back a frantic crowd of screaming Negro and white music fans in front of the Regal Theater. The headline read, 'Killed, By Hatred.' Frank held it up.

"I'm not sure, young fella."

"Mister, a Negro can be a gumshoe. It's not so uncommon."

"It is when they look thirteen years old." The guard stood and grabbed his key ring. "Visitor for division one!"

"Which inmate?" A guard on the other side of the powerful giant door.

"Ballard, Chauncey," the guard said.

"Let's go, young fella."

Frank stepped into a yard with chain-link fencing separating the inmates from the guards, who were brutally heckled as they exercised. One fell as he ran laps with his battalion.

"Retire that asshole," shouted a prisoner. Laughter rang out. The guards mostly ignored it.

Miller remained silent as Frank followed him across the yard to a guard outpost in front of a tunnel. The dormitory structure was two floors high, and as wide as a city block. The building was gray. Miller approached a large steel gate and held up his key. Frank watched as two men in the security booth pulled levers releasing the giant iron. Miller turned the lock with his key, joined by another guard in the same position from the other side.

"All these keys are a pain in the ass," the inside guard said.

"Blame it on Tony Accardo," Miller said. "The Outfit thinks they can take over this place, too."

Loud-voiced white men from down the hall shouted commands. The clanging of large iron cascaded throughout the cavernous tunnels, three in all, each leading to the hellhole that was Division One, Cook County Jail. He followed Miller into the tunnel and walked in near darkness to where, before he could see anything, he smelled feet and ass. Hundreds of feet and asses. Frank remembered the Meat Locker, and how his despair was interrupted by his chance encounter with Elliot in a place not that different, only smaller, and without so many dangerous folks.

Frank and Miller walked down the long, dank hall through the maximum security dormitory. He turned the key, opened the door, and the smell of broken humanity came over him. The narrow corridor with rows of tiny cells on each side was barely lit. It was dank, like a cave. Men cried out in sadness, or insanity, lashing out at those who laid them to rest behind iron bars, not in steel and concrete, but in their own hollowed out bodies and absconded consciousnesses. Long, gangly arms reached out and grabbed at Frank. The whispers and pleas of the damned filled his ears.

"Help me out, brother," one said, reaching out to Frank with talons for fingernails. "Help me get word to my people."

Another babbled in his cell as he sat forward, drooling on himself.

"Down this way," Miller said, as he flipped through cell keys. "Visitor for you, Ballard."

"Nobody wants to see me."

"Ballard," Frank said.

Chauncey turned slowly to him. He was bearded. His kinky hair was no longer hard brushed into a wave pattern, but overgrown and unkempt. He was graying. He looked gaunt. He wasn't present. Gone was the defiance. He was subdued. The state had him, same as Elliot mentioned. Miller opened the cell.

"You've got ten minutes."

Miller stepped out of the cell and waited outside.

"How you holding up in here," Frank said, watching Ballard's insane eyes.

"Like a nigger who killed a white woman. What do you want?"

"I need to ask you about Margaret McAlpin."

"I knew her as Margaret Thorne. You smoke?"

"If you're up for a conversation," Frank said, raising a fresh pack of Luckies he had the sense to grab for trade when he purchased the newspaper. Chauncey read the newspaper headline and laughed, softly.

"What happened?" Chauncey laughed.

"Bombing happened. Took out everyone on the block, damned near. He's barely alive."

"Caprice?"

Frank nodded. Chauncey cracked a smile, which widened into a pleased grin. Frank remembered Sissy Ellison's face as they told her she'd never see her sister Willow again.

"I ain't got a problem with you," Frank said. "I been locked up myself."

"Is that how you found Caprice?"

"I think he found me. We tied up in the same thing, with the same lady."

"Margaret."

"I'll be honest with you," Frank said. "I'm new at this. I'm frightened to death, but there's a lot more at stake than some money, or some foolishness in politics or crime. They're killing us wholesale, Ballard. Now, I know what it takes, alright? Maybe you need a favor on the outside. You still a man. You still got to have some life business."

Chauncey waved his hand.

"You can think of me. I'll owe you a favor."

"What you gonna do with my favor? Get me a Yoo-Hoo from down at the corner store?"

Frank was flummoxed.

"Caprice send you in here to torture me with kindness?" Chauncey straightened himself and lit a smoke. "She threw Black and Tan parties in the Belt when we were all in business school in the Loop."

"What's a black and tan party?"

Chauncey shook his head at Frank and smirked as he exhaled. His eyes seemed to light up behind the smoke.

"A get together, usually in some broad's flat, where you pay to get in the door, so you have a good chance of balling with a colored."

"Folks do that?"

Chauncey nodded. As he smoked and spoke, he seemed to grow more alive. At the business school, she passed around the privileges in the job placement department. She had the look, and that accent and manner worked on everyone. Her friends and folks who listened to her got the cushy assignments. If she didn't like you, they couldn't find you anything. If you were Negro, she pimped you out."

"What are you saying?"

"If you were colored, and you could fuck—"

Frank recoiled.

"—you became a special friend. That's how I met the McAlpins."

"You mean, both of them."

Chauncey nodded, slowly. "The second time, Old Man McAlpin brought his old lady."

"Who you killed."

"They never proved that. Instead of overreacting, she got them both laid. McAlpin was so impressed, he couldn't stop coming around. He was obsessed with Margaret's gumption. How driven at life she was. She became the maid."

"And Margaret was married to him not too long afterward."

"Once Margaret had control of the ships from Costas Cartage, the Black Belt got good reefer."

"Heroin as well?" Frank's jaw stiffened. "Which was why you killed that poor gal, Willow Ellison?"

"The aitch was me and her brother, branching out on our own, because the blonde didn't want us to make any money that didn't involve my penis."

"Her brother?"

Chauncey took another drag of his cigarette staring squarely into Frank's eyes.

"He's the one y'all threw me in the trunk with." Chauncey exhaled.

"Hold on a second," Frank said. "You're saying that Alistair Williams is Margaret's brother?"

"Her real daddy, that fella in the British Navy? That was Alistair Williams's father. His mother lived on the West End. A Jamaican castoff. Hear Alistair tell of it, she was a singer who also sewed dresses, something like that. Alistair found Margaret once he emigrated to Chicago fair and square, and she got him in the house as the driver."

The cell door rolled open. Miller wasted no time.

"That's it, boys."

Miller tapped Frank gently by the arm, but the Big Man didn't need convincing. He followed the guard out into the corridor.

"Fuquay," Chauncey said.

Frank turned around. He was immediately transfixed by Chauncey's stare, which was evil, as purely as Frank had ever seen in a man before.

"Best to your man, Caprice," Chauncey said.

Chauncey chuckled as smoke escaped his teeth. A chill fell down Frank's spine which he carried past every lost soul locked in that place and out into the Lincoln Town Car, where Leonidas took one look at him and nearly gasped.

"You alright, Big Guy?"

Frank didn't know how to say he'd never be alright again. Not without sounding like a kid.

"I need to get Uncle Buster to the boss."

Frank's hands trembled. Leo geared the Lincoln and pulled off.

CHAPTER 32

Uncle Buster was wearing a robe and slippers and reading the paper in Miss Margaret's living room. The hi-fi played jazz. She sat in a sculpted wood and leather chair, legs crossed, her foot swinging in the air to time. She was lively, and vibrant. She had rhythm. Margaret noticed Frank standing there, staring. He felt embarrassed. She turned down the music.

"Francis," she said.

"Uncle Buster," Frank said. "Time to go see Elliot."

Uncle Buster stood. "I better get some clothes on."

"You'll find new things for you hanging in the chifforobe, Nathan."

"Nathan, she called him," Frank whispered to Leo, who chuckled and went down the hall. Buster walked over.

"What'd they say?"

"Elliot is in big trouble."

"That boy," Buster said. "He just don't listen."

Buster walked away. The living room dropped a few degrees. Frank stood by the door.

"You're a guest, Francis," Margaret said.

Frank took off his hat and shoes before he sat on the couch. Margaret watched him the entire time.

"How is he," Margaret asked.

"He'll live," Frank said. "Unless everyone keeps helping him."

"I feel that's a pointed comment."

Frank stepped toward her and lowered his head, and his voice.

"Everywhere I turn folks say a lot about you Miss Margaret. So much, it's hard to sort what's spiteful from what's fair. I try to stay out of it."

"How wise of you."

"A woman in your position has to do a lot to keep all these fellas off you."

"Go on."

"The boss appreciates when I do my homework. When I follow through, you understand?"

"I don't believe I do." Margaret sat up, lit a cigarette, and crossed her legs.

"I know how all this began," Frank said. "At the business school in the loop. And your parties."

Margaret looked away, smiling. "You've visited Cook County jail."

"Yes, ma'am."

"Perhaps Elliot will present you with a merit badge," Margaret said. "Junior shamus."

"Perhaps I wind up a hot interview after all this, and I mention Alistair Williams' parentage."

Margaret took a slow drag before matching eyes with Frank. "I imagine that'd put some sand in the gears."

"It might, ma'am."

"And what am I to do for your discretion?"

Frank took off his hat. "Don't sell out the boss, Margaret. Don't give him up, not to the Negroes, or the Outfit, or the coppers. No one. He wouldn't give you up. Not for anything. Not in a million years. He hasn't."

Margaret looked away. "No, he hasn't."

"Elliot keeps me out of the street stuff," Frank said. "He won't discuss it, but to warn me away from it. He wouldn't say much about Chauncey Ballard, but I could see in his eyes he felt bad for the fella."

"Chauncey certainly doesn't feel bad for him."

"No," Frank said. "But he doesn't have to. That's how the boss is."

"You're unreal, Francis."

"I didn't go digging around anything the boss doesn't already know, and I didn't ask. Ballard gave it up. I didn't believe it was true until I caught your tell."

"I don't have any tell."

"The way you look away, and say something smart, Miss Margaret, means I got you in a lie."

Margaret shook her head.

"My sister does it, too."

"You have a sister."

"A little sister," Frank said. "Francine."

"Francis, and Francine." Margaret stared at Frank with wonderment.

"Miss Margaret, I spent lots of time with Elliot this year, speeding around from city to city, fighting with folks, chasing down those who hurt other people. I know he seems angry at everything, and he'd take the world down with him, but as long as I've known him, the man's only ever tried to do the right thing. Don't leverage him. Just ask him to help you."

"Leverage him? Francis, what are you on about?"

"The FBI told me you have the kind of problems you could use Elliot to get out of. Maybe just ask him to help you. He would."

"He would."

"Help your friends, leverage your enemies. That's what the boss says."

"That's what the boss says."

"That way, when the game is over, no one is mad who didn't have it coming."

Margaret smirked.

"Half-Negro Lao Tzu, that one. Very well. You have my allegiance. Shall we take an oath? Cut our fingers and press them together. You'll have to accept white blood. I'm afraid it's all I have."

"Miss Margaret, c'mon now."

"Francis," Margaret said, and she extinguished her butt in the ashtray. "I may not ever know what to do with Elliot Caprice, but I know I don't want to leverage him, or whatever you're on about. So, you violated my privacy for nothing."

"It's not so private if Chauncey Ballard has the goods on you, ma'am. I hope you're not mad at me for saying it."

"No," Margaret said, and she sighed. "This pickle I'm in I pulled out of the jar myself. I wouldn't sell Elliot out, but we're surrounded, all of us."

"The boss will know what to do," Frank said. "Keep faith."

Uncle Buster walked in wearing new flannel, black corduroy jeans, and a nice brown sweater. He looked handsome.

"Looking sharp, Nathan," Margaret said.

Buster nodded. "I'm ready."

Leo walked up behind him. "I'll get you in the car, Mr. Caprice."

Leo and Buster walked out the door. Frank stood in the vestibule. Margaret walked over.

"Francis, does Elliot speak of me?"

"He does," Frank said. "Not in such ways. Nicely. He smiles."

"Really?"

"He said he understands why you're mad all the time, and that you're dangerous because you're so pretty, the rage doesn't show until it's too late."

Margaret grinned, and pulled the door open.

"You weren't going to turn him over anyhow, were you?"

"He's worth more alive."

"You frighten me, Miss Margaret."

"Yes, well, you bean farmers scare quite easily."

CHAPTER 33

Elliot walked into Joe's Deluxe on South State Street. Hap Hinshaw, his old war corporal, was seated at the mahogany bar. He looked like a straight, with his brown high and tight, and bushy cop mustache. He was heavier than his days in the service, which meant the work was easier. As a ranking detective in the Black Belt, he was the power over angry, adventurous Negroes and not the babysitter of them, as he had been in Patton's 3rd Army. He was enjoying his status, drinking and absorbing Negro elite culture out in the open, even as he possessed the power to undo it. At least he was a down-ass white boy, who loved him some Negroes, queers 'n all.

"Mixie!"

Elliot brushed the snow off his olive drab woolen. The pretty, big legged coat check girl with hazel eyes and slightly crooked teeth took it off of him. He tipped her more than she'd make that night, kissed her on the cheek, then whispered in her ear something which made her blush. Hap chuckled. Elliot sat next to him and caught the eye of the bartender.

"Show off."

"Figure she's starved for attention."

The main room swelled with patrons of different hues. Everyone wanted a good seat for the drag trio, all the way from France, including all the queer ofays who found shelter and security within the Black Belt, where they wouldn't have to be closeted, not with their sexuality nor their respect for colored folks who, in harboring them in their joints and parties, had the power to free them, for a time, from living after the world's opinion. A colored butch in a bandoleer and a high-and-tight grabbed a white Betty Boop around the waist, kissed her deeply and squeezed her ass. Betty slipped out of her grasp with a giggle and sauntered over to a large black leather booth to take an order. She was ignored by an ofay who looked like the Illinois State's Attorney as he gently made out with a Puerto Rican from Humboldt Park with the body of a swim team captain, their kisses like soft brush strokes on a forbidden canvas. So many shades and gender configurations huddled in fleeting expression of desire's truth. Everyone played their little pretend games on the South Side of Chicago in 1948. Elliot Caprice was no exception.

The dapper bartender with the chocolate-rose skin of the Masai glided over.

"Hey, now, Sunshine." He laid his hand atop Elliot's.

"Sugar."

"I'm gonna pay that girl to burn that damned coat. War's over, Sunshine. Tom and tonic?"

Elliot nodded and sat. Sugar went to his work.

"Where's your Miss Ann?"

"She'll be here," Hap said.

"How she slow-draggin' and so damned uptight?"

"Some of us work during the day."

"Now you sound like that old man down in Southville."

Sugar brought over his drink. Elliot squeezed the lime into it and hoisted it to his lips. He knocked it back, sat it down, and tapped on the rim of the glass. Sugar shook his head and took to his work once more. He returned with more Old Tom, less tonic. Elliot squeezed the lime and raised the glass.

"You want another? I got it."

"Can't. On tonight."

Elliot looked at him. "Where's your uniform?"

"Training supervision. Flattening feets."

"How many foot soldiers does Chicago need?"

"The Outfit claimed the entire class of '46, damned near. Killing 'em, some. Bribing 'em, mostly."

Elliot watched hurt escape the edges of Hap's eyes.

"See," Elliot said. He slapped the bar. Old Tom entered the conversation. "That's why I can't do it, Hap."

Sugar brought Elliot another Old Tom.

"You can't do it, but you took the exam."

"I took the exam to hush up you and your colored girlfriend."

"Nadine isn't my girlfriend," Hap said. "Goddamnit, Elliot, you of all people would be perfect at it. You see how quickly I advanced in three years. Bars, already."

"Why then are you stuck working the Black Belt, huh? Indiana boy. Decorated veteran of the European theater. Walking the slums of the South Side."

Elliot lifted his drink.

"You're incorruptible, so you get to work the Black Belt. That's how they do an honest man in Chicago."

Before he could sip the last of his gin with barely a hint of tonic, two wide-bodied, sharp-suited colored men in fedoras burst through the door. Patrons complained about the sudden blast of winter air. The big fella on the right wearing brown looked around before he made eyes with Sugar Styles. Sugar ran to the end of the bar closest to the main room, looked, ran back and nodded to him. Brown turned toward the door and waved someone in.

From the cold walked a tall, doe-eyed man. He could pass. He had Elliot's shade, but more favored an older, slouchier white man. He had a thin mustache. He wore a topcoat over his gray double-breasted suit. He stepped in two-tone black and white shoes. Crowned with a short-brim Dobbs atop his balding head, he was dressed like a funeral director.

"Detective Hinshaw. You serving and protecting in Joe's Deluxe?"

"I was just leaving," Hap said.

"Then push on, constable. Those wrongs aren't going to right themselves."

Elliot averted his gaze, but a moment late.

"Hey. Don't I know you?"

He sipped his drink. Blue leaned in and grabbed his arm, spilled his liquor, a hanging offense.

"The man said, 'Don't he know you?'"

Brown stepped between Elliot and Hap. Impossibly, Joe's Deluxe fell even quieter. Elliot spun around on his stool. A metallic flick. A bit of blood to assist Brown's present moment awareness. Blue's shoulders tensed. A click. Elliot's .32 was in the Negro boss man's gut. Just like that, Elliot Caprice had the jump on the most influential Negro in Chicago's colored underworld.

Again.

"You still alive," Teddy Roe said. He swatted Brown and Blue away.

Elliot didn't speak. Hap raised his badge.

"This man is my friend, and a veteran, and if he says you don't know him, Teddy—"

"I know him, Hap," Elliot said.

"See? Me and this man go back, Hinshaw." Teddy grinned. "Caprice, right? Uncle owns his own land in Beanville?"

Murmured laughter grew from the crowd.

"Southville," Elliot said, quickly, crisply.

"What he grow again?"

Elliot felt the eyes. Always eyes, all over him.

"String beans."

The crowd laughed.

"Roseland Boys lend me money at two extra points because I gotta pay the colored man's tax to the Jew. We can all thank our friend Giveadam Jones for that. Gave it up to Izzy Rabinowitz the night he was strung up. Wish he gave-a-damn about them two points."

Laughs.

"Money ain't even clean, charges Negroes a premium, anyhow."

Gasps.

"Still won't bring it to me himself. Ain't coming to the Black Belt no more, he says. Maybe it ain't Kosher, I don't know. I do like me some pig's feet once in a while."

Elliot's thighs seized. His belly felt hot at the bottom. It was starting, same as all the fights with the other colored soldiers. Same as the cops in Champagne-Urbana. The point of no return.

"Every week, the Black Belt pays up to Rabinowitz, on time. Tend to our mutual business, tip-top. Izzy Rabinowitz only sends his nigger, the teenaged bean farmer, in his uncle's stolen pickup truck, with our cash."

"Oohs," and "Ahs," and "Whats."

"We saw him every weekend. He's their Shabbos goy, they call it. It's how the Hebes say house nigger."

Elliot felt the ire around him rise to where it crackled in his ears. Side jokes. Teeth sucking. Someone touched his miscegenated hair, which meant it was getting out of hand.

"Teddy Roe, head nigger in charge of where the streets ain't paved," Elliot said. "Didn't know King Oscar DePriest's leash ran that long. Better get a collar with a tag, before Hap Hinshaw writes you a citation."

The room turned quiet. No one, ever, came for Teddy Roe. That's why Elliot had to.

"You can get fucked up, poppin' cute in Joe's Deluxe, Lightskin."

"How's it working the Nash-Kelly political machine for your shekels, Teddy? Didn't know your red ass had Irish in you. Or perhaps it does, now."

A few snickers from the crowd drew a rebuke from Teddy's body men. Otherwise, it was as quiet as a mortician's cold room.

"You couldn't possibly be here to wear blue like your buddy Detective Hinshaw, could you? Insane as you are?"

"Just passing through after Europe."

"Europe? Ain't the war over, Elliot Caprice? Or are you helping Izzy Rabinowitz build Israel?"

Everyone laughed except Teddy and Elliot. Sugar Styles held his breath. Hap Hinshaw stepped forward to intervene, but Elliot raised his glass and snickered, ending it.

"Teddy Roe," he said. "Nice seeing you."

"Elliot Caprice," Roe said. "The craziest half-nigger in the Belt. You out of the game, huh?"

"No string beans," Elliot said. "No short paper. Swear on my uncle's pick-up truck."

Teddy extended his hand to Elliot, which drew immediate notice around the bar. Elliot accepted, granting him clout in the Black Belt. Once again, he walked the streets of Chicago, marked with the stink of a kingpin. Teddy slipped away, with his entourage, who stole little glimpses of Elliot, their faces contorted in wonder who he was, and how much power he may hold. The stares reminded him of Izzy Rabinowitz in Doc's clinic all those years ago. Uncle Buster was right, damn him. Always hungry eyes, wherever he went, and the hungriest eyes were always Negro.

Hap stared at him. "You could've told me you know Teddy Roe."

"Everyone knows him." Elliot looked away.

Elliot reached into his pocket for his billfold. He was eager to skate.

"Gotta settle up, Sugar."

"Money's no good here anymore, Sunshine."

Sugar pointed to where Teddy Roe, most influential Negro in Chicago, bar none, enjoyed the drag show as if he could give a shit what was between the performer's legs.

"Dare I say, it won't be for some time."

As Hap Hinshaw finished his beer, Elliot felt tightness in his chest.

"Take the physical, Elliot."

"No, Hap," he said. "I'm not joining the damned cops."

"Just try it. They're taking anyone."

He heard the sound of air rushing, followed by a click, before it started again. His face felt hot. His chest hurt something fierce. He couldn't lift his left arm, which felt cold at the wrist. For some reason, he heard his uncle snoring.

He slowly opened the one eye that wasn't bandaged. He knew he wasn't dead because he looked out onto Lake Michigan. Seagulls chased ferry boats to and from Benton Harbor. He ached in his chest. His face hurt. Buster Caprice was asleep in the chair next to him, snoring so loudly it reached across dimensions. Elliot reached for the mask over his face with his bad arm, but it was cuffed to the bedrail. Yanking on it hurt his chest like hell. He growled and shook his shackle. Buster sat up quickly. His eyes were bloodshot. He looked horrible. Elliot sighed in relief as his uncle gently removed the mask. He tried smiling, but everything hurt.

"Hi, Unk."

Buster stroked Elliot's face. He bit deeply into his bottom lip as he cried, softly.

"Hi, boy."

"Don't cry, Unk."

"I hate this city," Buster said, wiping his face. "She takes so much."

"She ain't so bad, after she kills you once or twice."

Elliot managed half a grin. Buster took his nephew into his arms.

"I love you, Unk."

"I love you, boy."

"Too much to die on you."

"I appreciate that."

CHAPTER 34

"Unk, where am I?"

"Michael Reese Hospital," Buster said.

"In Bronzeville?" Elliot shook his new bracelet.

"The FBI brought you here after the bombing."

"The bombing."

The memories returned. The fight with Michael Rabinowitz, over nothing but the changing times and their sway over the desperate. Elaine, whom he implicated, angrily, before she was nearly crushed. He didn't know whether she survived, although she seemed alive. He remembered a face full of floor, and wall. With blurred vision, he detected light. Red. Blue. Amber. An approaching ambulance, although much too soon. The strobing colors made his head hurt, like the rest of him. He tried pushing himself up, but his ribs let him down. He thought of combat in Germany, when peckerwoods weren't careful about colored soldiers clearing out before the bombing runs. He halfway writhed from under the large blocks of fallen wall, ceiling, and person, when a helpful ofay that looked much like the fella following him in Rockford, Illinois pulled him clear outside. A chorus of screaming onlookers, none colored, gaped at the three-story flaming mouth in the building. Smoke billowed through the decimated front entrance. The raging fires of hate burned down the block and even across the street. Cars were ruined. Lucille was buried under debris. He tried fighting back but two white coats held him on a gurney and cuffed him. He tried screaming at them but his throat felt like it was on fire. A siren's wail hailed from the distance.

"Go," the tail said to the white coats, and they took to their own vehicle, the typical black sedan no one but a Fed would drive.

Squad sirens grew in his ears. One engine company arrived, then another, all too late. He coughed blood. It hurt to breathe. He began to lose consciousness. One paramedic opened the ambulance doors before he helped slide him into the wagon. One lit a smoke as the other shut the doors, saying something to the effect he could see it coming, the way Negroes behave and all.

Then black.

Frank walked in sipping coffee from a paper cup. His jacket was off. His sleeves were rolled up. He looked as if he hadn't slept in days. When he saw Elliot he just stood there, straight and tall, smiling. His eyes watered.

"That's the way, boss." He wiped his face with the back of his hand.

Elliot pointed to his bandage.

"What happened to you?" It hurt so bad to talk.

"Southville has been under siege, damned near. A bunch of random attacks happened the same time as the bombing at the office, including the jail."

Elliot remembered the ledger he stole from Bradshaw's office. He tried sitting up, which was almost as agonizing as the truth: he may have absconded with evidence that brought the heat upon his friends. Frank Fuquay slipped his huge arm underneath him. Uncle Buster hurried over and placed pillows behind his back. Elliot coughed up something harsh before he got his wits.

"Lay it out for me, Big Man."

Frank Fuquay pulled a stenographer's notebook from his pocket, the kind Elliot suggested for his schoolwork. He flipped through a few sheets of math problems.

"About the time they attacked the office, someone attacked the jail. One casualty, Sheriff George, bullet to the gut, in hospital."

"Oh, no," Elliot said.

"Just prior, Deputy Ned arrested Eugene Brophy for fighting at the Seed and Supply with white folks he says were riled up by this pamphlet."

Frank went in his other pocket and produced the White Circle League handout.

"I'm pretty sure the same folks who burned down the roadhouse came for our place."

"Burned down the roadhouse?" Elliot coughed, violently. "Is Miss Betty?"

"It's alright," Buster said, handing him water. "She's staying with us until we figure out what's going on."

"Miss Betty's staying with us?" Elliot handed Buster back the glass. "Forget it, Unk. Let me die."

"They tossed the living room, the covered porch, and the barn, most likely, before they set fire to it, which ran off the workers, covering their tracks. The arsonists painted a large, white circle with a cross in it over the door, which I'm sure represents the folks who print those pamphlets, and the state police that trusts in that nonsense. I ain't figured out how the jailhouse hit fits into the mix yet, but I'm figuring on it." Frank flipped his notebook shut.

"I know how," Elliot said. "That's fine work, Frank. Don't let your studies slip."

"I haven't."

John Creamer walked in looking standard issue, except for his rich boy details: his dark suit was tailored. He wore his law school class ring, on the same hand as his Cartier watch. He couldn't possibly have a true friend amongst the FBI's rank and file. Wiggins trailed behind, like a small, angry dog.

"John," Elliot said.

"Caprice," Wiggins said. He held up the offending edition of the Chicago

Daily Defender. "Sorry for your loss."

"Just so's you know, Unk," Elliot said. "I ain't dead."

"There's a good boy."

A photo of Elaine lying in the hospital at Springfield General, bandaged, unconscious, ran in the side margin. "Clinging to life," read the caption.

"Kefauver reads the news, Caprice," Wiggins said. "He didn't appreciate that bit about him leaving you out to dry."

"Then he ought've not have done it."

Creamer turned to Uncle Buster. "Sir, there's a private dining hall here. Lovely food."

"I ain't hungry," Buster said.

"I'm in good hands," Elliot said, smiling at Frank.

"I could eat," Frank said.

"You could, always," said Uncle Buster, as he followed Frank out the door, staring John Creamer down the entire stretch.

"What gives, making me a prisoner?"

"It's so no one could kidnap you," John said. "Or worse. We need to talk."

"About why you've been following me?" Elliot coughed. "Or why you never show up before I get hurt?"

Elliot coughed again. Things moved around inside him that shouldn't. Creamer got him some water. He was kind. Elliot didn't like it. It felt like a con.

"We put a man on you since we picked up chatter on the wire that the Outfit considers you a risk to talk," Creamer said. "Elliot, you said Teddy Roe would come in, of his own volition."

"And he was, John," Elliot said. "Until that night in Bill Drury's garage."

"Until you ran," Wiggins said. "Once you did, Roe wouldn't comply. Said he didn't feel safe. Now we know, he helped you disappear."

Creamer folded his arms. "That's also why you wore the handcuff. We're not sure that we shouldn't arrest you."

"Teddy Roe never came in after you went on the lam," Wiggins said. "Sam Giancana plotted his murder on a boat out the Lake Calumet Marina."

Atop all his other ills, Elliot's stomach turned.

"The cops let the hit happen to him, right out in the open, where he's kingpin. The Outfit shut down the street to get him. How's that happen, if Negroes don't let it happen?"

"John, Teddy Roe ran his mouth on every mob-connected prosecutor he knew in Illinois to skate on killing Fat Lenny Caifano," Elliot said. "That's what did him in. No one knew he was going to talk to Kefauver."

"Someone knew," Wiggins said. "Other than you and Teddy Roe. That's how it wound up in the Chicago Bee."

Elliot hated Wiggins like a father-in-law who was right about everything.

"The chatter says they're coming to tidy you up next, and the Negro underworld is alright with it. Have you tangled with them?"

"I tangled with all of them, John. That's what happens when you're colored and you fight crime in the Black Belt. You get tangled."

"Come in," Creamer said. "Start with giving us Izzy Rabinowitz, who's responsible for half the bloodshed in your hometown."

"Bloodshed caused by Marion Bradshaw, whom you must know."

"We do," Creamer said. "He has some link to Roe, but his tracks are clean."

"That's because you don't know Negroes," Elliot said. "My man has pieced together an angle."

"Your man," John said, looking stern. "You mean the twenty-two-year-old felon?"

"Who has my back better than you did. I've got something that ties it all together, but I need out of this hospital and a few days."

"To cover your tracks," Wiggins said.

"To ensure you don't get anything incriminating on the Negro movement," Elliot said.

"The Outfit wants you dead for scrubbing evidence for Rabinowitz, and no one else. Your fellow Negro hoods are likely on a boat in that same marina with Giancana plotting how to kill you. Who could you possibly be loyal to, at this point?"

"You're talking about Frankie Freeman," Creamer said.

"Marion Bradshaw is her client. She's a serious attorney, and a good one. He also has something on Elaine Critchlow, who doesn't need any more problems, as I assume she isn't being protected by J. Edgar as well as I am."

"Two of our men are in the lobby of Springfield General," Wiggins said.

"Once good folks are clear, I've got what your masters need. Otherwise, you're not getting anything out of me that may harm the movement. If you take down a criminal or two, I figure that's what we criminals have coming to us."

"You amaze me, Caprice," Wiggins said. "Wherever they sell sausage and meatballs, or red beans and rice, everyone wants you dead, and you still want to bargain everything on your own terms. You've got three days. After that, we'll assume you're of no use to us."

Wiggins unlocked Elliot's cuff and walked out.

"What's going on? The damned streets are filled with fascists." Elliot held up the handbill. "The Illinois State Police half-operates like the Klan. They attacked my Uncle's land, John."

"How can I help?" John Creamer seemed sincere.

"Keep me dead for a while," he said. "I need to get out in front."

"We won't tell," John said. "You just stay low, and keep the body count down. I'll find out what the Bureau has on Bradshaw."

"I really want to know what's going on with his entanglement with Mikey Rab—"

Elliot stopped talking. He just sat still.

"I'm very sorry about your business partner, Elliot."

"He was a good man."

"He was," John said. "His father, not so much. Now, you really don't owe Izzy Rabinowitz anything."

John Creamer walked out.

When Frank and his uncle returned, he swung his legs out and sat on the bed, hurting but alive, and ready to put sail against the violent wind of his rectitude.

He just couldn't move so well, so his Uncle and Frank got him dressed. The FBI body man who followed him in Rockford helped him to the McAlpin Family town car. He said something about hanging in there. It was unexpected.

"Leo," Elliot said.

"Good to see you, Elliot."

"Where are we headed?"

"Mrs. McAlpin's," Leo said.

Elliot slowly turned to Frank.

"I thought on my feet, boss," he said, grinning awkwardly.

"It's alright, Frank," Elliot said. "Just as long as we leave before she becomes our new auntie."

Elliot cut his eyes toward Uncle Buster, who smirked as he held Elliot's hand.

Leo geared the Lincoln and pulled off.

CHAPTER 35

Nothing in Margaret McAlpin's master bath worked right. The sink stopper was built-in with a chrome lever. Elliot had to figure out how to turn on the water. He wanted to shave at least, before his meet with Jon Costas-McAlpin at the club. He'd shower, if he could figure out how to turn that on, or take a bath, but he was afraid to lie down again. He felt like dying. He opened the cabinet in search of some shave cream when he blacked out. He held onto the sink for stability, knocking over Margaret's fine porcelain lady schmutz canisters.

She walked in.

"I know you're angry with me, but must you take it out on the cosmetics?"

"Shtum," Elliot said.

Margaret went to him, sitting him atop her toilet. "You madman."

"I need to look presentable," Elliot said. "Can't let other Negroes see you weak. Not in Chicago."

Margaret found a man's shaving soap and brush in her lady's bureau. Elliot grinned.

"Mind your business," she said, before she opened the water and made suds. She lathered his face for him, deeply but gently.

"What's your gambit, hero?"

"The Top Hoodlum Program," Elliot said. "My man inside—"

"The one who helped you ruin my reputation?"

"Same. They're after Negro improvement groups, tracing the donor money back to its sources. That's gotta rankle a fat cat like T.R.M. Howard. He can't allow himself to be exposed to that much risk. He'll tango, I'm sure of it."

"If he meets with you," Margaret said. She began shaving him with the safety razor. "He's been Jon's chief opposer since the planning commission started. If this Bradshaw is his man, why will he play ball?"

"Because he can't afford to go down with Bradshaw and the Negro underworld. He's too big in the minds of the rank and file, same as Elijah Muhammad. The poor, worshipful elevator operators of the world have other options for heroes. You don't want to hear what the Bowties have to say anymore, go find a new kink. Better for them to cast out Bradshaw."

"You're willing to irk the RCNL, the Nation of Islam, and the entire Black Belt to destroy one man?"

"I better not find your name in that ledger of Bradshaw's, either."

Elliot lifted his chin to hers. Margaret continued shaving him.

"Assigned Detective Elliot N. Caprice," she said. "You should've been a firefighter. That way you could put out candles with water cannons."

"Swells like Howard can't afford to be associated with these Outfit tactics. Killing. Extortion. He plays it like Rockefeller. Muhammad plays it like a saint. Respectability is a tough con. It costs way too much to keep up."

"Lord," Margaret said. "Ain't that the truth."

Elliot grabbed Margaret's hand. "Now, what's yours?"

"My what?"

"Play, sister," Elliot said. "Why do you give a toss what's happening with me?"

"I have my own issues with the Negro underworld and I'm hoping for your help with them."

"I helped you enough," Elliot said. "And you know they won't listen to shit I have to say."

"Perhaps your ledger has something in there to help. A bit of leverage, perhaps."

"Margaret, you can just walk away."

She took water from the sink, splashed his face, wiped it with her hands, then dried it with a towel.

"There," she said. "Now you look good enough to die well."

Margaret lifted Elliot by his good shoulder, helping him to his feet.

"When you're all done in here, the tailor is waiting in the hall."

"Tailor?"

"Well, you can't go in the clothes they nearly killed you in, now can you?"

Something in him moved, not as a result of the bombing.

"Lady, why does it feel you're just some girl from Elgin, Illinois with a really good drama coach."

"Says the brokenhearted policeman who misses his badge."

Margaret left the bathroom. Elliot shook his head, and even that hurt too much.

The line of angry white folks stretched down the block. Ashcan fires were going, keeping hands and faces Ned Reilly didn't recognize warm, flames flickering in their harsh eyes as they cut them toward Negro field workers who arrived ready to hold their own. Suit-wearing white men fell in line with crackers. All chanted slogans related to keep America for Americans, whatever that meant. Women and children shouted back to the police, and each other. Negroes huddled up in smaller circles as they watched the play. The air felt electrified. All leveled mistrust, and scorn, at their neighbor.

Ned and Eugene approached the front door, only to be stopped by a uniform dick.

"Sorry Sheriff," he said, through his tight lips. "No one goes in as they're setting up."

"Deputy," Ned said. "So's he."

"Heard the colored fella took one in the gut," the cop said.

"That makes you acting sheriff, right, Dep?"

"Not around here, Eugene," Ned said. "Not tonight."

The hall doors opened. Southville's proletariat filed inside. It was open air, in a big hall with lacquered wood everywhere, and a long bench. Auctioneers showed up monthly to move livestock, so Human Resources may as well have been on the agenda. Ned noticed the bank's people seated on stage already, as was the leader of the Stateys, that jerk Meyer, in full uniform.

Whichever asshole the county elected to be president for two years banged the gavel. Now it seemed like a patriotic rally. War vets were paraded through the crowd with a color guard holding flags. They marched in lockstep through the back of the crowd toward the stage and took place underneath a giant-sized mural of George Washington, beautified, aglow in his divine power. Old Glory hung as large banners aside the American king, stars both in regular, and colonial configurations. Who Ned didn't notice was Izzy Rabinowitz, or any member of his Roseland Boys political block. Not even Abe Saperstein was there, and he normally was, but no Jews could be found, especially after the bombing that claimed Michael Rabinowitz, not to mention the foul reach of the White Circle League and their propaganda.

Once common matters were cleared off the agenda—new taxes, regulations for whatever—they moved on to hearings. Ned made Molly Duffy at the front door. She walked over to him, pushing past angry war veterans who sat in the seats near the aisles. A few shoving matches started in the back. In the balcony, Negroes remained in self-segregation, thin balm for the growing ache of uncertainty.

Everyone took their turn on the microphone. No one asked any questions. One white fella complained the labor force had enough of the hassles of the city fathers, he should be able to hire whomever he wished for the job at hand. After he sat down, another man stood up.

"White men need a labor union free from Jews and colored influence so we can set fair wage prices for white farmers."

The balcony of blacks shouted down the assertion. A crackpot ran toward the stage and yanked the microphone for himself, carrying on about using

American ideals to demand the government be returned to the white race, and he was for the ordinance because law, order, and stability needed to be ensured. A Negro ran to the stage and tried snatching the microphone. Members of the rank and file seized him and beat him down on the stage. Negroes emerged from the balcony to assist him, but Ned leaped to the stage and began shoving folks back.

"Get back to your seats," he said. "For Christ's sake, think about what's important."

"Tell them that," a Negro said, as he pointed out to the hostile crowd.

Molly Duffy was soon on stage, snatching the mic from one of the cops.

"I want to know what puts Duffy's Tavern on your dry list," she said, pointing at the County president, and Meyer. "Other than we enjoy serving Negroes in our establishment. I also want to know why, all of a sudden, everyone is worried over the price of wages when I know the pennies you pay, because your field hands pay it to me to drink their cares away. So, as a business owner, and as a lady born in this damned county, I need to know why, now, after Negroes have been here since you founded this rat hole for Frank Nitty, would this ordinance need passing?"

The crowd turned silent as a strawberry-blonde vision gave them what for.

"Thousands of people migrating North come through Southville. Some remain, others move on. All my years, it's never been the Negroes starting the ruckus. Negroes have, from time to time, continued the ruckus, and for that, the law is the law. Otherwise, you're all wrong for this, what you're about to do, and there will be a reckoning."

Ned stood up, he couldn't stand it anymore.

"I'm Acting Sheriff Reilly," he said. "These men feel we can't police our town. I'm taking deputies, same as Eugene here, to help this harvest. We're from here. We can make this work on our own. Vote down this ordinance, come on down to the jail and get yourself a badge, and stand up for what's right."

"What's the pay?"

Ned pointed to the white man in the back. "We need volunteers again this year. We don't have the budget yet. But we'll get it."

"This is why I pay taxes," another white man from the front shouted. "And fought for this country!"

"Negroes fought for this country, same as you white folks."

"More so!"

Shouting and shoving returned. Ned looked over at the board seats. Every face turned away from him. Ned put on his hat.

"Come on, Eugene," he said, before walking out the door, his new Negro deputy in tow. The rabble remained roused as Molly climbed down from the rostrum and joined them.

"Everyone's lost their minds," she said.

Out past the rabid throngs and into the street they went. Eugene made something stuck in the windshield. When he returned, he handed Ned Reilly a White Circle League pamphlet. The headline read LABOR BATTLES IN BEAN COUNTRY HARM WHITE FARMERS, in all capital letters, crudely printed, using far too many exclamation points.

"They mean to kill us all," Eugene said.

"We don't have to help them do it."

Molly snatched it away from Ned. "Motherfuckers."

"Have you heard from Frank, Miss Molly?"

"Not yet, Eugene." She shook her fist with the pamphlet balled up inside. "When I do, I'll have to tell him the crazies have taken our town."

Molly walked away, fuming, without looking at Ned.

"Molly," Ned said. "I didn't know what else to do."

Molly Duffy's shoulders slumped forward. She turned toward him.

"Then you weren't supposed to do anything, Ned."

Molly walked away. She didn't storm off, float away, or fade. Only dangled.

"Dep," Eugene said. "What do we do?"

"We better get back to the jail, Eugene. We're in for a rough night."

Ned watched Molly disappear around Pettingill Road. No one sweated and bled into Southville's soil more than her. If she was done with it all, Ned knew the entire county was lost.

CHAPTER 36

Elliot and Frank shambled through the kitchen of the Chicago Athletic Club, past gigantic soup pots as large as a man, and a long wall of burners where Negro chefs kept the fat cats fed. Workers couldn't believe the mad mulatto walked amongst them, a vengeful ghost. Out the service doors and into the private elevator lobby they stepped. The same attendant was on duty. He gasped as Frank helped Elliot into the car. The poor man frantically ran in behind them.

Frank propped Elliot up on the wall, then turned around and extended his hand to the elevator man.

"Hey, there. My name's Frank Fuquay," he said.

"Ralph Gibson." he said, shaking Frank's large mitt. Prior to pulling the lever to close the cage, he pulled the daily death edition from his box of newspapers.

"Mr. Caprice, how is it you're still alive?"

"I'm not."

Ralph pulled the lever. Up they ascended.

"McAlpin waiting on you again?"

"Amongst others."

The car stopped. Ralph opened the doors. Elliot paused just before stepping out. He stuck out his hand. The elevator man handed him the paper. He reached into his pocket for his pencil and looked for a place to sign.

"Would you make it out to 'Raphael?'"

"Show it to anyone else, I'll make you out to be a liar."

He took the paper and Elliot's hand and shook, too hard. Frank spirited Elliot away. Raphael smiled as he closed the gate and returned to the surface.

"I wouldn't mind if Uncle Buster put that article in the scrapbook."

"Dewey defeats Truman," Frank said.

Jon Costas-McAlpin intercepted the duo in the lobby in passionate relief.

"My friend," he said, taking Elliot's arm. "I feared they claimed you."

"Got too much piss and vinegar in me for all that."

Leo flanked Jon. He was all business.

"They're here," he said.

"What's all that Negro money look like up close, Leo?"

"Rarefied air."

"This way," Jon said.

At the opposite end of the hall was a private dining room. Leo opened the door after a sharp knock. Jon frickin' overdid it, with violinists, even. The foyer was almost the size of the farmhouse's living room. The walls were painted flat white with beautiful white plaster moldings. In an alcove trussed with pillars was an ebony wood phone table. Above them were one of two crystal chandeliers. The other was in the large dining room where Elliot made two elite Bowties holding point at the door. Elliot knew they must've been extra special because they wore tie-ons rather than clip-ons. A Negro in service dress—vest, shiny buttons, shiny shoes—took Jon's nod and cleared his throat before announcing them.

"Elliot Caprice, and Francis Fuquay."

Chairs turned outward. Glasses and tableware rattled.

"What the hell?"

Hard footsteps beat Turkish rugs until Frankie Freeman, attorney at law, marched out of the dining room and stood bemused at the dead man before her. Elliot stretched out his hand.

"Freeman. Didn't know you'd be here."

"I'd be here?" Freeman took his hand in both of hers, compulsively. She lowered her voice. "What in the holy hell, Caprice? You got nine lives?"

"I need a lot more than nine," he said. "This is my associate, Mr. Fuquay."

"Ma'am," Frank said. He doffed his cap. "Heard you on the radio the afternoon of the bombing. Those were kind words."

"Go on and scope out the seating arrangements, Big Man."

Frank stepped, but Elliot stopped him. "Almost done with his general equivalency. Eight grades in one year, this fella."

"What's your favorite subject?"

"All of 'em, ma'am." Frank smiled and left.

"It's good for a young buck to see Negros doing well with education."

Freeman's face broke into a long, disbelieving smile. "Are you going to tell me what's going on?"

"Get out from under Marion Bradshaw before I lower the hammer," Elliot said. "For the movement, you have to detach."

"Speculation, even from the nearly assassinated, is still only that."

"I have it cold that Marion Bradshaw leveraged diverse criminal interests to increase his own power, and that it led to the bombing that killed Attorney Michael Rabinowitz."

"You have evidence Bradshaw has colluded with organized crime."

"Evidence he's standing on underworld money and influence."

"And now he stands on the Negro movement."

"Which is how he's on the planning committee despite the lack of a controlling land stake. The white folks who all want to preserve their own stake are afraid to cross him, same as the rest of you Negroes in the movement."

"Feels as if you're preparing an indictment, Mister Man."

"Marion Bradshaw found himself with a measure of power granted to him by Negroes. Folks think he's here to do the right thing, but on the street, he has the Bowties to intimidate for him. He's got the Chicago Bee for Mike and Elaine."

"How is she?"

"I honestly don't know," Elliot said.

Freeman sighed, and took a seat on the tufted, red velvet couch. "I always wondered what the Negro Republicans over at the Bee wanted with the likes of me."

"Mikey got those eight families represented in his complaint to block Bradshaw's con until he could get out in front. That's why he contacted you. He needed an edge on Bradshaw. Elaine Critchlow said you introduced them."

Freeman grew sullen in a hurry.

"I gotta know, Frankie."

Freeman's tone finally softened.

"Bradshaw sucks everyone around him into his myopic view of racial stratification," Freeman said. "His desire is to be better than white people. If you're one of the Negroes he co-opts along his way to prominence, you should be happy he picked you."

"Elaine Critchlow kept correspondence with him, even before the lawsuit."

"Bradshaw held these networking socials for other Negroes in and around the capital. Teas. Meet and greets. Discussion groups. The value of the political scene hides in their cliques and cabals. If you don't know anyone, and you can't find acceptance, you're getting nowhere fast. It's one of the ways whites keep us out."

Elliot remembered Bradley University, the night he showed all those ofays he could speak their Queen's English right back at them.

"Negroes couldn't get in, especially women, so when he arrived with the right look, and all the right credentials and bona fides, we fell in line. The way he discussed things on the scene. It was fresh. He made us feel as if he saw us. You know the type, Caprice."

"Everyone remembers him from somewhere. No one can say for sure."

"He just seemed to have always been around. Ask about him, it's either a profusely kind word from some white person in authority who approves of him, or no actual comment. Cross him, and you see the other side of him."

"Would that side throw a bomb through Elaine Critchlow's window?"

"We figured he was tough enough to take on white folks, but where he found his voice is in barking down other Negroes. As he angled for himself, he got the right white folks to back him. Those at the mouth of the resource river."

Freeman nodded at Elliot before she pulled a handkerchief from her lapel pocket and wiped the corner of his lips of blood.

"You're high maintenance, Elliot Caprice." She let him keep the hanky. "The first few times he slipped up in business matters involving my small shop, I brushed it off as overcommitment. He was everywhere there was a microphone, but usually cut out on the work."

"The shiny new thing."

"He tried talking his way onto the NAACP Legal Defense Fund, but he didn't pass muster, and so he accused the local board of having it out for him. The Illinois delegation of Negro lawyers in the movement assembled for Brown v. Topeka. When he wasn't let on the team, he smeared Negro attorneys who were. If he didn't have so much white and Negro influence behind him, everyone would see he's a blowhard."

"He's a headhunter," Elliot said. "And he's moving up to take over the Planning Commission from guilty, rich white folks, and you helped him do it."

"No one in the Negro elite found reason to throw a colored man out for what a Negro woman would be disqualified for, so don't blame me he's got all the influence that makes the civil rights scene go 'round."

Elliot started coughing, violently. Freeman leapt to her feet, found a pitcher of water and a glass. Elliot waved her off.

"That ain't—" He tried righting himself. "—gonna help much."

Freeman put it all down and went to him.

"Listen, Freeman, we're caught in the same bowl of spaghetti. We gotta eat our way out, together. Bradshaw is bad news, and I'm going to find out what his jones for Michael Rabinowitz really was before this is over, but I'm telling you, the FBI is sniffing at the movement for Negro civil rights, and they're following dirty money from the Negro underworld back to it."

"It'd be a canard."

"It's meant as an excuse, Frankie. Marion Bradshaw is a conduit for bad money to mix in with civic funds, and I'd just bet the Negro underworld is in on it."

Frank stepped in the doorway. "Boss?"

Elliot replied with a nod. Frank split. Elliot tried standing but couldn't. Freeman stood and helped him up by the shoulder.

"These fellows see it as the movement for Negro male civil rights. They control the moral conscience of the conversation, as they speak the most, and loudest."

"They're the ones who get the ofays to respect you, so the doors open."

"Doors that other Negroes without the same privileges can't get into. Hammer away at that, and you got a case I can defend for Howard and Muhammad to pull the plug."

Elliot stuck out his hand. Freeman accepted it.

"And what do you want, Freeman? So badly you'd risk everything yourself?"

"Bullies ruin everything," Frankie said. "Now, you have to convince that room."

Elliot turned slowly toward the alcove of the dining room, accepting it as the point of no return, where his guts were the main course, and he was all set to spill them.

CHAPTER 37

He was lighter-skinned than everyone except Jon Costas-McAlpin, yet he was, arguably, the blackest man in the room. He was slight. Elliot put him at a buck thirty, soaking wet. He had a boyish, nondescript face, with soothing eyes, something like a cobra's. He spoke in a smooth, Georgian accent with a voice so soft, you'd almost forget that Bowties, all ready to kill and die at his command, stood behind his chair and at the door.

It was the kufi what bugged Elliot the most about Elijah Muhammad. Walking the streets of France after the war was where he first saw them, as he dropped alms at the destitute feet of a Franco-Arab, one of those who conquered North Africa from the African, but managed to lose Africa to the Caucasian. Simple, woven caps, with tiny bits of brightly colored thread, made by someone poor and desperate, to adorn the poor and desperate, yet Elijah Muhammad wore it as a crown. He was possessed of cosmic gumption, and a mind for the darker markets. His newspaper, Muhammad Speaks, was on every street corner, as were his eyes. There wasn't much he didn't know. The Bowties got all the gossip on the street, every cop knew that. They were the note takers. They guarded the gilded gates. Elijah Muhammad had numbers, muscle, and power.

Theodore Roosevelt Mason Howard was a natural polymath. Recognized at a young age for his great intellectual gifts by America's most well-intentioned white alternative spiritualists, the Seventh Day Adventists, they funded his education and taught him to be meddlesome. A surgeon and serial entrepreneur, by 1930 he rose to fame as the first Negro to have done just about everything, and so, spent of challenges, he relocated to Chicago to help Negroes rise in America. It was a different dream than Muhammad's, who was Bradshaw's Merlin. Or Sir Francis Walsingham. The guy was all spies and cohorts and unseen control. Should the Great Doctor T.R.M. Howard back away from thee, then so shall the sun, and the movement for Negro civil rights. This is who backed Bradshaw in the movement. The most powerful friend an activist Negro could have. Half of the Chicago Bee's advertising revenue came from Howard's businesses, or his causes. He was the mythical black swell. Howard put his money and clout behind the best and brightest in the Negro movement. When it was mighty useful folks, a la Fannie Lou Hamer, Howard was on the money. When he tapped the Marion Bradshaws, not so much. Power brokering is a tricky business.

His skin was cinnamon. He wore suits far too light for his shade. He was groomed in the typical style of the Negro activist: big, black-rimmed glasses, oddly-trimmed mustache, skinny tie. Elliot wondered if his glasses were prescription or proscribed. Elliot hated his voice. It sounded clipped, and restrained, as if he went to the same family physician as George Washington Carver. The sort of man who seemed incapable of offending just about anyone. Quiet power, like George Stingley's over Southville's right to law and order. Power that does its dirty work through indifference. It would take some convincing to get him to cut off Marion Bradshaw. The way he felt entitled to Frankie Freeman's attention suggested he liked himself a good protégé. She sat behind him.

"I thought this a practical joke," Howard said, pointing to Elliot as he took his seat. "Or stunt, perhaps like your young goons out in front of the building."

Freeman put the White Circle League handbill out on the table.

"Your young white thugs have been passing them out all over town."

"Our thugs aren't the pamphlet printing type," Leo said.

"You're going to hang that on me as well, Howard?" Costas leapt from his seat, ever the hot-blooded Greek. "I was never for the racial factions around the university campus project. If you remember, I resisted ethnic overtures from two different constituencies before the pressure began."

"Pressure you fell to," Muhammad said. "Before the carving up of the black man's land to give yourself some slack."

"Mister Muhammad, I inherited that land, and have been desperately attempting to unload it ever since."

"Return it to the black," Muhammad said.

"They left it a shit hole when they lost it the first time," Elliot said quietly, and to the ire of the Fruit of Islam standing guard behind him.

"Groups such as the White Circle League exert tremendous economic pressure upon the Negro people of Illinois." Dr. Howard sipped water. "They set the pot to boil, agitate on occasion, and wait until the average white citizen, caught up in the imbroglio, forces the Negro out though racial pogrom. Your own people have been guilty of this, Costas."

"They're not my people, Howard."

"They're Greek," Muhammad said. "You're Greek."

"I'm Greek, and Scots-Irish, born in Kenilworth."

The fat cats all laughed, relating with each other. It turned Elliot's stomach. Frankie Freeman didn't seem pleased, either.

Jon Costas pushed his soup away. "The Negro cabal you formed to take me on in the Planning Commission won't hold once what we've uncovered comes to light."

"How so?"

"Marion Bradshaw, your show pony, is mob connected up to his cold gills." Elliot drummed his fingers on the table. "I have material which proves it, and as no one likes me, I'm moving on from this particular consortium and taking my chances with the Negro press, who love them a good Elliot Caprice tale lately, boy, lemme tell y'all. What happens when I show them Bradshaw's ante up in the whole nasty racial mess is funded by death?"

Elijah sat silent for a moment, his hands touching in the form of a pyramid underneath his chin. "The brother is clever."

"It's the white man in me," Elliot said.

The Honorable Elijah Muhammad laughed. His men seemed not to understand how something such as that were possible. The dinner arrived. It was roasted Cornish hen. Elijah Muhammad pointed to the White Circle League pamphlet.

"These are not the words of men confident in their position. Those are."

Muhammad pointed to an FOI by the door, who handed Elliot an edition of Muhammad Speaks. Elliot's death made the cover, but only at the bottom, and in a very tiny column.

"My stock is sinking, Francis."

"It's your reluctance to take photos, boss. You gotta let 'em see you."

T.R.M. Howard turned toward Frankie Freeman and began furiously discussing something with her. Elliot pushed his plate away.

"Marion Bradshaw and the Muslim goons you assigned to him are strong-arming Negroes into giving up their land, which is a really bad thing. Wonder what the Martin Kings of the world would suggest about your movement. Maybe those newspapers, and nasty frickin' bean pies, sell less."

"You have proof?" Howard began to sweat, same as most colored big shots under pressure.

"What sort of proof did you need when you stood with Bradshaw and the Chicago Bee against Mikey Rabinowitz?"

Everyone in the room fell silent as Elliot hacked up a lung and clutched at his chest.

"It's obvious I didn't come here to fight," Elliot said. "The FBI watches me, always, for Kefauver. They watch me grow beans. That's how I know they're watching you. I have that, cold."

"This from the man who peddles Negroes to the Special Committee," Howard said.

"The brothers and sisters in the Nation are immune to such infiltrations."

Muhammad wouldn't eat, either.

"Actually, you have the most problems in all this, boss," Frank said.

"Marion Bradshaw works with one of your special ones," Elliot said. "Not one of the no-names, with the X, but an honest to goodness Muhammad. One of yours, I figure."

"We'll kill you for bearing false witness on the brother like that," said one of his goons.

Elijah Muhammad raised his finger to his lips. They stood perfectly still. Elliot felt it. He knew to cut it with the mouth and play it straight. He'd exhausted a powerful man's patience being petulant. Damn his piss and vinegar.

"Bradshaw's Muhammad has a black bottom lip, twitchy. The sort we'd narc up in the Department and send them back to you, as a plant. A stoolie."

Elijah Muhammad's eyes turned as cold as his smile. "Negro imps."

"When I was on the cops, I'd see them grab a guy from the gutter, get him a shower, haircut, take him around to the tailor and send him to you. He comes back for his money, or his fix, he spills his guts. Could be anyone, Brother Minister. Maybe these greasy niggers right here in this room with you."

Howard was out of his chair and shooting out his stack. "I insist you cease this, McAlpin! I won't be party to—"

"My friend," Jon said. "Are you sure you know what you're doing?"

Muhammad slapped the table, hard, causing everyone's glasses and plates to rattle. He stole the center for himself for almost a minute until he spoke again. No one said shit. Jon Costas-McAlpin kept his quiet, but Elliot could see he was observing, closely, how big swinging dicks in the Black Belt did it.

"You're saying the brother, Muhammad—"

"Smells like he's on da job," Elliot said. "With that twitch, it's either that or he's strung out."

Elijah Muhammad put his pyramid back under his chin and sighed, slowly. He closed his eyes and bowed his head. Elliot felt nervous. After a moment he slowly nodded, raised his hand, and the FOI all took to the doorways.

"We rescind our commitment to the Near West Side Improvement Association, Mister Howard. Good night to you."

Gone went the high king of a certain type of Negro.

"If you think that I'll just lie down and take your attacks—"

"Howard, goddamnit," Freeman said. She sat her fat cat in a seat and filled him with sense. "You need to hear what this man has to say. You have no idea what's at stake."

"If it's as you say, present it at the planning commission."

"He has too many of the other committees too frightened to intervene," Frankie said. "If he comes out on top at session, he'll hold the Chicago movement in his pocket."

"In comes the FBI, and you won't have a leg to stand on."

"I won't be seen tearing down a Negro who, in my estimation, stands to do well for Negroes, Caprice."

"You piece of trash, Michael Rabinowitz is dead. Mose Boysaw, dead. My uncle's farm attacked, but you don't have to bear those costs."

"Present your evidence at the planning commission," Howard said. "Make it stick, and I'll disavow him. Otherwise, if Negro economic progress is to be possible, we must all play by the rules. I must be an honest businessman."

"Then you shouldn't be in Chicago."

Elliot shook his head at him as Howard left to hedge his bets.

Freeman stepped over.

"I tried," Frankie said. "You have to make it stick."

"How?"

"Connect him to something big," Freeman said. "You know the stakes, Caprice. Look at the cash pile. See you at the Commission. I hope you find something."

She hurried out behind T.R.M. Howard.

Elliot bristled as he put on his hat.

"Leo, may I bother you for one more ride?"

"Sure, Elliot. Where to?"

"Springfield. I need my car."

CHAPTER 38

He woke in his Hyde Park flat to the kitchen phone ringing. It had better not be Bill Drury. That one bit of intel had him all hopped up. He dug up Elliot's number, goddamned detective. Nadine had a few hours before she was on shift. Elliot didn't want to wake her. He hopped out of bed, couldn't find his robe, so he took himself naked to the kitchen, where it was colder, and answered.

"Caprice Famil—" It happened when he was really tired, forgetting where he was. "Detective Caprice."

"Sunshine," Sugar Styles said.

"Sugar?"

"I need a hand," Sugar said, his voice quivering. "Get on over to Joe's Deluxe."

Sugar hung up before Elliot could say anything. He knew what that meant. Again, conscripted into some powerful man's mess. He went back to bed, to kiss her before it was back out into the street to do something he shouldn't.

"Don't wake me when you come back from your right-quick with that fink, Drury."

"I ain't pulling some right-quick, Nadine." He hugged her close to him, pressing his crotch into her rear.

"You need to leave, don't you?"

"Just lemme put the spoons away, right quick."

Elliot cuddled her once more. She had a spot between her chin and neck where his nose fit, just right.

"Mm, hm," she said. "Bye. Tell Bill Drury he's a fink."

"I'm not going to see Drury, Nadine," Elliot said.

"Goodbye, Elliot."

Elliot got dressed questioning why he was most attracted to mean women who minded his business for him.

An icy rain began that blew sideways in his face as he marched up the block. He pulled down his eight-panel and pulled up the collar on his pea coat. By the time he hit Joe's no one was inside except Sugar, who was covered in blood, speaking on the phone.

"Holy shit," Elliot said. He drew his service revolver. "Sugar what's going on."

"Sunshine," he said. "You gotta come with me."

He pulled Elliot out into the back of the club and into the alley, through a loading dock, to a back stairway headed up. Elliot pulled his badge from his pocket and clipped it to the front of his coat. He took the lead from Sugar, who pointed to the open door at the top of the stairs. It was the back porch door to a nice apartment, which opened to a kitchen which was modern, and well-kitted. A young man, immaculately dressed, stood at the phone, frantically dialing a number.

"Emergency services said they're on their way, mama!"

"I said call the fire department," said a woman from the other side of a door. "Call his friends."

Elliot trained his sights on a back bedroom. The door was cracked. There was a boy peering inside. He was small. He was in his underwear and a t-shirt. It was hot. Elliot pulled the boy away from the door and into the kitchen.

"Hey, fella," he said. "You probably don't want to go in there. What's going on?"

"My father is in there with my mom," the boy said. He didn't cry. He seemed more curious about the matter. "She's a nurse. She's going to save him."

The boy's brother ran over. He slapped the boy. "Mom said stay out."

"All of you, outside," Elliot said. "Sugar, help them."

"Come with me, guys," Sugar said. "Let's take it next door."

Teddy Roe walked in, pacing, smoking. He had blood on his sleeves. Sugar lured the kids away. Elliot entered the room to see, standing over a large, strong bodied, nude man, a nude woman all of 30, covered in blood and whatever else she got all over herself fighting for the man's life. She screamed at him, over and over, to help her, not leave her. Elliot went to her, expecting her hysterical. She pushed him off her. He fell to the floor.

"Get out," she said. "I'm a surgical nurse."

"Ma'am," he said. "I'm Assigned Detective Elliot N…"

"Go keep my sons safe. There're nothing but criminals in this building."

"Ma'am, stop. Let me help. I have training."

"I train who trains you," she said. "Get out of my bedroom."

She returned to early, aggressive, vigorous resuscitation. Elliot remembered it from the academy, how to tend to a gunshot wound to the head. Elliot closed the door. Teddy stood before him, arms folded.

"My brother-in-law?"

"Teddy—" Elliot was still stunned. "I'm sorry."

The woman in the next room, who fought the losing battle, howled in a way that made the gods take notice of the sadness they cause mankind. Sugar ran to her, as did Teddy. Elliot remained in the kitchen. The boys sat on the back steps until their maternal uncles arrived. They also weren't gentle characters.

"Caprice," Teddy said, as he walked into the kitchen. "We need to keep this quiet."

"Teddy, I'm calling this in."

"You can't."

"That man is dead. His wife and kids have been in contact with the scene."

"They'll be alright," Teddy said. "They're tough. They're young."

"Teddy, those kids are traumatized. That little boy was in the doorway the entire time. Right outside that door. Oh, my God."

Elliot reached for the phone and felt Teddy's revolver at the back of his head.

"Don't make it two losses for me tonight, Lightskin."

Elliot trembled. "Teddy, this is wrong."

"Bourbon is your thing, right?" Teddy pleaded with his eyes. "Four Roses good?"

"If I have to," Elliot said.

Joe made a fortune selling furs—both warm and hot—and parlayed them into his nightclub that specialized in making room for folks. Joe Hughes controlled the weigh station, his basement, where access required trust at the highest levels of crime. Those who enter leave entrusted with the secrets of the criminal underbelly of Chicago. Violate the rules of strict confidence and confidentiality, and you would lie down there with the empties.

"My sister's father-in-law," Teddy said. "He's a big man in the city. Runs firehouses, as a colored."

"Another Negro first, 'eh." Elliot shook his head. "I'm so tired of us."

"You can do a lot of things running a couple of firehouses."

"He's a fence," Elliot said.

"My brother-in-law grew up in that shit. Once he couldn't take it anymore, he went the other way from the family, straight and narrow. Guess it caught up with him."

"Teddy, if I don't report this, I have to carry it."

"Lightskin," Teddy said. "Listen to reason for me. I can't let this get out. I have a reputation to protect. The Outfit is gunning for me."

Sugar walked over, sobbing, but changed into his work attire. "Elliot, you got a message. Someone named Bill Drury."

"The crime writer?" Teddy shook his head. "Are you insane, Caprice?"

"Kefauver is cutting me loose soon. I know it. I need an out."

"You get caught telling your tales, you're dead."

"I'm just going to see what he says," Elliot said. "Just be prepared to funnel me facts. Enough to titillate, but not incriminate."

"And for that, you got my back?"

"I'll get my man Creamer to make sure you stay out of it."

He headed for the door.

"Sugar," he said. "The little guy."

"He's a smart kid," Teddy said. "We'll all look after him."

"Elliot," Leo said. "We're here."

CHAPTER 39

He opened his eyes to the office building, the place where it all nearly ended. The police roped off the scene, including Elliot's pride and joy, the precious Lucille, she a rocket amongst eighty-eights. He found his keys in his coat pocket, pulled them out, exited the Lincoln, and ran his hand down the soot and ash atop her front hood. The windshield was cracked.

"I'm sorry, honey," he said. "I'll get Amos to fix it."

"Good luck, Caprice."

"Thanks, Leo."

Leo pointed to Frank. "Your young leg man here knows a thing or two."

"Smart, too," Elliot said. "Only needs one more grade to pass his equivalency."

"We'll set the stage at the commission. Be careful."

"Later, Leo." Frank doffed his cap.

"Leg man, huh?"

"He's just being nice, boss."

"Mm, hm."

He dusted off the door lock, inserted his key, and opened the door. Frank walked over. Elliot put the key into the ignition.

"I'm sorry I let 'em do you dirty, Lucille."

He turned the key. He wasn't truly worried.

Sure enough, there were men in the lobby of Springfield General who didn't give Elliot and Frank any guff, but a nod.

"Jon Creamer called ahead," Frank said.

"Cover our flank for a tail," Elliot said. "Those jamokes want their noses in everything."

They took the elevator to the private room she had on the second floor. She was behind a curtain, crying, as nurses attended to her. She sounded miserable. Frank couldn't handle it and stepped out the room, but Elliot wouldn't leave. He knew he'd never hurt as bad as she, no matter how he ached for his friend, her once true love and intended.

The nurses spiked her fluids with a syringe of calm-her-down. As they left, Elliot looked away. He gave her a moment to collect herself, as if she ever really would.

"Elaine?"

"Elliot? Is that you?"

Elliot peered around the curtain. Elaine was treated for burns on much of her body.

"Oh no, Elaine."

"I thought you were dead," she said.

"The FBI got me out," Elliot said. "They've been following me. I need to know what happened between you and Bradshaw."

"Why? You think it's him?"

"It's looking so. Level with me."

"Bradshaw was interesting. He had everyone else all figured out. Sometimes he made things happen. Most times, he was all talk. After his neighborhood association made it into the press, he asked if I'd be interested in working for him. I told him no, thanks. At the next function, half the folks in the room were against me. People I had been knowing since college."

"Sounds like his emmoh."

"I was at a CORE meeting in Springfield when a nephew of one of the

Maxwell Street Eight came to me. He came home on leave to find his aunt's home vandalized, her windows broken. Beer bottles in the gutter. Needles in the ashcans."

"He bears false witness against you." Elliot thought of the Negro Underworld and their rage at him and Margaret.

"Someone robs and kills your aunt in her apartment while you're headed back to fight in Korea." Elaine shut her eyes. "He's a monster, Elliot. Bradshaw goes after people until he can find the thing that makes them hurt, and he presses on it until you relent or mount a defense. I worked hard to get to where I am. Now I'm some colored Jezebel who chases after white men."

Elaine sniffed, gritted her teeth, and put her head back.

"I can't cry. It'll burn my skin."

"So, neither of you knew Izzy Rabinowitz's money was floating around with Bradshaw?"

"Not until you found out."

Elliot's stomach sank. "This seems targeted Elaine. Why did he hate Mikey so much?"

"I don't know," Elaine said. "But it's personal. Be careful, Elliot. He hates you, too. I can't talk anymore. It hurts. I'm sorry."

"Okay," Elliot said, softly. "You went after him. That's why you two were in separate offices."

"I told Michael I could take him myself. He gave me my space. I almost got him. He fights…"

Elaine held on to her last note as her body gave in to the narcotic.

"Dirty," Elliot said. "Just like the goyim."

Elliot put on his hat, closed the curtain behind her, and stepped into the hall where he found Frank crying silently, his head on the wall. Elliot walked over to him.

"You alright, Big Man?"

Frank nodded.

"I promise, Frank, we'll see our way through this. Chin up, now."

Elliot patted him on the back. Frank wiped his face.

"Now, help me down the stairs. We need to slip these Feds."

"Where're we headed?"

"The jail," Elliot said. "To take back what everyone was looking for."

CHAPTER 40

Elliot swatted Frank away when he opened the door and tried helping him out the car. Eugene opened the jailhouse door for him. He didn't acknowledge Ned sitting at his desk so much as collapse in a chair in front of him.

"I heard about the hit on the jail. Are you—"

"I'm fine," Ned said. "A helluva lot better than you."

"Georgie still in hospital?"

"No," Ned said. "With his Ma."

Ned put his hand on Elliot's shoulder. It wasn't their normal thing.

"Get me some evidence, will you?"

Ned opened his desk drawer, producing the bottle of Blanton's. Elliot closed his eyes, hoping to blink away the pain in his guts. When it didn't work, he tried subduing them with good hooch, hoping no one noticed his blood falling back into the amber. He wanted to die, and wished he had, but that would mean the secrets in the ledger would die with him. He figured a look inside justified the expense of the Reaper's time.

"That book I gave you," Elliot said.

Eugene stood. "It's in the gun safe. I'll get it."

Eugene walked away. Elliot leaned in closer.

"Ned, you sure you know what you're doing? Eugene is wild."

"He's not afraid, either," Ned said. "And he listens. Seems to never want you on his bad side, or Frank there on his conscience."

"Eugene gets the job done," Frank said. Eugene produced the ledger.

"My guess is a separate squad hit your place," Ned said.

"They were looking for this," Elliot said, holding up the book. "Whoever did it."

"These jamokes are state cops. The one I blasted off of Frank over at Miss Betty's was wearing a mask."

"No fooling. Same ones?"

"I shot the asshole who tried baiting you in a fight for Eugene."

"You're gonna take a lot of heat putting down a state boy."

"Heroic law enforcement officer dies in fire in Negro shanty. His wife will get a medal from the governor."

"That still doesn't sort what happened here," Eugene said. "No way the state cops did this. Not with their faces covered."

"As sure as I'm colored, so was that fella I snatched the mask from, Elliot," Frank said. "Even his gait, and his build, seemed like one of us."

"The mask was the same type as the Stateys that torched Betty's place." Ned finished his pour.

Elliot shook his head. "I need the rest of these names figured out."

"Rabinowitz could tell you," Ned said.

"Izzy is mixed up somehow. His money is inside that book."

"You're not suggesting he has anything to do with it?"

"Naw, Ned, I don't think that. I think Izzy turned up the heat on the Short Paper War, and I found the reason why." Elliot pointed to the ledger. "Izzy has been angling for repatriation, ever since Benny Siegel washed the first bag of money with Peter Bergson at the Yishuv Laundromat."

"Elliot's FBI folks told me Mr. Rabinowitz rests easier Elliot is dead," Frank said. "Not to suggest he'd hurt his own child—"

Elliot stood, because he had to, but then sat, because his body said so.

"We need an outsider," Elliot said.

"Who? Looks like everyone you know is in on it," Ned said.

"Not everyone." Elliot smirked.

"Who?"

"The Turk, Frank," Ned said. "How bad do you need to know, Elliot? I mean, Jeez, you're friends with the frickin' FBI."

"Who just kept me handcuffed to a bed for a week, Ned." Elliot ran his fingers through his hair. "Listen here, you know everything George is doing. How much good it can bring to Negroes and communities like ours, right?"

Ned nodded, and pointed to Eugene. "Change is a bitch."

"Something in this book got Mikey Rabinowitz killed, and is likely the reason Marion Bradshaw is one step ahead of me. George's movement is in danger."

"And so are the people in it," Ned said. "I knew Mike Rabinowitz. He tried out for baseball."

"Mikey liked baseball?"

"Could pitch," Ned said. "Wore his glasses on the mound. Coach Ventress—"

"The Rhetoric teacher?"

"Same. He said Mike made the team. He would have started him."

"What happened?"

"His father," Ned said. He stared into his own cup. "It's always fathers, isn't it?"

Elliot rose from his chair, with Frank's help. "Lend me Eugene for a few hours."

"To do what?"

"Go knocking on doors in Rockford." Elliot half-smiled.

Ned sighed, tipped his coffee cup of bourbon, and swallowed hard. "Go ahead. Don't break him. He's my first and only deputy."

Eugene got the door.

"Make sure the badge shows, Eugene," Ned said. "Remember where you're from."

Eugene nodded. Frank patted him on the back. Eugene closed the door behind them.

It must've been those crackers at the 19th Hole's worst nightmare to see Elliot Caprice returned with two crazy Negroes, one a sheriff's deputy a few counties over. Frank Fuquay had Cyclops, cynical bartender of the working man, dial Chester's number with his face. They stood outside until he arrived, with Gimp.

"You want your asses whooped, don't you, Big Black?"

Frank squared up, sidestepped the first punch from Gimp, and stunned him with a perfect right hook off the right jab. Eugene snuck up to him and laid him out, good-night, with the butt of his Southville-issue shotgun. Gimp was asleep before he hit pavement.

"You been hanging down at the auto yard with Amos, Frank?"

"He showed me some stuff," he said.

"Don't kill anyone."

"Don't worry." The Big Man tipped his hat.

"Let's take a ride," Elliot said to Chester. "Keys."

Chester gave them right up. He knew the score. Eugene helped him into his own back seat.

"First off," Elliot said, with his finger in Chester's face, from the front seat of the man's car, as he was sandwiched between Frank and Eugene. "We're going to discuss Mose Boysaw. I made you leaving the area the night he was killed, in that Buick, and that terrible hat."

"Naw, I ain't killed him," Chester said. "He was my cousin."

"C'man." Elliot removed the finger.

"Moses Boysaw was my mama's people."

"Your cousin?"

"Second, once removed," Chester said. "So, of course I didn't kill him."

"Every man is your brother, until the rent is due."

"He came up with my auntie, who's really my Mama's cousin. I hear it from everyone, my mama, his mama, his lady. 'Get Mose some work.' 'Help Mose out.' He won't work, tho'. Not a straight."

"That's how he was. Sees you have it, thinks getting it is as easy as taking it from you. Like the Turk, and Izzy's territory."

"Well, he found something of ours he ought not have wanted." Chester's voice broke.

Elliot felt badly for wishing he didn't feel badly for an asshole. He held up the ledger.

"This contains Roseland Boys money, as well as the Negro underworld's, I'm sure. I need to know who else."

"What do you need to know that for," Chester said. "Other than a reason to hang yourself?"

"The bombing that took my friend has something to do with it. So, I need his eyeballs, and his pencil."

"Why should he?"

Elliot got back in his face, dead cousin or not.

"So he can make sure his name isn't in it, and the names of anyone he wants dead are."

Chester grinned, showing that gold tooth. "You bring it upon yourself, the way these Negroes and ofays do you. You got everyone fooled, Elliot Caprice. The Chicago Police, the Outfit. They think you're some rage-possessed nigger. I know you ain't nuthin' but guilty white folks inside."

"Name his price."

"Oh, he will," Chester said. "Expect it to cost big. This particular troll exacts a very particular toll."

"I need this yesterday," Elliot said.

"You also need it like a hole in the head. Ain't no way Rabinowitz's kid is worth that much to you."

"It's wrong what these bastards are doing to poor folk to build some goddamned college campus for white folks."

Chester shook his head. "Even your trouble is uppity. I'll be in touch."

Everyone got out of the car. Chester climbed into his own driver's seat.

"Frank," Elliot said.

Frank Fuquay grabbed Gimp underneath his shoulders. Eugene grabbed his feet and in the back seat he went.

"Much obliged," Chester said, and he pulled off without closing the door first. Elliot watched his headlights fade in the distance.

"Now what?" Eugene kept watch on the street as they walked to Lucille.

"I'm going to sleep," Elliot said. "I have to bury my friend in the morning."

CHAPTER 41

Aside from Teddy Roe, with whom his tense friendship still counted, Joe Hughes was the only trustworthy member of the Negro underworld Elliot knew enough to trust, except his trust came at a price, as did everything in the Black Belt, marked up to include colored people's tax. In Bronzeville, your tax collectors were also colored, and it'd take a while to get those dollars back to the treasury if they had anything to do with it. In Chicago, it was called having big shoulders, big enough to scrub all that black into bronze, and if that made your shoulders bigger than the Negroes who didn't scrub as much or as well, you go with what works in the City That Works.

Joe was stout, as he preferred to evidence his largesse rather than offer it. He favored Elliot, wearing a gray pinstripe three-piece four sizes larger. They careened down the stairs after Sugar Styles, in bartender's bowtie and slacks, lost his grip on Elliot's good shoulder. He collapsed into the beer room. Elliot was delirious at that point, shouting curses and screaming in pain.

"Goddamnit, Sugar," Joe said. "Shut that half-nigger up."

Sugar went to him. "You see the man."

"What's that got to do with me and my business?" Joe looked up the stairs, then back around the room, frantically. "I'm tired of being caught up in his shit."

"He called me," Teddy Roe said, as he stepped, smoking a short, from the shadows.

"I ain't mean nothing by it, Teddy," Joe said. He walked up to Teddy, whispering. "Word is, he's a stool-pigeon."

"He's one of us," Sugar said.

"He police, Teddy," Joe said. "He can end here, and this Kefauver nonsense ends with him."

Teddy went to Elliot, who was laid out atop crates of empties.

"What if we called your lady?"

"I can't, Teddy," Elliot said. "I can't involve her."

"Rabinowitz, then," Teddy said. "He's got the juice."

"No," Elliot said. "Never again."

The Outfit's surgeon came over to the crates. He was octoroon, with a twitch, and he walked as if one leg was shorter than the other.

"This fella was in the Great War," Teddy said. "He knows his stuff."

"You're not Outfit, are you?" Elliot coughed.

"I'm a rogue, sir," he said. "Charles Wright, at your service."

"Stop him from bleeding, then get him the hell out of here." Joe made himself scarce as he went up the stairs to the main room.

Teddy Roe shoved a fist full of cash into the Surgeon's smock pocket, and slipped Elliot some well-folded bills, discreetly, into the pocket of the shirt he wore to meet Nadine's parents.

"Very well," the Surgeon said. "If I put back three-fifths of him, that'll be enough, no?"

The Surgeon snickered. Elliot was sure he was going to die at the hands of the uppity colored butcher who had one leg shorter than the other.

The Yellow Westclox moonbeam made noise again.

⁂

Elliot rose on the third day he was back from hospital, with his Uncle, Frank Fuquay, and the toiling workers who sweated under the hot fall sky, and at the chastening rod of Miss Betty, who Uncle Buster wished had her essaroh back. She didn't like scrapple, either.

Elliot stepped into the kitchen. Uncle Buster was in the fields already. Frank slept in the bed because he earned the day off sending in his final general equivalency test to the state. Miss Betty was in the kitchen doing the books, checking expenses against the haul from the yard, grousing about the money they paid the hands.

"Whathatchasaythere, Miss Betty?"

She got up from her work, grabbed the percolator and poured him a cup.

"Miss Betty," Elliot said, also wishing she had her essaroh back. "I can fix my own coffee."

"Sit down, Elliot Caprice," she said. "I ain't gonna have you dying while I'm here."

He didn't deserve comfort. He was alive. He was lucky to have that.

"Miss Betty, cut it out, aight?"

"The hell's your problem?"

Elliot looked away. "They sitting shiva. The funeral is today."

Betty looked at him and shook her head. "Honestly, boy, I don't know how you got yourself insinuated with those people."

"Doc is Unk's best friend."

"Shapiro has been my friend longer than you, and your uncle," Betty said. "I mean them folk, period."

"Jews."

"I don't understand them," she said. "Never have. Doc pays out the nose to do his work for free, his cousin would slit your throat for a dollar. They got your back, until they don't. You blind to them folks, Elliot Caprice. You ain't gotta love everyone who was kind to you once."

"Who else do I love?"

Chester walked past the kitchen window.

"What is he doing here?"

Elliot went out the front door. The previous day's edition of the Chicago Daily Defender was on the porch. He stepped over it as he made Chester near a column, playing it cool.

"Lightskin."

"Chester," he said. Elliot approached him. He looked tired. "You aight?"

"The man's daughter is a wildcat," he said. "He had us hustling in the street until 4am to find her."

"Wayward?"

"Not all the way there," he said. "Mama's gone. You know how it is when a man don't know how to raise a child."

"Yeah, I know."

Chester handed Elliot the ledger. There were several pieces of paper stuck between the pages, some taped into sections. It had lines drawn across. It seemed like law enforcement work.

"This is more than I expected," Elliot said.

"You come to the man, expect a man's job."

"What's the man's toll?"

"You'll see."

Chester pointed to the evidence, then tipped his awful bowler hat and sauntered down the porch stairs. Elliot could feel himself being recruited. He took the ledger back inside and sat in the living room, where he went through the tangle of exotic facts and figures. The Turk's scribbles and notations were a patchwork quilt of dirty money. His acquaintances stood out. The Jones Family, in honor of Giveadam, which is as they insisted it be listed, was in for thousands, as was Joe Hughes, proprietor of Joe's Deluxe. Sugar Styles was in, under his actual name, Aloysius Green, for at least half Joe Hughes' stake. These were the men in the Black Belt who carried clout, and the money of the less heeled, who weren't allowed in the middle-class colored reindeer games, same as the Maxwell Street Eight.

After that it was all short paper, collected across the Belt. Izzy Rabinowitz, Jewish short paper king and big donor to *Eretz-Israel*, had his money mixed in with the saps and simps in Chicagoland's religious rhetoric set. It was the Dead Sea Scrolls. It was the Lost Gospel of Thomas. It was everything Frankie Freeman, the Chicago Daily Defender, and the Top Hoodlum

Program could want.

The Turk was nice enough to include a list of references he couldn't explain. A few business names. Obscured symbols. The tell the Turk was indeed a foreigner were in his references to underworld Negroes, which included awkward spellings, and bigoted word associations used commonly, as if someone taught him the word 'schvartze' first and then backtracked to explaining colored folk's humanity. Elliot consulted the list, sure he'd find other members of social improvement groups down the line. At the top of the larger donors list, a name stood out, in for fifty grand, a name which rankled him.

Upstairs in Frank's room, which used to be his room, were all the dirty books he'd hide, and the Latin dictionary he kept from Catechism, which came in handy translating Roman sex poetry. Frank woke up.

"Sorry Big Man," Elliot said. "I know you were up late."

Elliot left him in bed and went back downstairs. As he flipped pages, Frank sat with him, yawning. He read through the Turk's markings.

"C. Albus Fotus," he said, as he ran his finger across the margin. "You recognize him?"

"It ain't a him," Elliot said. "Not if I remember my Latin."

Elliot found Albus in the dictionary and showed it to Frank.

"Bright, clear, favorable, aus—"

"Auspicious."

"I was gonna say that, Boss." Frank continued. "Favorable, auspicious, fortunate."

"White."

Frank's face came off the page frozen in amazement. "Boss. Noooo."

"You can look up fodus yourself, and I'm pretty sure the 'c' goes for circulus."

"Like, circle?"

Elliot nodded.

"Boss, what do we do?"

"Go to Chicago," Elliot said. "To the Negro underworld's doorstep."

CHAPTER 42

The day Mikey Rabinowitz was laid to rest according to Jewish tradition, on a lovely Indian Summer day in a cemetery that provided for numerous denominations, although not races, Elliot wore his basic black suit with a white shirt and skinny black tie. The Negroes of the movement had to pay their respects from the fringes. Elliot looked Jewish enough to stand by father and mother.

Izzy wept somberly at Rebecca Rabinowitz's side. Silent tears streamed down her veiled face. Elliot had never really met her, but knew she took an interest in him by Izzy's admonishments, i.e., "Rebecca says I should fire you," and such. He wouldn't look at her. Rebecca Rabinowitz went in her handbag, pulled out a blue yarmulke, and handed it to Elliot. It had a hairpin like colored girls use in their styles. He found that funny. Elliot's hands shook. Izzy took it from him and pinned it on.

"It was Mikey's," Izzy said. "He wore it for his graduation from law school."

Elliot could see Rebecca staring at him through the veil. He couldn't tell if she was smiling or crying. He averted his gaze again.

"You shouldn't be out," Izzy said.

"I'll die on my feet, thank you kindly." Elliot sucked back more tears. "I'm sorry, Izzy. I tried to save him."

Izzy looked at his shoes.

"Everything happened so fast."

"Kid, it was a bomb. Shtum."

Although his equilibrium was shot, his hearing hadn't fully returned to his right ear, and he was still jumpy, he willed himself to stand by them, same as when their son stood with him in St. Louis.

Michael Sasha Rabinowitz, Attorney at Law, a man who never saw a Negro problem he couldn't fix with a lawsuit against some white folks, was dead. His daddy was no good, yet an abundance of good flowed from him. In the unfair tangle that is creation, Isadora Rabinowitz, the Jewish strong man of the Midwest who wouldn't let a Negro in his house, won the respect of Negroes across America. He only had to lose his baby boy and his family's last hope in the process. In the end, only Negroes could say they sacrificed so much, and it's the sacrifice that binds us, tribal mores be damned.

They sat in the backyard together, Elliot and Izzy, at the wooden picnic table, where Elliot carved his initials, got a smack and his pay docked. Elliot couldn't look at him. Izzy stared at the stars as Elliot laid out the case. Izzy would never get into Israel, as he had always dreamed, should the inconvenient intersections laid out by the Turk come to light. If Frankie Freeman got ahold of it, the Top Hoodlum Program would enter and thwart his repatriation dreams. All he worked for, and all his reckless sacrifices, including the Short Paper War, would be for nothing. Izzy was too smart. He knew the angles were closed off. He wouldn't be much trouble.

"You told Bradshaw about short paper in Southville?"

"He had bonafides," Izzy said. "Found me through your buddy, Giveadam."

"So, Bradshaw is connected-connected. Who's backing him?"

"Hard to tell," Izzy said. "I figured it was the Turk."

"You always figure its him, Izzy. It's myopic."

"You're the one who went to college, not me."

"He knows what makes you tick, Bradshaw," Elliot said, looking down at the table. "He knows what makes you mad."

"And what's that?"

"You have a hard on for Negroes who have it better than you," Elliot said. "I've always seen it. It doesn't bug me. It's Chicagoland. Everyone here is obligated to be a bigot. But it made you weak to Bradshaw's play."

Izzy had no comeback. "So, kid," he said. "What now?"

"I'm going to cast Bradshaw into the light, once I know the facts. If you pull out of the St. Louis Land Clearance deal, you'll be clear. The cash you gave him, you're out that, but Bradshaw will go down."

"Not good enough."

"Man, you're finished and you know it. You were when I saw you in Doc's clinic the night I returned."

Izzy didn't say a word.

"I was wrong about everything leading up to now. I don't know how I'm gonna live that down."

"Bury him," Izzy said.

"And then what?" Elliot shook his head. "I still gotta find a way to keep the farm going. You? You got what you need. Get out of here. Give Rebecca what she deserves."

"I lose everything then, huh?"

"Not everything," Elliot said, and he did not waver in his stare.

Izzy snickered after he smirked. "Always on your terms."

"Now the Rabinowitz name is synonymous with the movement to free Negroes. You have all the respect you need to be an upstanding person in the eyes of everyone. Enjoy Israel."

Elliot rose and stuck out his hand. Izzy looked at it.

"Still the best," Izzy said.

"You'll ever know," Elliot said. "Deal?"

Izzy took Elliot's hand and squeezed, hard. "That's some slick shit they teach over at the Chicago Athletic Club."

It gave Elliot a chill.

"See you in the funny papers."

Elliot split toward the gate.

"Thanks for coming to the funeral," Izzy said. "He loved you."

Elliot turned around.

"We started talking again."

"Yeah?" Elliot smiled.

Izzy nodded. "He told me he wanted to fire you seven times per day? I told him, for me, it was eight."

Izzy winked at him. Elliot wanted to hug him, which was something he never felt before, but instead went out the gate.

CHAPTER 43

The Planning Commission emergency meeting Jon Costas-McAlpin called was at seven 'o clock, as most ethnics liked a free meal on the government what exploited their poor people's labor. Bronzeville was balmy that evening. Frank cruised slowly along 47th Street, streaking Lucille's hood with red neon, blinking amber, and black progress. He passed the Regal Theater. The marquee read:

Anniversary Extravaganza

The Platters

47th and South Park is where, if you stood there long enough, you'd find any Negro you thought you'd never see again, or hoped you'd never see, if you compromised your career and social standing as Elliot had. The last thing he wanted was a confrontation with the Negro underworld, many of them his old cohorts. He was reluctant to accept them as tribe and kept the Black Belt's criminal power blocks at bay by keeping his nose to law and order, no matter his arrest record was a bit of playing all sides to the middle. Now he needed the underworld to understand they were headed for ruin running with Bradshaw, regardless of Elliot's next move. He needed them to understand the entire score, not just what Marion's respectable colored activist clout meant in their quest for legitimacy.

He stood in the alley behind Joe's. It smelled the same back there as it did inside; haughty, with hints of Negro perspiration. Frank remained in the car as Elliot got out. The McAlpin town car pulled up. Margaret got out, one long, beautiful leg at a time.

"I still don't know the play," Margaret said.

"Neither do I," Elliot said. "Need folks to tell their truths first."

"How do you know they'll tell them to you?"

Elliot cut his eyes downward.

"I know enough of them already," he said. "They'll give me the rest."

"So," Margaret said, grabbing her compact from her purse. "I'm to be your snowflake in this endeavor."

"My what?"

"Snowflake," Margaret said, with a sneer. "I'm playing the role of your white bitch."

Elliot grabbed her hands with one of his, stopping her from opening the compact.

"After I go in, order a drink and talk whomever's behind the bar into letting you past to pee. You're white. They'll let you."

"Alright."

"Get downstairs, and just listen. You'll know."

"I'll know, hm?"

Elliot nodded slowly. "These guys aren't here because they're the brightest. That's why they clustered around Teddy Roe. He didn't have half the strength of Izzy, but he knew all the plays. Led like a colored man, fought like a white man. That's why Giancana had to kill him. Imagine that, big shot of the Chicago mob, needed to off a Negro boss to get his stars and bars."

"Those are big names," Margaret said.

"Not as big as the name McAlpin," Elliot said. "The Black Belt is where get in where you fit in was invented. You'll know."

Margaret opened the compact and checked herself. "We're even after this."

Elliot scoffed.

"I mean your fee," she said. "You never came to collect it."

"Maybe I'm still gonna."

Elliot walked toward the alley, where he made a right and descended upon Joe's Deluxe's loading dock. He pushed the black doorbell button. Loud chimes went off behind the door. In a moment, it opened. Sugar Styles stood before Elliot wearing a black suit and emerald green tie. His jacket lining was emerald green. His socks were green. Sugar Styles was forced to move in circles that were beneath him, and he was quick to put a bullet in a detractor, hence colors signaled to those around him what was important to him, which was green. Not colored, or queer, to be harassed and browbeaten. A man, about his green. See that and Sugar wouldn't shoot you in the face. That was Chitown shit.

"Hey, there," he said.

"Sugar," Elliot said. "You came up in the world since I last saw you."

"The power of information," Sugar said. Elliot stepped away from the door. Sugar closed it and spun around.

"You know what it is, Sunshine."

Elliot nodded, opened his coat, and showed Sugar he was unarmed.

"Folks remember you as a grudge holder." Sugar patted him around. "This the second time we thought you dead, and a guy beating those odds, twice, has a vendetta."

"Got me there. So, whatsatchasay there, Sugar Styles?"

"I say you and me need to get on the same page." Sugar looked around the corner. "What we have between us."

"We don't have anything between us, Sugar." Elliot took off his coat.

"These fellas," Sugar said. "They don't know me like you do."

"You mean, they'll accept it if you don't talk about it."

"I'm saying, they don't know I was some kin to Teddy Roe."

"How not?"

"He didn't want it to get out about me," Sugar said. "My cousin loved me, Elliot."

"I know he did. He loved a lot of us."

"The motherfucking Chicago Bee is gonna get someone fucked up, royal, and all for the cover price of a nickel."

"It's Bradshaw," Elliot said. "He's telling tales to those Negro conservatives. Those jamokes were two-faced against the Pullman Porters but praise every Negro entrepreneur as the second coming. Where the hell does Bradshaw come from, Sugar?"

Sugar shook his head. "I'm the one put it together. God knows, I was only trying to help the boy."

"Who?"

"Marion. He came looking to be staked on a land trust deal. He did it right, just like we do it in Chicago. The university was in his pocket because he was on academic scholarship, and most Negroes can't get that. He had the moral conscience, with the movement. He had a plan to build black wealth to balance out the white."

"You've always been the smart one, Sugar. You know that's all bullshit."

"As I said, I was only trying to help the lad."

"Sugar, Marion Bradshaw killed my friend and you know something about it."

"Sunshine," Sugar said. "You already know."

"What?"

"That night," Sugar said. "The boys. Teddy's nephews."

Elliot remembered it. The two boys that were left stricken and traumatized by their father's suicide. He had always wondered what happened to them.

"The little boy," Elliot said. "What of him?"

"He got lost in the Belt," Sugar said. "No one has found him since. It was when the eldest boy went back to college."

"University of Illinois? In Champaign?"

"Same," Sugar said. His eyes watered. Elliot wondered why Champaign-Urbana, Illinois was, for him, always the mouth of hell.

"Teddy promised to help look after him. I did. Everyone did, but those boys were left with our cousin, and she just couldn't get it together after that. She took back to drinking and running in the street. We all wild in the family, Sunshine. We just—"

"Forgot about him?"

Sugar nodded. "David."

"What's his brother's name?"

Sugar began to cry. "Marion."

Elliot felt his face get hot.

"David loved books. Ronnie would leave him at the library, as long as he wanted, but she started forgetting to pick him up. He liked the Carnegie, over on the West side. He'd take the bus himself after everyone started whiting on him, leaving him to look out the window, wondering if his cousins gave a shit about him anymore. Ain't nobody gonna make no trouble for Teddy Roe's nephew, we figured."

"They killed Teddy," Elliot said, remembering it occurred during the Alastair Williams Affair.

"Marion thinks it's for talking to you," Sugar said. "And agreeing to testify for your man Kefauver."

"No wonder he hates me," Elliot said. "I stayed on the lam after I got shot. No one knew if I was dead or alive. He thinks I whited on Teddy. Why did he skate, Sugar? I had my man in the Bureau looking after him."

"Teddy ran after we all figured you were dead, Elliot. He knew he was under the gun, so he had to lie low."

"If Marion is a Roe, how does no one know?"

"We all lost touch with him after he got back to school. Last we heard, he had an academic scholarship from the Seventh Day Adventists."

"Which is how he met T.R.M. Howard," Elliot said. "Hit him with the poor, orphaned rap."

"On a speaking tour, on a white college campus." Sugar shook his head.

"Where the Black Muslims recruit."

"He was away at college, relying upon the Adventists for support, because the Black Belt whited on him."

"Christ," Elliot said. "On the cross. That's how he knows me and my stories. He got them from you bums."

"Marion digs for dirt to hold against you later, Elliot. He ingratiates himself until you can't shake him off. Once you try—"

"He smears you to the Belt until your rep is shit," Elliot said. "And you can't operate, because who's going to argue with Robin Hood's nephew. But that's grammar school shit. Family or no, you got taken."

"The Muhammads put their money in his real estate play. They're big on that, buying up land, most time from other coloreds. You don't want to not pay the Muslims. You need muscle to push back."

"And Teddy is gone," Elliot said. "Sugar, how has Marion's support not run out."

"The Belt is eager to legitimize. They see Marion as their sherpa. He's in with T.R.M. Howard, and all the organizations. He plays like he's clean."

"So, he can bring respectability."

"And the politics. You know the white folks only like certain Negroes. He's the Negro they like, and those eight families your attorney got ahold of? Those are just honest to goodness, poor folks in the Belt. Not scoundrels like us. They're going to get rolled. That'll be our downfall."

"I can help that," Margaret said. She stepped from the shadows.

"The white widow, herself," Sugar said, gawking. "Sunshine, you're ever filled with surprises."

"Tell your crew that Marion Bradshaw, nephew or no, has them all exposed to a downfall," Margaret said. "My power extends up through the planning commission. Leave Bradshaw, and I'll let you ride along with me in my own private real estate trust, which is kept secure and separate from the McAlpin Family Trust. Then you won't need Bradshaw."

"And Margaret is also going to buy out those eight families," Elliot said, glancing at her. "At fair market value, plus ten—"

Margaret side-eyed him back. "Yes. Of course." If looks could kill.

"That way, you guys make out with a better investment than what you lost on Costas Cartage's weed trade. A rising tide lifts all boats."

Sugar smiled and nodded. "I can carry that back to everyone."

Elliot took Margaret aside. "Pull the trigger."

Margaret stared into his eyes, longingly. Elliot pushed her gently back toward Sugar.

"You have my word," she said.

"That's not worth much to the Belt. Not since Alphabet City."

"Add mine to it," Elliot said. "I'll keep my mouth shut. That should be enough, shouldn't it, Sugar?"

Sugar and Elliot stared at each other. Sugar relented.

"I'll let them know."

Elliot accepted Margaret's arm. He shook his head as he walked out the back door with the white woman the Black Belt loved to hate.

"Was that satisfactory to you, your lordship?"

"You did good, Snowflake."

Leo pulled up. Margaret took advantage of Elliot's weakened defenses and kissed him. When she let him go he could barely breathe, which he figured is how she preferred him.

"We could take them all on," she said. "We could run this whole city."

"I like the city fine how it is."

"All it's ever done is try to kill you."

"At least it tries."

"See you at the commission meeting."

"You're showing up?"

"I want to see what I spent my inheritance on," she said, and she slithered into the car, gams 'n all.

CHAPTER 44

Elliot and Frank parked at the far end of the large lot and walked toward Navy Pier's Main Hall. He cataloged the ethnicities in attendance by the car brands they preferred.

Negroes drove Fords more than any other brand for Henry hired their cousins straight out of 10th grade. Hank Ford shot his mouth off at the government, a lot, and made big, publicly subsidized promises with his angry mouth. Like George S. Patton, the Ford Motor Company knew what everyone else ignored about Negroes and, soon, every Negro family had at least one Ford in the driveway, and a Cousin So-and-so who could fix it for barter.

The Polish rode in Mercurys, likely to differentiate themselves from Negroes, but usually for the opposite reasons, as Mercurys were made in Detroit, and the Polaks had superior numbers in the automotive game, unless they were the kind of Polish folks who lived and loved Negroes, in which case, it was still a Ford. Polish folks weren't proud of their cars as much as their craftsmanship, which was like most anything for them in Chicago, since they were the quietly powerful workforce Chicago relied upon since 1850.

The Italians rode in Cadillacs, as long as they were middle-class, and at least two cousins removed from the Melrose Park mob contingent, which represented the Dago arm of the university project. Elliot enjoyed busting the balls of newly minted white Italians coming and going through the Black Belt when he'd pull them over after running a plate. At least twice he kept some pol or civic leader on the side of the road, explaining to his truly white wife he had no idea Uncle Carmine's wedding gift was stolen.

The Irish came in government cars, since they somehow made the city forget they were the thumb-breakers for Al Capone going back to Dion O'Banion. They slowly retook power over the Italians in the city when they left the Dagos what was left of the Outfit and sent their grandkids to the police academies and law schools in the City. That's the power that saw fit to build a new campus funded for some, by all. They had power. True power. The sort Teddy Roe once had, before Giancana whacked him, which Chicago's Irish cop contingent allowed to happen.

John Creamer, himself one of Chicago's sanitized Irish contingent, stood at the door of the elegant ballroom that smelled like stale feet since it slept Navy conscripts who were headed off to war. Mikey once took classes in that ballroom to pass his Juris Doctorate, watching with envy those who responded to their own yearning by signing up and taking it hard to Hitler. He didn't get to fight the way he wanted to. Elliot would fight for him, in the manner Elaine Critchlow intended.

"Got something for you," John said. He handed him a lovely edition of Kahil Gibran's The Prophet, bound in black cloth.

"I read it," Elliot said, as he accepted it.

"It's a first edition."

"So's my copy, ofay."

Elliot pulled out a folded sheet of paper with which Creamer bookmarked the chapter Friendship.

"The University's Bursar's office ran some numbers for us," John said. "Up until nineteen-forty seven, Marion Bradshaw's tuition was paid for by his mother, in cash."

"That's his Uncle Teddy's money," Elliot said.

"Bradshaw and Teddy Roe were related?"

Elliot shook his head, wondering why his law enforcement pals were always the last to know anything.

"What happened to her?"

"She dies of exposure in nineteen forty-nine."

"They still call a broken heart and an empty liquor cabinet *exposure*?"

"An A. Green—"

"Cousin Sugar is the bag man."

"—paid for one whole year, until nineteen-fifty."

"When Teddy was lying low, hemorrhaging money."

"Guess he couldn't keep up with Bradshaw's education. He's almost kicked out of school until, luckily, he receives a grant."

John Creamer handed Elliot a cancelled business check, made out to the university, from WCL Publications.

"WCL," Elliot said. "Imagine that."

"They paid up until his law degree."

"I just found the White Circle League in Bradshaw's ledger book."

"They had him from day one," John said. "He wouldn't have been able to get his law degree without them."

"Does Doc Howard know?"

"It isn't anything anyone would know," John said.

Elliot handed John Creamer his notes on Bradshaw's operation, but not the ledger book.

"Elliot," Creamer said. "What's this?"

"All you're getting."

"Oh, no," Creamer said. "We had a deal."

"Bradshaw's ship is set to sink today," Elliot said. "Get ready to catch the rats that run off the deck."

"Elliot," John Creamer said. "Damn you."

Half the remaining Negro underworld power brokers walked past Elliot and Creamer and entered the ballroom. Giveadam's fine ass sister, Justine, walked in looking better than everyone else, and just as racially ambiguous. She cut her eyes at Elliot. He remembered Uncle Buster's advice: "Try not to get your honey where you make your money."

Sugar Styles kept it low key, making slight eye contact with Elliot before walking inside. The play was on.

Joe Hughes showed up dressed like a damned Spanish peacock, in blue gabardine and equally tacky blue Florsheim Imperials.

"Ain't this some shit?" Joe laughed, looking nervous. "How the hell you alive, boy?"

Elliot muffed him into a phone booth and shut the door.

"Be cool, baby," Joe said.

"Cool?" Elliot pulled him closer. "Last I heard your voice, it was you suggesting I die in your basement."

"Desperate times, desperate measures," Joe said. "Good to see you back in form."

"Do I look *in form,* jackass? Sugar give you the play?"

"Yeah," Joe said. "You got it all laid out?"

Elliot nodded, sadly. "Shame about his people, Bradshaw."

"That fool will bring us all down, Elliot. Better the way you got it planned. If we do it, we gonna get him on his front porch."

"He's mine," Elliot said. "He's cost me too much. You got it?"

Joe Hughes got it. Elliot opened the phone booth, pulled his brim, and went inside.

Elliot took a seat near the rafters where he stood underneath the gilded dome's large mural, which was some majestic scene painted in honor of the Emancipation Proclamation, an original copy of which burned up along with the First City. Before the St. Lawrence Seaway brought thousands of jobs, and the Chicago Fire Department arrived to train their peaceful troops, American might expanded, and state power retooled, and those who fought the Axis found education, as long as they were white. With so many new entrants to whiteness, all the races packed into the auction priming for a grab at whatever what was left.

A few Negroes who didn't appear to be well-heeled took seats on the other side of the balcony. Elliot made his Negro underworld folks filing in next to the Grecian contingent, likely a few insane popes in attendance. Elliot made eye contact with Sugar Styles, who nodded that he was in. Margaret McAlpin was now walking down the aisle to take her seat by the Greek, Leonidas, and their entire contingent, who whistled and catcalled her. She waved to them and winked like a hard broad.

The Polish, Irish, and remaining Italian sets were ready to go. Marion Bradshaw strutted up, his twitchy Muhammad guarding him. He sat in with the Negroes. Sugar Styles patted him on the back. Even from the cheap seats, he seemed pompous.

The Greek began the proceedings.

"Regularly, we have all met together in the hopes of easing tensions around the University campus improvement projects."

The crowd was already belligerent.

"It is important that we trust the other improvement groups to know their constituencies best, including the Polish/Slavic—"

Who paid little attention.

"The Greek."

Who shouted as if they owned the place.

"The Irish, and Italian."

No one gave a shit.

"And, the Negro."

Elliot made T.R.M. Howard walk in with Frankie Freeman and take a seat behind Bradshaw. Frankie looked up at the rafters. Frank waved at her until Elliot popped him on the shoulder.

"We're laying low, Big Man."

"Sorry, Boss."

Jon Costas-McAlpin started doing his thing, explaining facts, figures, and making mild assertions of the criminality of each and every contingent.

"We are all feeling the effects of organized crime upon our fair city, and those of us who hold legitimate business interests—"

Angry voices shouted the Greek down, en masse. He wasn't eloquent, just wealthy and well-intentioned.

"We need order and structure to bring economic opportunity to the surrounding neighborhood, not disorder, mayhem, and intimidation, as evidenced by Marion Bradshaw's Near West Side Improvement Association."

Negrodom was outraged, all except Marion Bradshaw's criminal tribe, who watched him as he stepped up to the podium. T.R.M. Howard and Frankie Freeman sat expressionless.

"Watch, Frank," Elliot whispered. "He can't resist the microphone."

Bradshaw cleared his throat, as if he intended to start singing.

"Apparently, there's been talk of bullying, on the part of the Negro, toward the white contingent, who don't want a Negro to have anything a white man didn't move out of first, just to charge us three times the rent after we move in."

The Negro quarter testified mannerly, but the Negro underworld didn't take its eyes off Bradshaw. Neither did the Greeks.

"Whites should recognize we have the numbers now to determine, for ourselves, what the Black Belt is worth, and how to get all its worth, for the black."

Elliot's ears pricked up. The sergeant at arms took back the microphone and handed it to Jon. Marion Bradshaw sat. T.R.M. Howard patted him on the back. Frankie Freeman looked up at Elliot.

"Forgive me, for I am but a simple Greek," Jon said. The crowd howled in disagreement. "I've inherited slums that represents each and every ethnicity in this room. We know how our poorer children live. This university campus gives Chicago's citizens the hope of public education, of which my competitor from the Negro contingent knows, full well, the benefits. As he entered this same institution long ago, when he decided to obtain a juris doctorate, a noble pursuit for anyone, Negro or otherwise."

All agreed.

"What's more, Mr. Bradshaw is fortunate enough to receive the patronage of many of the city's elite citizens, such as Dr. T.R.M. Howard, who also opposes me on the commission."

Applause went out from the Negro quarter, some enthusiastic, some polite.

"We, who uphold the public trust for our constituencies who were not gifted as much as we, hold control of land and property. We must share it. For those who have been given much, we must ask for them to provide in kind. Andrew Carnegie himself did no less bequeathing America its libraries."

Marion Bradshaw stood up, feigning agreement, and clapping for Costas-McAlpin, just to get him off the deck.

"Marion Bradshaw, attorney at law, is a firebrand in his community, representing poor and well-heeled Negro alike."

His base applauded him.

"And why wouldn't he," the Greek said. "He carries on the tradition of his uncle, that great statesman, Theodore Roe, numbers kingpin of the Black Belt."

Murmurs of noble conceits bubbled up from the crowd, as if just about every Tom, Dick, and Harry in there wasn't crooked. The room got hot. Bradshaw stood up and attempted to quell his tribe by demonstrably waving Costas-McAlpin off.

"Theodore Roe, outlaw, suspect in countless crimes, including the murder of Fat Lenny Ciafano."

Bradshaw snatched the microphone, flustered. Costas-McAlpin relented, easily, playing into it.

"Here it comes, Frank." Elliot sat up on his haunches.

"Here what comes?"

"When Chicago gets Windy."

"I was an orphan," Bradshaw said. "Happy to have been granted any kindness. Many covered my tuition, as I received an academic scholarship, as well as several grants from wealthy institutions, many who are willing to help the Negro quarter come to prominence."

"That's where he let the White Circle League in," Frank said. "They had him from jump."

"Grants aren't charity, Frank. It's influence."

Frank nodded.

Once Bradshaw went on about his bona fides, the moment unraveled. Negroes who backed Bradshaw were off their feet defending him. Jon took the microphone back.

"The Chicago quid pro quo is not foreign fauna, my friend."

Laughter. Stillness.

"My family's attorney, Michael Rabinowitz, was assassinated as he was tracking payments in and out of his neighborhood improvement association."

Bradshaw snatched back the mic. "Michael Rabinowitz, while a dear friend, and a friend to the Negro movement for civil rights—"

Elliot wanted to kill Bradshaw.

"—lost his life because of his father, a Shylock, and a gangster, who once held sway on the same streets you intend to bulldoze, has enemies. Great ones. It's unfortunate, but same as emancipation, and the War of 1812, none of this is the Negro's fault."

The room erupted in laughter, although a man was dead. Bradshaw knew how to work the microphone.

"Is it your fault the eight families who are named in the complaint against your Near West Side Improvement Association—"

Costas-McAlpin pointed to the balcony, where the Maxwell Street Eight sat.

"—are being browbeaten and intimidated by the black Muslims, who have resorted to mafia tactics to force them to comply with your wishes, Bradshaw?"

"What mafia tactics would the Negro know, had not the ethnic white taught it to him? It appears as if Costas-McAlpin wishes to make me mayor of Chicago, as well as the cause of all the Negro's problems."

The crowd laughed as he continued on with his rap.

"Not all of them, Marion," Jon said. "Just money laundering, extortion, murder, and racketeering, as observed by the FBI's Top Hoodlum Program."

Frankie Freeman shot Elliot a look upward. Elliot showed her the ledger book, with a nod.

"Marion Bradshaw is an egalitarian, at heart. He offers investment opportunities to his detractors, and even his community's mortal enemies. He's a Good Samaritan, as good as a Samaritan's reputation allows, anyhow. His even-handed, racial perspective comes because he accepts investment from anywhere, including those who would harm the heroes of Negroes, such as Attorney Michael Rabinowitz, whose beginnings were on Maxwell Street, with many of you."

The crowd applauded.

"Bradshaw takes whatever he can get to help his constituents in the Black Belt. And himself, as he did when he took advantage of smaller investors, all young Negro professionals, men and women, and such, struggling to maintain their place in the economy and the movement that may achieve for them, equality."

"Holy shit, Frank," Elliot said. "The Greek is burying him."

"Marion Bradshaw is out for Marion Bradshaw. It is safe speculation he is aware of the murder of Michael Rabinowitz. I have seen his books, which we've obtained and had decoded through elite law enforcement at our disposal."

"Elite," Frank said. "He paid you a compliment, Boss."

Elliot bristled. "I'll send him a box of Fannie May."

Margaret waved. The Sergeant at arms brought her a microphone. She stood.

"I am Margaret Thorne-McAlpin. Many of you know me for my charitable trust for Negro policing."

Boos. Hisses. Catcalls.

"I may attest to this evidence, and will surely provide it to the fine officers of the Ladies' Bureau of the Chicago Police Department…"

Margaret raised her voice at the end, as a school marm might, and she waved the ruffians all back in their seats. She continued, ignoring the uproarious laughter and crude jokes.

"My private foundation has chosen to assist, therefore, to help weed out the corruption that challenges the University project, which is for the good of the city's population, overall. Greek, Roman, Negro, Slavic, all rising together until the City of Chicago treats its Negro citizens as its equals in the business sector—"

"Fuck me in the face," Elliot said. "She's straight-up gaming them Negroes."

"I miss Mississippi sometimes, Boss."

Margaret continued to spin gold.

"Negro families, such as my new friends represented here, will forever be vulnerable at the whims of a city that saves little for their labor, but spends much to resist their false fears of replacement. The McAlpin Family says pay those shekels to the working man."

Fuquay scooted forward in his chair.

"To the eight families we are assisting, please, stand up."

They did so.

"These poor, unaware homeowners have suffered, unimaginably—"

"There it is," Elliot said.

"—for being Negro, and they have the McAlpin family's fullest support in getting their property back, and their lives back on track. Please don't thank me, for I have done well in my life."

It was white girl church at that point. She held the moment by the throat, and she was squeezing.

"Please, thank my familial cohort, the Greek!"

The entire tribe rose to their feet, followed by the Poles. Those first to the city, the Negro, then the Irish, and the Italian, remained seated, and stared at Bradshaw. T.R.M. Howard rose from his seat, coldly looked away from Marion, and walked out with a dignified air. Frankie Freeman pursued. Bradshaw tried snatching the microphone from Margaret, but Leonidas stepped forward. He was met by Twitchy Muhammad. A contingent of

Jews came in, angry, as no one told them about the meeting. The Poles said something in Polish, likely asking whether all roads into Damascus must go through Jerusalem.

"Don't manhandle him," Jon said. "Sergeant at arms, if you please?"

The flatfoots in attendance pulled batons and stepped toward the belligerent, who settled down, enough to return their eyes to the stage. Margaret continued.

"Please, a most honorable mention to our hero, from the rafters, the valiant detective, Elliot Caprice."

Each and every eye went to the service balcony. Elliot sank into his seat. Frank took off his hat and began to stand up. Elliot slapped him on the arm. Frank stayed put.

Margaret went on. "He who saved my life from two murderers in my midst, which you all know full well. His undercover work here was exemplary."

The room made no noise.

"Boss?"

"Shtum, Frank."

The Greek grabbed the microphone from Margaret, who realized she stepped where she shitted. She slinked back down into her seat.

"Yes, thank you to Elliot Caprice," Jon said. "Who has joined me to root out corruption in the project, as well as in the neighborhood planning sector."

Elliot thought he died, which was tough, as he was already dead.

"Take a bow, Elliot!" Jon raised his hand in salute.

"Christ," Elliot said, to the Angel of Death. "All the way up, on the frickin' cross. Frank."

"Yeah, Boss."

"Maybe you should warm up Lucille."

"Good idea."

Elliot rose from his seat as Frank dashed. Bradshaw stared death up at him. Elliot stared back, as the entire ballroom saw him stick out his trigger finger toward Marion, who was swarmed by the sausage-finger contingent, who demanded answers for his fuckery. Muhammad and Bradshaw pushed through the hostile crowd. Twitchy was aggressive. An Outfit tough took a sucker dip into his jacket, and Muhammad shot him. The crowd went up. The CPD moved in as Muhammad and Bradshaw ran out the back-adjoining door.

"Goddamnit," Elliot said, as he made it down the balcony, through the panicked crowd, passing a visibly angry Mattie Smith and Vernon Jarrett.

"You stay loving those white folks, Caprice," Jarrett said. Elliot slapped his pad and pencil out of his hand again.

Outside, Elliot watched as Bradshaw and Muhammad escaped into a black Ford driven by another Bowtie. As they peeled away, Frank pulled up.

"Get in, Boss." Elliot did so. "Tail them?"

"No," Elliot said.

"No?"

Elliot pointed to the crowd of ethnic power players mulling about the green, as the Chicago Police Department emptied pockets, checked credentials, and took advantage of the disturbance. The trench coats, led by Creamer and Wiggins, hemmed up each and every mob connected member of the planning commission. City tow trucks arrived, as did paddy wagons.

"They don't call it the windy city for nothing."

"Nope," Elliot said. "Let's go home, Frank."

CHAPTER 45

His first dime was in the pool of his own blood at his feet. He dropped it when he blacked out standing up. He reached into his pocket for another, but that one fell. That meant the nerves in his body were wacky. He was going into shock. He reached down into the puddle, found the dime, only to realize it was the engagement ring he picked up from the Jews in the Diamond District in the Loop. Abe Saperstein called ahead for him to make sure he'd get a good deal. Abe knew every Jew in Chicago worth knowing. The cut was lovely, and the color quite clear, but with a loupe, an imperfection could be made out at its center. The diamond broker knocked down the price, over clarity. Elliot hit Abe up for advice on how to get Uncle Buster to Chicago to meet her folks, because Nadine's folks were high-class, and they'd need to have their society friends over.

And he missed him.

Abe said, "Just ask, boychik."

May as well scale Gibraltar.

"She'll hate you," he said to himself, before he grabbed another dime, climbed up the phone, and dialed.

"Operator."

"Thomas Maisel, in Woodlawn."

"One moment."

The phone rang twice.

"Yeah."

"Put the man on."

"To whom are you referring?"

"Teddy Roe, who Ma Bell knows as Theodore Maisel. Hand him the phone."

"Who's this?"

"Lightskin," Elliot said.

Seconds passed like hours.

"Still alive, hunh, young buck?"

"For a few more minutes." Elliot's voice was hoarse.

"Give it to me."

"I'm shot right through my left shoulder. Been bleeding bad for an hour."

"How bad?"

"Bad enough I'm gonna die if I don't stop talking."

"Where are you?"

"A phone booth outside the Dagos' housing projects."

"Crew's on the way, Lightskin. Hang tight."

Elliot slid down the phone booth to his ass, a bold brush stroke of his crimson painted behind him.

"Get up, boy."

"I just sat down, old man."

"Elliot…" Doc Shapiro said.

***

Elliot opened one eye. Uncle Buster stood at the end of his bed, Doc Shapiro behind him.

"You forgot Doc was comin'," Buster said.

Elliot sat up. His heart was racing. He moaned and grabbed his head. Doc Shapiro laid him down.

"If you're still getting headaches…"

"More people die in hospitals than anywhere else."

Buster chuckled. Doc got Elliot to his feet.

"I just need some coffee."

Elliot wandered down the hallway to the kitchen. Buster and Doc followed. Doc gently pushed Elliot into a chair Buster pulled out for him. Doc poured Elliot some coffee.

"Is this what it feels like to have a mommy and a daddy?"

"Don't joke, boy."

The phone in the kitchen rang. Elliot answered.

"Caprice Family Farm," Elliot said. "Now found at your local grocer."

"Elliot," John Creamer said.

"John. You got a line on Bradshaw?"

"No," he said. "But he couldn't have gotten far."

"Look here, you still got men on detail at Springfield General? I hoped to get word on Elaine Critchlow."

"A man claiming to be her brother checked her out of the hospital. She refused further protection. That was yesterday morning. She's gone."

He didn't know he had a thing deep in his heart for Elaine until he was forced to keep it to himself.

"Thanks, John."

"Come in," John said. "Help us take the rest of them down."

"Best to your family, John."

Elliot hung up. He heard the sound of a buggy coming up the gravel access road. The bell rang. Everyone tried to help him.

"Lemme alone, y'all. I got it."

Elliot stepped to the door and opened it. It was the postman, with the mail of the day.

"Need you to sign for this one," he said, and handed Elliot a clipboard with a card on it.

Elliot pulled a pen from the table by the front door, signed it, and handed it back to him.

"Good to see you—"

"Yeah, yeah. Thanks."

Elliot smiled tightly and shut the door. It was a certified letter from the state Board of Education. Uncle Buster walked in the room.

"Unk, what day is it?"

"Monday. Thanksgiving's this Thursday."

"What we got planned?"

"Nuthin," Buster said. "Seem like"

"—now's not the time, yeah, yeah."

"If you feeling up to it, we can put sum'n together."

Elliot looked at the envelope.

"Yeah. I'm up to it."

CHAPTER 46

Percy was asleep in Elliot's chair by the fireplace as the horse races at Balmoral were on the radio. Frank Fuquay, in apron, and Miss Betty, sans apron, fought in the kitchen over Mamie's reheat instructions. Elliot was clean and coiffed and folding white cloth napkins, again, from the S&H Green Stamp folks. The matching tablecloth was already down. The doorbell rang. Elliot went to answer. It was George, this time with Deputy Ned Reilly, who looked a bit sleepless.

"You sure you can eat, Georgie?" Elliot chuckled, but it was hollow. George was exhausted, and moving slowly, supported by Ned Reilly, Southville's only true white hat.

"Hey, Ned."

"Elliot," Ned said. They shook hands. Ned produced a magnum of Blanton's Special Reserve before he sat George on the couch.

"Ned, you shouldn't have. This is too much."

"Not at all," Ned said. "Thanks for the invitation."

As Elliot put the bottle on the mahogany bar cart, George shook his head.

"Ned—"

"There're five more bottles in evidence, Georgie. Prosecutor only needs one."

"Lord, help me."

Uncle Buster came down the stairs in his snazzier flannel shirt and brown corduroy pants.

"Is that the shirt Margaret gave you?" Elliot laughed.

"Don't you sass me on the farmer's holiday, boy."

Frank kept checking the bone-in spiral ham Buster ordered at the last minute from Mamie's. She was happy to oblige. Even threw in a whole roasted chicken for Doc Shapiro, who bought his daily coffee from her even though nothing was Kosher in her greasy spoon but the salt she used to pickle pigs' feet.

"It's still cold. What temperature should the oven be?"

"Two-fifty."

Ned shared a drink with Buster and Shapiro. Elliot sat closely to George, who stared at him.

"Don't," he said.

Elliot pulled out the handbill from the White Circle League, a crudely composed and printed cry for help from those unable to admit the gravest mistake.

"It's not your fault," George said, sounding weary but confident.

"You were right in the alley behind Abe's, Georgie. I'm living in a moment created from my boyhood choices."

"That would mean life is hell," George said. "And I don't believe that."

"That's because all your choices were made for you," Elliot said. "Which is why you don't know how to duck."

Elliot and George looked at each other, laid up together, somehow on the same side although not from within the same purpose.

"Negroes deserve an America, too, Elliot."

Elliot nodded.

"There's already a Negro America, Georgie. No one notices it because it works the same as all the others."

Frank sat across from Elliot.

"Y'all," he said. "The Big Man has completed his equivalency exams."

"Hey, now," Uncle Buster said.

Doc patted him on the shoulder.

"Now you gotta get into college," Miss Betty said, and she passed him the first plate. Frank sat it in front of Elliot. The Big Man made eye contact. Before he could form words, Elliot winked and tendered him a slight nod.

"Those who know better, do better, Frank."

Frank nodded back.

Miss Betty gave everyone a generous portion before she sat herself between Percy and Uncle Buster. All bowed their heads. The ham was still a bit cold. No one minded.

He stood alone at the sink, doing dishes in an attempt to think beyond his nagging aches and pains, those new as well as those which lingered in reminder of the dangers of dogged insistence. He wondered of Elaine. What was she doing? Where could she have gone? He was so busy pushing against his own stone, he never really got to know her. She gave her man her permission to help Doc Shapiro and George Stingley rescue him, and he was off like a rocket. Why hadn't he asked for her mother's name? Why didn't he know her, when she saved him?

The phone rang. He picked up the receiver.

"Caprice Fam—"

"Hey," Molly said.

"Hey, there, Molly. I know I'm late, but there were a lot of dishes. I'm sure you're tired. I'll help bar back so you can get out of there."

Molly made a squeal.

"Come on down to the tavern, Caprice."

It was Marion Bradshaw. He sounded maniacal.

"I'll have a drink with your white bitch until you get here."

The line went dead. Elliot hung up. Frank walked in reading the Gibran Elliot received from John Creamer.

"Need some help with the dishes?"

"I gotta get down to Duffy's."

"Boss, why don't you just tell her you love her?"

Elliot's heart broke into a hundred pieces.

"Don't ever change, Frank."

"Not until you do, Boss."

Elliot grabbed Frank for dear life and hugged him. He whispered in his ear.

"I'm gonna go see Molly."

"Okay, Boss."

Frank grabbed the dishrag from him and got to work.

Elliot slipped out the side door, ran to the ruins of the family's barn, and pulled up the charred floorboards from the tack room. He reached inside the hole, found his field safe, and pulled his US Army issue 1911A .45 and two clips. Lucille waited for him down the gravel access road, which he walked slowly, and deliberately, so his uncle wouldn't hear his footsteps. Elliot started her up, but turned down the radio. Frank had it to WKEI, who reported that a few Negro townships in the farm belt were under attack by rioting whites.

CHAPTER 47

Past Pettingill, it was all brown and orange skies. Cars were overturned. Storefronts along Main were looted by Negro and white rioters. His boyhood fears returned. Elliot watched as Negro and white fought bitterly, barehanded, or wielding the bottles they enjoyed as they let off steam on the biggest party night of the year. Christmas was for the kids. New Year's Eve was for the lovers, but the weekend after Thanksgiving was when working people earned their rest, relaxation, and exhalation, and instead, them ofays were using it to run the table. The bank, the League, and the racist faction of the Illinois State Police had conspired to terrorize landowners for months, impressing upon them the burden of land through the tyranny of lax law and depressed jobs, ensuring the bloodiest harvest yet.

Pick-up trucks with loudspeakers tuned to the Vatican's Huey P. Long, Cardinal Mahoney, blasted on ten. The Cardinal decried the sinful ways of the Jew, and the Nigger, who ate into the economic opportunities of poor, struggling white Americans, except the Negro who beat the white boy senseless with the bottle of corn wasn't seeking political discourse but release, from the tension held in bodies made to work in the fields all day long, and make babies for the remainder of the night, and yearn for those few days per year where they could feel the illusion of freedom. White folks figured they could make Negroes dead whenever they wanted. White folks would learn better that night.

Elliot piloted Lucille through the inferno. He made out friend and neighbor, turning on each other. Even the Stateys had trouble with the crowds, likely regretting their decision to serve and protect the White Circle League's business interests. Elliot turned past Abe Saperstein's, who was outside his shop swinging his baseball bat. His head was bloodied. A crowd of white folks menaced him with taunts against Jews. Elliot parked his car and got out waving the 1911. They dispersed. Elliot took Abe and put him in the car.

"I need to lock up my shop!"

"Abe," Elliot said. "Let me take you to Doc's."

"It's worse this time, Boychik," Abe said, bleeding and crying.

Elliot hit the hammer and sped to Doc's private entrance in the alley. He took Abe inside as Doc continued his preparations. Elliot went to him.

"First patient," Elliot said. "Abe, when you're not bleeding, help Doc. I may be sending back wounded."

"Where are you going?" Shapiro reached out to him. "Stay here, boychik."

"Doc," Elliot said. "They've got Molly."

Doc nodded, but his eyes were saddened.

Elliot walked out, his 1911 in front of him, as he avoided skirmishes that placed the whites on the losing side. Negroes mean-mugged him as he approached the door to Duffy's Tavern. He stepped inside. Molly stood behind the bar as Muhammad held her at gunpoint. Hard luck Negro patrons were hiding inside.

"You good, Molly?"

"I'm good," she said.

"It wasn't enough for you to destroy everyone's life, Bradshaw. You had to destroy my town."

"I brought your town progress."

"Whose progress," Elliot asked him, as he trained his sights on Bradshaw. "You fools never ask where the power in empowerment comes from."

"It comes from Negro ingenuity."

"It comes from labor, you moron. Look around you. What do you think this is all about?"

The riot raged outside. Bradshaw snatched Molly from behind the counter and dragged her to the front of the bar. "Then why take up with these Devils? Hm?"

"She's a devil, alright—"

"Elliot Caprice," Molly said.

Muhammad fired a shot at Elliot's feet.

"I've heard enough," Muhammad said. "Get the dough."

"What dough?" Elliot wondered which man to shoot first.

"That ledger you stole, you didn't want to know everything that was inside." Bradshaw pulled Molly into him and grabbed her around the waist, where he fondled her boob. "My backers are exacting. They invested in me. In the future of America. I've made assurances."

"Assurances you backed with Negro pain and suffering."

"You've got it, don't you?" Bradshaw feigned hurting Molly. "Your harvest came in. Let's go over to your house. See your uncle, and your leg man, and the old whore from the essaroh."

"Betty Bridges would snatch your soul from you herself, punk."

A herd of the angry broke through the door. Elliot put two in Twitchy Muhammad's chest before his eyes lit up and he realized his end was then. He let out a sympathetic shot from atop the bar, grazing a patron. Bradshaw, who must've never seen a man opened up before, hesitated in the moment, and Molly grabbed a bottle of rum and smashed it against his temple. Along with the wallop, he had to contend with the duck shotgun Molly kept behind the bar. She let off one shot that missed him. She tried blasting him at the door as he slipped away.

"Put that thing away, will you?"

"Get after him!"

"Call Ned Reilly," Elliot said. "And maybe the National Guard."

Elliot ran out.

CHAPTER 48

Elliot followed Marion outside, where black and white cut grievances into each other's flesh in the rain and mud. There were, at least, one hundred men all fighting with whatever they found to waylay their opposer, and Bradshaw ran into the crowd, frightened. Folks grabbed at him, so he began firing wildly, catching rioters unawares, which increased the frenzy. Elliot took aim, but a herd of angry, drunken bodies stormed the scene. Molly stepped outside.

"No," Elliot said. "Get back on the phone."

"Who am I calling, Elliot?" Molly shook her head at the horror.

Elliot made Bradshaw trying the doors down Main Street. He yanked at Spats Culpepper's door handle but went down hard after buck shot went off and knocked out the window.

"Get on," said Spat's wife, Nanette, in headscarf and muumuu, as she stepped out her tailor shop holding the steel. Bradshaw tried turning around to run, but she fired again, putting him on his face. He crawled himself out of the dirt and, as he scrambled toward Doc Shapiro's clinic, he fired, catching Nanette in the throat. Spats ran screaming out the tailor shop with two pistols, firing at anything that moved. The state police arrived, slogging through the Sugartown mud. Spats didn't care. He continued screaming and firing until the dicks unloaded on him, taking his life in the doorway, scant feet from where his wife bled out.

Bradshaw took off down the block. Elliot pushed through the rioters to a clearing on the strip. A lump of a man holding a sickle punched Elliot in his bad shoulder. He went down like a ton of bricks. The Negro raised his sickle before the bottom part of his jaw blew off. He fell backward, as did Eugene Brophy, who knew what to do when it mattered. He got to his feet and helped Elliot, who pointed at the Negroes aligned against the whites, those who didn't realize they weren't winning.

"Eugene, everyone is nuts. We have to hold the line."

"I got you, Caprice."

"Molly is keeping a bunch of folks safe at the tavern. Get going." Elliot slapped him on the cheek. "Southville took a chance on you."

"I understand."

Elliot shambled forward in the mud, toward where Marion Bradshaw limped toward Doc's front door.

"How many Negroes have to die before you do, Marion?"

Marion broke out the glass of the clinic door with his gun handle and stepped inside. Elliot stepped through the window, the back of Bradshaw's skull in his sight.

"Was it worth it, destroying my town?"

"Destroying you was worth it," he said. "All your tales. All your valuable little secrets. You discard people when you're done with them. That's how you killed my uncle."

"I went to the FBI and told them Teddy was off the list."

"You're a liar."

"It was the deal, Marion. I was half-dead in the basement of Joe's, and your uncle helped me get out of Chicago. I took my secrets with me to spare the Black Belt Kefauver's aggression. It was Giveadam Jones who got him killed."

Bradshaw raised the gun at a Negro boy. Abe ran to him and took him in his arms.

"Look at all the well-intentioned Jews, helping Negroes."

"Giveadam shared a cell with Sam Giancana at Leavenworth," Elliot said, wondering if he should rush him. "The asshole couldn't help but trick on the whole Black Belt. Told a dago with a seventh-grade education all about Bronzeville. Of course, that peacock made himself the star of the story. The policy banks and numbers joints. The paradise we made out of unpaved streets. And he told Giancana that Teddy was the man to beat."

"The Joneses treated me like family."

"Then why did the White Circle League pay your tuition?"

Marion Bradshaw froze. "You know?"

"The FBI knows. That's what you Negroes do, Bradshaw. You want to be better than white folks, without actually doing anything better than white folks. Teddy shot his mouth off keeping up with the Joneses but kept his charity a secret. That was his true wealth, Marion. And he didn't share it with you."

"Shut up!"

"Teddy Roe made great starts but lousy finishes, same as he did with bringing order to the Black Belt. Being Robin Hood is fun, until someone has to pay the milk man. Or babysit your little brother."

"They all hate you," he said. "There's no where you can go, Caprice. Here, or Chicago. It's over."

"I never had any friends in the Belt. Just occasionally friendly competitors. Michael Rabinowitz and Elaine Critchlow were my friends, and I'll never see them again because of you."

Elliot walked up to him. Bradshaw fired his gun, over and over, to gasps from the room, and impotent clicks.

"What was I thinking?" Elliot shook his head as he grabbed his collar. "You're no daisy at all."

Elliot belted him. Bradshaw fell to the floor. Abe and Doc stood over him. Marion Bradshaw was finished.

"Caprice," Eugene said, standing in the doorway.

"Goddamnit, Eugene. What did I tell you?"

"Molly sent me here," he said. Bradshaw lay prone. "Guess you handled that one, huh?"

"Did Ned officially deputize you?"

"Just this morning."

Elliot stood over Bradshaw, triumphant in absolutely nothing.

"Do your duty and arrest him."

Eugene pulled his handcuffs.

"The black man in America will have a nation, Caprice," Bradshaw said, laughing, and crying, and laughing.

Elliot fished into his pocket for a hand rolled, found his Zippo, and lit up.

"We already have one," Elliot said. "You were doing it wrong."

Elliot opened the door and walked out.

CHAPTER 49

He leaned onto cars as he struggled to stand, much less walk. As he approached Duffy's tavern, he made a crowd out front. The whites finally accepted that they lost the battle. Many had dispersed. The state police needed reinforcements.

"There he is," one said.

"Hey there, light skin," another said. "You alright? You look hurt."

His body had nothing left to give Negroes. Nothing for the altar of shame for possessing what they lacked, which was whiteness, which wasn't anything at all, really. It blended, the white. It mixed well with everything, if they just allowed it, finally. He knew it from within his own blood, which ran in the Sugartown mud and rain.

One man ran up and swung for Elliot's face. Elliot shot him in the shoulder. The rest seized him. He was dragged into the muddied street in front of Duffy's and thrown down. More Negroes realized what was happening and stood around, taunting him. A few Negroes from town shouted for them to stop, but most stood by, watching black crush semi-black, for not being black enough, or perhaps a bit too much.

The first blow struck his face. It tasted like the Champagne-Urbana Police Department.

"Who do you think you are?"

"You think you're better than us?"

"You think you're something special?"

The taunts were the same, Negro, white, or otherwise. Around the fourth punch, the lights dimmed. Elliot stopped trying. In his heart, the hurt had already come long before, when none of them could tell he loved them far too much, as Negroes, to fight against them. What's more, if Negroes wouldn't have him, with whiteness as no alternative, he didn't want to live anyhow. The harvest came through. Uncle Buster had Miss Betty, and Frank, who had a future.

He tasted his own blood and thought, "It's okay."

One of the Negroes rifled through his pockets as he lay still. Another pulled a blade. That's when he met his end, once Molly perforated him at the belly with the duck gun from under the bar.

"Piss and vinegar," Elliot said, in his head, as she pulled the second trigger, catching one Negro in the face. Others scattered, but more arrived. That's when they learned Molly could reload, with the quickness.

Eugene Brophy ran down the sidewalk, revolver drawn. One of the rioters shot. Eugene shot back and hit him. Molly swung the butt of the shotgun wildly in the crowd as Negro men descended upon her. Elliot stood up and shot one man in the back of his head. Another tackled him and raised a bottle.

Buster Caprice had the shotgun from the barn in his hands, smoking, as the man flew three feet, onto his back, life leaking from him.

"Get up, boy."

He gave Elliot his hand. Some of the Negroes arrived packing. Elliot wasted no time, firing shots back at those who would accept their abundance, and slit their throats. Buster and Elliot, back to back, fighting for their place in the world. They couldn't have him. Not his uncle. Not another damned soul.

Buster missed one of the rioters on his flank and was seized. Elliot grabbed him, pulled him down, and cradled him as two men jumped them. He covered the old man up in his arms, doing the best he could to shield him from the blows. Frank Fuquay ran over with Ned Reilly, who brandished a shotgun. Frank pulled Uncle Buster out of the mud. Elliot staggered to his feet.

"Get off the street," Ned said. "Now."

The Illinois State Police arrived, in full force. They lobbed tear gas canisters at black and white alike. They marched in rows of five, firing upon anyone within range. As the mob dispersed in terror, the White Circle League's loudspeakers wailed on.

"I'm getting you to a hospital," Frank said.

"You do and you're fired."

Molly threw open the tavern door. Uncle Buster, Ned, Frank Fuquay, and Elliot ducked inside. Frank locked it behind them.

"Where's Bradshaw?"

"Doc Shapiro is treating him at the clinic. Abe Saperstein is keeping the shotgun on him."

White boys were more apportioned with weapons, but they didn't have the numbers. The harvest brought Negroes to Southville by the thousands. Desperate folk, just passing through, with no relation to the land, and therefore no reason to give white folks the benefit of the doubt, had been hearing how they were less than human for months. In the rainy murk of the heartland, red ribbons streaked through black mud, white hate, and green envy. Negroes finally knew what Southville ofays really thought of them and it was too late to take it back. The White Circle League sold one too many wolf tickets. Negroes would sit quietly in the balcony no longer.

Molly wandered over to the bar, exhausted, and grabbed the bottle of Blanton's Reserve she kept for Elliot. She uncorked it, poured herself a shot, and enjoyed it. She poured another, leaving it on the bar, reached into the cooler and found a Nehi, uncapped it, and sat them together on the bar before slipping away in the back. Elliot rose from his seat, took to his pour, and sipped slowly. Frank walked over and sat. He tipped his Nehi—Grape, for Molly understood Negroes like flavors—and raised it in salute.

"Some harvest, huh, Boss?"

Frank patted Elliot on the shoulder. He must've been feeling froggy, because he lifted Elliot's bourbon, put it to his lips, and then regretted it, making the worst face the young buck had in him. Elliot took it from him, downed it, then turned the glass over.

"Let her out slow, Frank." He winked.

Elliot walked to the window and looked outside. Negroes and ofays, all laid out in the mud, proving Molly Duffy's point, a debate that cost Southville Mose Boysaw, and the Culpeppers, and Little Mikey Rabinowitz, who spoke up for Elliot when no one else did.

Ned opened the back door to a familiar sound. It was Sheriff George Stingley, still nursing his wounds, driving the police cruiser, loudspeaker attached, cranked up to drown out the White Circle League.

"Southville, this is your sheriff," he said. "I am one of you, born and raised here. Many of you knew my father, when he'd grant shelter and God's word to anyone who found themselves in dire straits. The Stingleys have stood for law, order, justice and forgiveness in this town, alongside you, all of you, no matter our criminal beginnings, since its founding. We were Negroes here before the migration. We met you upon your arrival."

Molly stepped from the storeroom and looked out the window.

"We have come together, in this forsaken place, not to forsake ourselves, but to claim a piece of the good, green earth for those of us who wish to tread meekly amongst our brethren and sistren, no matter their race. To find balance, in as much as we remain imbalanced by forces who deceive us into believing we are enemies, when we have lived, and loved, and stood for each other as long as my father, Right Reverend George Stingley, Sr., enjoyed you in his congregation. And that was since the beginning. Before Frank Nitty, and Isadora Rabinowitz, and the Illinois State Police."

Elliot stepped out the door and walked to the car. George was in his house clothes. He looked terrible, hunched over, addled, but he would stand. Elliot grabbed a shotgun out of the back of the cruiser and held post next to him. Frank and Molly stepped outside.

"For months, we have endured the onslaught of evil from those who do not live in our community, who do not know us, and who do not share the same stakes for our land as we do. We stand where we, the discarded of Illinois, decided to make a way. We have been here a long time, since Southville's dubious founding. We have survived Alfonse Capone, the Dust Bowl, the flash floods, the boll weevil, and the migration, walking, from wherever we began as individuals, until we became a tribe, as uneasy as we may be in our tribal obligations."

Ned Reilly walked over to the League's nightmare loudspeaker car, shot out a window, opened the door, and yanked enough out of the dashboard to cease the White Circle League's sermon.

"All of you, be it the white, the Negro, or the Jew, came here in desperation and found ease, although we are no promised land. We know this. We do not care. We are Southville. If you do not wish to open your life to the sanctity of God, Mother Nature, and kin, do not come here, for the only purchase you will find is the gutter, and the only community you'll find is with the dead, as these poor souls here."

George pointed to the mounting dead, and then those living, and then those in authority.

"God's law rules my home, and my church."

Ned walked up to George, square jawed, defiant but hurting badly. Eugene stood next to him, solid in the pocket.

"My law rules Southville County. Collect your dead, go home, and come to church on Sunday."

George pulled a shotgun from the back seat and held it high. Ned Reilly took off his badge and handed it back to him. Eugene reached for his own badge, but Ned pushed his hand away.

"I'll order another one, Eugene."

"Welp, looks as if y'all got some law now," Elliot said. He tossed Eugene the shotgun. "Make sure they pay you something."

Eugene nodded.

"Bring Lucille on when you come home, Frank. It's parked in the alley behind Doc's."

"You don't want a ride?"

"Naw."

"Let me go get the car, Boss. You're a wreck."

"Born that way, Big Man." Elliot waved. "C-ya later, Molly."

"Fix my bar," she said. "You promised."

He walked away, through the mud, and the dead, and their blood, and their now dead lies. His work was done, he was still alive, and he'd get the hell out of there before the Gods realized it. Elliot Caprice wanted to walk home, one last time, before the world knew he defied death. Perhaps then, Negroes would let him sleep.

Elliot Nathan Caprice, a mulatto, a bastard, who took his lumps and gave them right back, walked past the bodies in the gutter, straight to his Uncle's house, and took to his covered porch, where he'd slept as a child. Despite the sadness and the blood, his harvest was a boon. The gods favored him, it seemed. The only exchange was, on occasion, someone else's business would need minding. What they, and the Negro underworld, and now the White Circle League hadn't accounted for was, if it was wrong, and it happened in front of him, that made it Elliot Caprice's business, which he was exceedingly better at minding, more's the pity.

CHAPTER 50

Most of the operating bean fields were spared in the holocaust that plagued Southville proper, but the riots claimed enough farms for the National Guard to release a company to patrol unincorporated county. Bands of men, maybe white, perhaps not, attacked Buster's neighbors. Homes were ransacked. Bandits made off with equipment. Livestock was maimed or killed. As area farmers saw the Caprice's lights on, they ran to them for shelter. Buster didn't hold them to their years-long rumor mongering, and deceitful, unneighborly behavior. He welcomed them inside, to Miss Betty's chagrin, and held space for them until they felt safe enough to head back to their ruined lives. Nearly the next day, signs from the bank went up in quite a few farmhouse front yards. Uncle Buster had checkmate. It arrived at the same moment as his pity. Miss Betty, of course, pointed out his victory to him, but Uncle Buster didn't pay it any attention. It didn't help the string beans grow. It didn't get her off his back to fix up the place.

Sure as the sun rose the day following what the Chicago Bee themed Red Harvest, Southville County Savings and Loan was open, eagerly providing relief and assistance to landowner and business owner alike, little of which the Negro race represented anymore, once economic sabotage upended Spats's Haberdashery, and Boots' Barber Shop, and Miss Betty's SRO. No Guests. No Vacancies. No nothing.

Mamie's survived, which was good news, because Elliot didn't find Miss Betty's cooking much better than his uncle's. She was in the kitchen all set to pound some meat into shoe leather when Uncle Buster invaded his covered porch. He was enjoying a smoke and a good read when the old man snuck in, lowered his voice, and convinced Elliot he himself wanted to eat his once ex-lady friend Mamie's mud fish, right in front of his old time used to be, Betty Bridges.

Elliot was loath to leave the house, especially with the press still mulling around, but Uncle Buster wouldn't get out his face. He enjoyed a short nip off some Blanton's before he stepped into the kitchen, black eight-panel in hand, black pea coat, black mood. Buster and Miss Betty were at the table going over facts and figures related to her insurance claim. Elliot felt where his respect had grown for the woman who bought the land across from his farm, because she could, and didn't plant anything there but space between her and the Caprice men.

"I'm going."

"Take Frank with you."

"Frank is studying."

"I'm not studying." The Big Man walked into the kitchen.

"You are, too, studying. You have entrance exams." Elliot put on his hat.

"It's alright if you want to be left alone," Frank said. "He's being mercurial, Uncle Buster."

"Good word choice, mercurial," Elliot said, tipping his brim. "Because I am."

Frank smiled and nodded. "Hopefully not so much you don't bring back cobbler."

"I'll get you cobbler, Frank," Elliot said. "Unk, I'm going by my lonely. If you wanna eat, that's how it's coming."

"Fine," Buster said. "Make sure you don't get—"

"End pieces."

"There's a good boy. Be careful."

"Be easy."

"And maybe find out where she gettin' her produce from, hear?"

"Let the boy get on, Nathan," Betty said. "Don't see why her damned catfish is so special, anyhow."

Elliot stepped out the door, wondering how Uncle Buster would finish the meal without injury.

As he piloted Lucille through the destruction on Main Street, he saw the most viable property was snapped up by the bank, near immediately. There was a new sign above Abe Saperstein's busted-out pharmacy. Walgreen's would claim the corner after all. The day Elliot closed his bank accounts with those vipers for good he saw Abe, seated with the bank man, hat in hand. He looked like Uncle Buster had when Elliot found him at Miss Betty's: gaunt and tired, with a thousand-yard stare. He hadn't been able to reopen. Illinois State property tax bills were coming due. Two generations of his family lived above his pharmacy. None of it mattered. He was as busted out as Miss Betty, who declined their vile offers of bank financing, and took her accounts to Chicago First National with Elliot, at Margaret McAlpin's advice, and introduction. It was the only manner of repayment he'd allow. The white widow convinced him he needed help with minding the books and his privacy, since everyone in the Negro and white worlds was watching. Giancana had to feel him thumping around Chicago for a second time since he was supposedly dead, and the Negro rags were of no help, especially not Mattie Smith, or that blowhard Vernon Jarrett, who had been nosing around at the Jailhouse and the county seat, asking questions about him. What was troubling was the disappearance of the White Circle League from the scene once Bradshaw wound up behind bars. It was as if they were never there. No more sedition via radio shows in bean country. No more influence over the Southville County Seat. Perhaps Elliot beat them. He knew they wouldn't remain beaten. He knew they'd be sore.

Elliot arrived at Mamie's expecting a bit less competition for the good pieces, but didn't expect the complete abandonment of her restaurant by the Negro migrant labor who fought so hard, so quickly, and for so very little. They flew from the bloodiest harvest in Southville history on toward their next means of survival. Be they from the bean fields of Southville County, or the onion farms of South Holland, or the corn fields out where Illinois met Indiana, all only ever toiled in Chicago's shadow, watching, waiting, and praying for their moment to get in where they may fit in.

Elliot understood the feeling. Once, from the porch, on a day when the wind and the rain, and the turning of the sun all happened just right, nature cleared up that dirty, industrial horizon just enough for Elliot to barely make out, in the hazy, rotting onion mist, the great titan city's steel spires sprouting in the distance, offering him the notion he could himself stand tall, and strong, and singular, if only he got the hell off that old man's bean farm. And so, he did.

Mamie was ready with his uncle's order when he walked in.

"These ain't y'all's string beans."

"Next season, Miss Mamie."

"Betty still at your place?"

Elliot nodded.

"They were always good together," Mamie said.

Elliot watched Mamie's husband, in the kitchen, chopping dead fish. He silently wished he wasn't too much of a bull in a china shop. Perhaps he could be Molly Duffy's forever bar back, or still on the job, with Nadine.

Mamie came out the cash register with Elliot's change off his twenty.

"Keep it."

"Child," she said, shaking her head, and putting the change in the coffee can by the register.

"See you next Tuesday, Miss Mamie."

He tugged his brim and angled toward the door, when his stomach sank at the sight of Frankie Muse Freeman, standing in the doorway, horn-rimmed glasses, smart scarf around her head, tan winter woolen. Elliot almost dropped his uncle's catfish.

"I tried to reach you by phone."

"I had the line pulled out after Izzy Rabinowitz told on himself," Elliot said.

"Don't you find that unprofessional? You're the last one left standing at Rabinowitz and Associates."

"I wasn't in the law profession. They put my name on the door to be nice. Elaine Critchlow was the last member of the firm."

Frankie looked away, found something and returned.

"You have a responsibility to the public."

"I have a responsibility to get this catfish home. Take care, Freeman."

Elliot tried walking past her, but she touched him on the shoulder.

"Elliot," she said. "Please."

"My uncle don't like his dinner getting cold."

"Five minutes."

Elliot scratched his head underneath his hat. Everything in the bag was smelling so good.

"Walk with me."

Elliot walked out the door and toward Lucille, parked on the dirt and gravel round, which the town never got around to paving. Frankie followed him.

"You said you and Elaine had social club business together."

"Yes," Frankie said.

"So, Bradshaw connected all of us through you."

"It's regrettable, but Negroes socialize in ways that help us survive our oppression."

"You ever consider if being forced upon each other is the oppression?" Elliot stopped and glared at her.

"I've been in touch with the FBI." Freeman looked cold.

"Oh?"

"You have a lot of friends in different places."

"Not very good ones. Always getting me shot. Or my office exploded."

"They took Marion Bradshaw."

"As you knew they were gonna," Elliot said. "What's the problem? He's out of the movement, isn't he?"

"The FBI will use this to suppress efforts all over the country."

"Then play it straight." Elliot opened the car door and put the bag inside. "And throw out the bums. You got two more minutes."

"Thank you."

Elliot didn't say anything.

"The McAlpins told me it was your suggestion." Freeman bundled herself in the December chill. "The retainer came right on time."

"I told them you do good work, and it wouldn't be fair if you lost your backing."

"They've asked me to take over for Michael Rabinowitz on the Maxwell Street Eight case."

"Mikey wasn't working that case. He just signed off on everything. It was Elaine. It was all her work."

Freeman stared at Elliot as he stared at his shoes.

"The Eight told me to thank you."

"I didn't do anything." Elliot opened Lucille's door. "Take care, Freeman. Try the soup at the Chicago Athletic Club sometime."

Before he got in, Freeman grabbed his hand, not forcefully, but not gracefully.

"Your people need you, Elliot."

"I've only ever been too much or not enough for us, but now we all need me."

"I need you," Freeman said. "I admit it. You saw the plays I didn't. You showed me where the movement is exposed."

Elliot watched Freeman's face as it contorted around the truth.

"You showed me where it can be brought down. From within. From among our own."

Elliot took his hand back and put it on her shoulder.

"Negroes want to be left alone, Freeman. To have it all, or to have none of it. Our choice. You find a movement for that, I'll let y'all march me around until my feet hurt. Goodbye."

Elliot hopped into Lucille and pulled the door shut. Freeman just stood there. He rolled down the window.

"Since you're here, you may as well get the catfish."

"I'm sorry you lost your friends, Elliot." Freeman cracked a dim smile.

"They don't tell you about the cost of freedom before y'all go signing up your lives to the movement, huh?"

Frankie somehow found quiet. Elliot wouldn't use it as the upper hand.

"The phone man comes out next week. Maybe I give you the number."

Frankie nodded.

"Something doesn't feel right to you, you give me a call. Avoid bothering me during growing season. My uncle is a hard screw."

Elliot started Lucille.

"I hope you had a good harvest, after all."

"If that social network of yours finds word about Elaine, I'd be happy to know she's alright."

Frankie tended a silent nod.

"You be well, Frankie Muse Freeman."

Elliot rolled up the window and pulled away, watching Freeman watch him from his rear view. Elliot turned on the radio to distract himself. It was set to WKEI. For Negroes, by Negroes.

When he returned to the house he brought the catfish to the table, told everyone good night, and excused himself. On his bed he sat in the dark, quiet and still, same as in country for Patton, or on stakeouts for the Chicago Police Department. Or in his bedroom, dressed for mischief, waiting for Uncle Buster to begin snoring.

He listened to Miss Betty and Frank Fuquay, and Uncle Buster enjoy dinner, and the sweet relief of each other's company, and wonder aloud if everything would be alright, or if they would be. Conversation stopped for a while after that, until Frank asked Miss Betty to pass the cobbler.

Elliot Caprice was halfway to worrying about everyone again before a yawn broke his consciousness. Sleep, his most elusive lover, was finally upon him. He undressed, crawled into his bunk, pulled his army blanket over himself, and took a fair shot at a good night's rest. He knew he better enjoy it.

Negroes never allowed him to sleep for long.

—fin

ACKNOWLEDGEMENTS

Nick Petrie showed me how not to play myself.

Jim E'Toile showed me how not to play anyone else.

Lots of folks come and go. Rich Yaker taught me that's right.

My older brother Walter reminds me of my older brother, Walter, also not

Easy to love, but they cut my meat for me, and I ate, and I am here.

Erika Green-Swafford, Rori Flynn, Rob Hines, and Ann-Marie Johnson.

Peter Carlaftes ruined me for other publishers, and editors.

Missy Haas, Dan Hardin, Allison Davis, and their peers at DWT.

Christian Bevaqua, Michael Sasha King, Bill Podger, and all my gurus.

Daniel II helps his dad a great deal.

All my SF/BAY/MARIN/BERKLEY/OAKTOWN crew.

John, and CJ, who both are very good to me.

Yes, indeedy, you're my sweetie.

The Washington Heights neighborhood of the great City of Chicago.

John Laymon Gardner, Jr. (1945-1981)

Rosalita Annette Gant (1947-1993)

John Laymon Gardner, III (1965-1994)